SAND,
SEQUINS &
SILICONE

SAND, SEQUINS & SILICONE

PIA MIA

wattpad books

FRAYED PAGES

Published in Canada by Wattpad WEBTOON Book Group,
a division of Wattpad WEBTOON Studios, Inc.
36 Wellington Street E., Toronto, ON M5E 1C7

www.wattpad.com

First Frayed Pages x Wattpad Books edition: May 2024

www.frayedpagesmedia.com

ISBN 978-1-99885-476-9 (Trade Paperback)
ISBN 978-1-99885-477-6 (eBook)

Library and Archives Canada Cataloguing in Publication and U.S. Library of
Congress Cataloging in Publication information is available upon request.

Printed and bound in Canada

1 3 5 7 9 10 8 6 4 2

Cover design by Emily Wittig
Cover image © amedeoemaja via Shutterstock
Typesetting by Delaney Anderson

For the lovers, the dreamers, and the truth seekers.

To Angela and Peter, your unwavering belief in my dreams and guidance throughout my journey have been my pillars of strength. Thank you for being by my side every step of the way.

1

Butterflies flutter in my belly to the beat of my new song as our Sprinter pulls up at the top of the red carpet. Except I can see through the tinted windows this carpet isn't red—it's pink to match the huge promo posters hanging all over the downtown building.

My face, glittering in full glam makeup, reigns over everyone below.

As "Princess" continues to play loudly through the Los Angeles night air, a crowd of fans holding homemade signs screams wildly, cell phones poised, ready to capture the big moment. They're ushered back by fierce-looking security guards while, behind them, camera lights flash at VIP guests posing in front of the press wall.

Any second now all eyes will be on me.

This is *my* moment.

I've worked my entire life for this.

"Oh my god!" Maya, one of my best friends, squeals from the seat beside me. She taps her phone screen and her eyes sparkle like diamonds. "It's passed a million streams already, Princess!"

Those butterflies take flight in my belly again. *You bet it did.* It was impossible to sleep last night—we were all so glued to our screens watching the streams add up after the song's midnight release.

"Oh, I've got a good feeling about this song . . ." Valerie, my other bestie, says, eyes sparkling.

I've got a good feeling about it too. I only wish this wasn't all so bittersweet. My heart is still broken, and the song reminds me of what I've lost to get here. Shaking off the shadows of these feelings, I force myself to stay present, to soak up every bit of goodness happening right now.

"Princess?" Kimi, my manager, sits forward. "Are you ready?"

"*So* ready."

My hands slide over my custom-made champagne-pink Chanel dress, as if to check they're all still there, every last twinkling Swarovski crystal. It *has* to be perfect. Photos from tonight will be all over the internet tomorrow, and if there's one thing I've learned about Hollywood, it's that appearance is *everything* if you want to make it. One bad photo and I'll be crucified. Insecurity bubbles up but I breathe it out; I can't let anything ruin this moment.

The limo door opens and sound floods in, pulsing inside my chest.

"You look amazing, babe!" Valerie gives my hand one last squeeze.

"After four hours of hair and makeup, I should freaking hope so," Maya mutters, and we laugh together as I scoot across the seat to the door.

Between video calls and phone interviews with radio stations across the country, the house had been manic all day with a swarm of stylists and makeup artists making me look flawless. *Hot and empowered*, that was the vibe we were going for with this song. And honestly, we did *good*. I didn't get a chance to go down to the beach this morning with the girls like I normally would, but with the excitement of staying up through the early hours to share "Princess" with my fans for the first time and the anticipation of my first big release party tonight, it's been easy to forget the sand and sea and replace it with glitz and glam just this once.

Take each day as it comes and make sure to enjoy every second, my lawyer told me when I signed my record deal. Well, that's exactly what I'm here to do.

Enjoy. Every. Second.

And I deserve to. It took so long to find a record label that truly understands me, that vibes with my style and recognizes me for the dedicated artist I am without taking advantage of my prior naïveté. So much so that I almost lost hope my work would ever get this attention. But now, as I step out of the Sprinter onto the baby-pink carpet and smile up at five hundred awestruck fans, happiness fills me until I'm warm like the sun.

This party's a celebration of all the crap I went through to get here—and all the doors that are about to open up for me, with or without *his* help. I'm doing this on my own.

And *god*, I hope he sees me win.

I bask in the buzz from the crowd lining the entrance, pausing to take pictures and give out hugs.

"Too much time on the fans, Princess," Kimi murmurs beside me as I lean in for another selfie with one of the screaming girls. "Remember, we've got to stick to schedule. This is a big night for you so let's be sure to stay on track."

"Oh my god, I love you so much! I've been following you for years!" a girl gushes as I sign her poster, and, *seriously*, how could anyone say there's such a thing as spending too much time on the fans?

My fans are why I'm here tonight—the reason any of us are here, Kimi included. They're the ones who listen to my story through my songs, who sing along with my lyrics, and genuinely *care* about the work I put out into the world. According to the rules set by my manager, I'm supposed to simply smile and walk by them as if that doesn't even matter to me? As if they don't matter to me?

Screw that. I love these people.

"Hey! Thanks so much for coming!" I lean in for a photo with another fan.

Kimi gives a deep sigh and stares pointedly to hurry me along, but it's her job to do that. Deep down, she knows how much this moment means to me.

People think that in Hollywood you're handed everything on a plate, and everything is glitz and glamour without any hardships, but when you've fought for your voice like I have, you know that couldn't be further from the truth. And even if, like me, you work hard, put in the hours, and sacrifice your whole entire comfort zone, at the end of the day, if luck isn't on your side, you're left in the dark while someone else takes the spotlight. Not to mention, I have zero nepotism as an advantage; I have gained my success completely on my own. Glittering moments like these—*screaming fans* like these—you can't take them for granted, and I never, ever would.

After all, in just one night, everything can go away.

"Princess! Why isn't your boyfriend with you?" a member of the press calls from behind his camera. His greedy expression tells me everything I need to know about him. He gets off on asking inappropriate personal questions at carpeted events in hopes of getting a viral-worthy reaction. *Not today.*

Maya grips my arm and leans in close. "You don't have to answer that," she whispers, and with one gentle tug she moves me on.

A twinge of heartache overtakes me for a second, and my smile drops.

But then I look up at the huge building in front of me, the area full of people who've turned out to celebrate my success, and I remind myself once again, this night is all *mine*. I'm not here because of him, and he's not by my side when I need him the most.

When I was eight years old and working as a wedding singer in Guam, I used to close my eyes and pretend I was singing to my own crowd. I wished every day for *this* life.

And now here I am, in a custom fucking Chanel dress, my name in shining lights, my own song blasting through the speakers for all of downtown Los Angeles to hear, and six-figure streams racking up on my new song in less than twenty-four hours.

What's a little *heartache* when I've put in so much hustle along the way?

I stride along the pink carpet with my head held high, smiling for every camera I pass. While the bustle of celebs and friends hurry me on from the VIP area, I wave at more fans. On my walk up to the press wall, I even do a little dance in time with the music, exactly how we planned.

In fact, it's better than I ever dreamed.

And that's exactly why I'm not prepared when my eyes lock with his across the crowded carpet.

Through the VIP crowd, amid all the pink shimmering lights, I catch a blood-pumping flash of ocean blue. I'd recognize those eyes anywhere. They pull me back to him like the tide every time.

"Princess! Princess!"

"Princess, over here!"

Photographers call out around me, and my body works on autopilot as I pose and flash my teeth, that *perfect* Hollywood smile. *He* knows it's not real. He's one of the few people in this sequin-and-silicone world who's seen the girl I am under the surface, behind closed doors. He knows me—the real me.

The corner of his lips twitch into an almost grin as his eyes slide over me from head to toe, making my skin burn hot with the memory of his touch.

And then, just as I'm imagining the possibility that he got my invitation and came back for *me*, a manicured hand lands on his shoulder and the stunning brunette beside him whispers something in his ear. I had always imagined that we would celebrate these moments together, like we had fantasized about so many times.

All that hot blood pumping through me immediately runs cold.

What is he doing here anyway?

And why the hell did he bring *another girl*? We were never the kind of people to hurt each other on purpose.

"Princess! I love your dress!"

"Princess! Smile this way for me!"

"Princess! Congratulations on the new song—how does it feel to be back?"

With adrenaline powering fast through my veins, I pull my eyes away from them and make the choice to stand tall for the ones who *really* matter.

"How does it feel?" I repeat the question back. "It feels like the first step on a brand-new journey. A move in the right direction."

Away from him, I remind myself.

Because that's the thing about Hollywood. Beneath all the glitter, there's a whole lot of glue: the secrets that bind people together; the betrayals that make heartache stick inside you. It's true you have to work hard to make it here. But with the right people by your side, you can build your own fresh start. As long as there's love—and maybe a little bit of luck—there's always, *always* hope.

I smile at the crowd, and this time, it's from the heart.

Because, yes, I am the Princess. Just like my song.

This is my fuckin' life and I'm going to fuckin' live it.

2

Two hours before the pink carpet

The final rays of sunlight sting my eyes as I pose against the wall of the balcony for Maya. Behind us, the shimmering ocean rolls over the California sand, and I close my eyes and tilt my chin up to breathe in the air that reminds me of home.

"Perfect! Hold that pose!" Maya instructs.

Valerie's pouring drinks for us inside, and I hear the *clink* of ice hitting glass right as the phone camera snaps another shot. There's still a half hour left until the car—sorry, *Sprinter*—arrives to sweep us off to Hollywood for tonight's event. I asked for some alone time with my girls before the big night out. There's something about hearing our laughter as the waves crash against the shore that makes it easy to remember there's a wide-open world of possibility out there, and we're lucky to have found ourselves living in this reality. And, sure, pregaming in an oceanfront Malibu beach house was half the reason I rented this place for my release weekend anyway.

"Hot!" Maya hypes me up with a little dance as she steps forward, the sun hitting her long auburn hair and making her green eyes really pop. "Seriously, this Chanel dress was made for golden hour."

"This dress was made for *me*," I say proudly, catching my reflection in the sliding glass doors as I walk over to see the photo. Each tiny pink crystal glints as I move, highlighting my petite curves and sun-kissed tan.

"See? *Ah-mazing*." Maya taps to zoom in on the image. She just walked at Paris Fashion Week, and her modeling career is absolutely taking off. Her unique features make her fascinating to look at, and her charisma is next-level. She's a natural in front of the camera and she always gets the best angles. "Shit, they should hire me to work behind the camera too."

"Maybe we should hire you to be our personal Instagram photographer," I tease.

"As if! This is *Maya Brown*—honey, people should be taking pictures of *her*." Valerie laughs as she steps onto the balcony and hands each of us a drink.

"Of course you would have your own custom ice cubes!" Maya dips a red-painted stiletto nail into the glass to tilt the huge block of ice with a *Princess* logo etched into it.

"Duh. Is there any other way to drink Don Julio Real than on the rocks—correction, a custom-made rock?"

"We are Hollywood royalty after all," Valerie adds as she snaps a picture of her drink. "Anyway, can we take some more photos? We've got a stunning Malibu beach house here and I need something cute to put on my Instagram!"

A few minutes later, when we walk back into the house, our stylists are just leaving. When my makeup artist, Angel, catches sight of us, his eyes pop with a huge smile.

"Wow! You guys look so gorgeous!"

"Couldn't have done it without you," I remind him, and he swats the compliment away with a high-pitched laugh.

"Are you bringing dates tonight?"

"No way—"

"Hell, no—"

"No, thank you."

Valerie, Maya, and I scrunch up our noses at each other as we answer in sync. Then, at Angel's stunned expression, we burst out laughing.

"We're *so* over guys," Val explains.

With a nod, Maya adds, "They're always trippin'. We have no time for them."

Angel's eyes land on me. "Who needs a date when you're all so damn cool on your own?"

"Right?" I take a sip of my drink as I pass the huge island in the center of the kitchen.

"She's the fuckin' *Princess*," Val says with a pout.

"Guys need to step up their game and figure out how to treat us first. It's like, we're not here to teach you—you should already *know*." I shrug. "It's pretty simple."

"Exactly." Angel smiles. "Okay, I'm gonna leave you girls to it. Have the *best* night, and congrats again, Princess!"

"Thanks, Angel. Love you."

In the lounge, Maya's hooked her phone up to the speakers and put her playlist on loud. She's dancing with Val for her Instagram story and tugs me by the arm to join in. Val is the ultimate it-girl—her classy but modern vibe screams old money, and she's become such a trendsetter online. Me, Val, and Maya are the ultimate trio.

"Oh my god, did you see Blake's post earlier?" Val asks as she scrolls back through her feed. "He was training—here, look!" Finding the photo, she flips her phone around for us to see. The guy onscreen is *built*, posing topless in his gym shorts in front of a locker-room mirror.

"He's *so* hot," Maya and I say together, and Maya practically drools as she zooms in on the image.

"Is he single?" she asks.

I push her shoulder playfully. "Throwback to, like, five seconds ago. We have no time for guys, remember . . . ?"

"Hey, how's it going in here?" a deep male voice interrupts.

We turn to find my other manager, Wayne, looking fresh in a dark suit, pocketing his cell phone as he walks into the kitchen. He's the other half of my management team, and even though he's gorgeous and has the perfect temperament, as well as a successful roster of the hottest stars for at least a decade, he's strictly off-limits as an option to any of us. But that doesn't stop the girls from whistling as they step up to greet him.

"It's not like you to be looking all polished and smart, Wayne." Maya rubs a hand over his shaved head.

"You're kidding, right?" It's rare to see him looking anything but.

"He even went for the good cologne too," Val teases. "You and Kimi got a hot 'business meeting' after the party or something?"

Wayne shakes his head with a tight jaw. He hates it when we tease him about Kimi. The two of them are so over the top with their professionalism it's like nothing can ruffle their feathers.

Ignoring the question, he asks with a sigh, "Are we ready?"

"Nope." Valerie hands him one of the glasses waiting on the island. "Here's your drink."

"Thanks." He takes a swig then twists an arm to glance at his Apple Watch.

"You're behind, Wayne," I say. "It's about to be a crazy night."

"*I'm* ready," he corrects me. "What do you have left to do?"

"Well, I need to use the bathroom," Maya answers for me, dabbing at her red lips, which have faded a little from sipping her drink.

"I'll come with."

"I'm uploading that story to Instagram!" Val calls as we walk off.

"Don't forget to tag Chanel!" I call back, pointing at my dress.

The bathroom's as luxe as the rest of the house. I lean in front of the enormous mirror to check my makeup. My hair looks perfect, crimped blonde extensions piled high on my head and a crystal tiara perched delicately on top. Sparkling lips, dewy with gloss, pop as I pout at my reflection, and with a flutter of my long lashes I know I'm ready for my big moment.

"Is Jessie coming tonight?" Maya asks.

"Yeah. She finished her finals yesterday so she's flying down from San Francisco. She'll be here in time for the after-party. I have a driver picking her up from LAX."

"Love that girl," Maya says, popping her lips as well. "Can't wait to hang out with her later."

I love her too. I've been best friends with Jessie since we were four years old. We met in kindergarten, and though our lives took totally different paths after I left Guam—she's studying to be a biologist and likes to stay out of the spotlight—we both ended up here in California. After eighteen years, I still talk to her every day. She's the one person who gets where I'm from and how hard this whole world can be. She's the one person I can truly trust in this chaotic life I have now.

"Who needs fair-weather friends when I've got you three, solid as a fucking rock, right?" I say as Maya hitches her black bodycon dress up to adjust her panties.

"Exactly. Ride or die, babe."

I notice the unmistakable flash of red silk and hide a smile. If there's one thing I've learned from nights out with Maya Brown, it's that she only wears *those* panties—the superhot Agent Provocateur ones, silky red with delicate lace detailing—when she's planning to get fucked so good the story alone will leave us all red in the face.

No time for guys, my ass . . .

I'm about to make a joke and ask who the lucky man is when Maya finishes adjusting her dress and turns to look at me, her eyes suddenly serious. "Princess, I know this is a really big, important night for you and you're playing it cool, but how are you really feeling . . . about John?" she asks.

My throat dries up. "I'm doing okay." I look down as I run a finger across the edge of the marble countertop. "I love when you guys are here and we can all be together. I'm trying, you know, to be okay?"

Maya nods, still watching me closely.

"And at least he and I don't hate each other," I continue. "It's more like this voice inside my head saying, *Damn, did I make a mistake and fuck this up so bad . . . is this going to be the biggest regret of your life?* It's just that kind of thing on a loop at the moment. I wish it would go away, but it's a little harder to forget about it when I'm alone."

Maya reaches out to stroke my arm. "I get it, but you didn't fuck it up. He did," she says. "That's why my motto is always fuck it and move on."

I chuckle with her. "Yep, we've always been the same."

And we have. Usually my bounce-back game is pretty solid. This is the first time in my life I've ever felt this way about a guy. Maybe I never knew real love before him—but now I'm learning heartache too. It's a constant back-of-the-mind sadness I can't shake, a creeping sense of loneliness reminding me that this time it's for real and we won't be getting back together. I would be lying if I said I didn't think about him multiple times a day. Even the smallest of things remind me of him. Maybe he's the one who got away, and I'll smile and pretend like that doesn't even matter anymore. It's for the best . . . isn't it?

But I don't want to let anyone else know the dark thoughts clouding my head. At least not tonight. People only see what they want to see, and right now, from the outside looking in, my success should be the only thing that matters.

If only it was that simple.

"I don't know what's going on with me."

Maya reaches out for a hug. Before she can speak, a loud knock steals our attention.

"Princess?" Wayne's voice sounds through the door. "Security called. The cars are here."

"Hey," Maya whispers, flashing me a smile as she pulls back. "You got this, okay? Fuck *him*. This is *your* night, and you deserve to enjoy every goddamn second."

She says it with so much power I believe it in my heart.

Outside, we find Kimi giving instructions to the driver. Behind it, two more black cars hold our security team and another car waits for Wayne at the end of the sweeping driveway.

"All right," he says before the three of us get in the back. "Kimi's taking you to the release party so I'll go on ahead and do a walk-through of the club, check everything's good for later tonight."

"Thanks, Wayne."

He smiles back at me, dark eyes shining with pride. "You look great, Princess."

"So do you, Wayne!" Val calls from inside the car.

"It's never-ending." Wayne sighs wearily. "I'll see you later, okay?"

"Sure." I grin. "Can't wait."

Inside the Sprinter, I ease carefully into the seat so as not to ruin my outfit.

"All good?" Maya checks one final time.

Staring around at the pink star lights on the ceiling and tequila and champagne bottles lined up in ice buckets up front, I'm stupidly happy. This is fucking sick. I'm an island girl about to head out to my release party in Hollywood, living the dream in the spotlight, making a career doing what I love the most, and I've got my best girls by my side. And he's already in the rearview mirror.

I'm doing okay. I'm trying hard. I'm not letting anything hold me back.

"Better than good," I say, squeezing Maya's hand. "I'm great. It's *go time!*"

Two hours later, when we pull up in front of Delilah, the club booked for the after-party, it looks like things are already crazy busy. Crowds of fans wait on Santa Monica Boulevard to greet us, and as our car pulls up out front, I notice the long line of people waiting to get inside too. We booked the whole venue, exclusive access only, so unless any of their names are on the VIP guest list or they have promoter connections, they won't be getting past security tonight.

"Look—Princess!"

The people outside the club form a sea of pink, wearing T-shirts and hoodies with the tiara logo and the word *Princess* printed across the front—my first batch of merch for the release.

"Oh my god! That's so cute!" I clutch my heart, wishing I could go out there and take photos with each and every one of them. But as security ushers the group of fans back and Wayne appears at the window, I already know that won't be an option.

"Hey, girls," he says as he slides open the door. Immediately, the fans' screams pierce the air, making it difficult to hear his next words. "How was the release party?"

"Fucking incredible," Valerie answers, her voice barely audible, and when Wayne looks to Kimi for confirmation, she nods.

"It went really well. The press couldn't get enough of her. Speaking of . . ."

Cameras flash through every window as more paparazzi crowd the car.

"Sounds great." Wayne grins at me. "Now, let's get to the real party, right?"

"Tequila, baby!" Maya hoots as she steps out, and the fans erupt even louder.

"Photos first!" Kimi calls as we get out of the car.

Like always, we stand together and hold our heads high for a few shots, the three of us linking arms as we pose for the nonstop flash of camera lights.

All the screaming faces are a thrill to see, and I lift my hand in a wave as I pass them by, but with security packed so tight up against us and Wayne and Kimi moving at such a fast pace, there's no time to even pause for a selfie.

Inside the club, the atmosphere's electric, bodies grinding on the dance floor and groups gathered at the bar. "Princess" plays loudly through the speakers when the DJ announces my arrival, and eyes follow us from every corner as security escorts us through the venue.

"Shit, look at this décor!" Val points up at the ceiling of the main room where hundreds of enormous pink balloons filled with gold glitter float through the smoke-filled air on thick ribbons. Each one catches the light from the dance floor and glows as if it's luminescent.

"And the screens!" Maya adds in excitement. The massive LEDs are playing rolling clips from the visualizer we put out for the song. *Too* fucking cool.

"This party is fucking insane!" I can't stop grinning.

Kimi smiles. "You know we got you."

We make our way to our table, and I cheer when I see the bottle servers lined up holding champagne bottles and Real with sparklers that fizzle and flare like bright streams of starry light.

The area's been roped off just for us, and even though everyone got in here by invitation only, there's still a crowd of people dancing around the ropes and pushing forward in the hope of catching my eye and starting a conversation. But with security guarding the table from any unwanted guests, only one person steals my attention for real. As Jessie stands up from her seat, eyes wide with amazement and looking a little out of her depth already, Maya and I let out squeals and rush forward, pulling her into a hug.

"You made it!"

"Wouldn't have missed it for the world," she shouts over the thump of music as she wraps her arms around my neck. "Seriously, Princess, this is the coolest night of my life, and it's not even *my* night!" She leans over to hug Maya too. "It's crazy, right?"

"I love this!" Maya grabs at Jessie's pastel-blue halter dress in approval.

"Thanks!"

It's clear from her rosy cheeks that Jessie's flattered. I guess it's not every day a biology student who spends all week in a lab coat gets complimented on her wardrobe by an international supermodel. This lifestyle's wild, and even though by ridiculous Hollywood standards Jessie shouldn't fit in, she somehow just *does*. She's the type of person who can adapt to any situation; she mixes in so fast I always tell her it's her superpower. Not only is she such a girl's girl, but she also has a heart of pure gold and is effortlessly gorgeous and doesn't realize it.

"Jessie!" From behind us, Valerie drops her arms over our shoulders. "Glad you could make it, girl! And, hey, congrats on finishing your finals! I'd buy you a drink, but . . ." She points to the center of the table where there are endless bottles of every kind of liquor we could need, plus champagne.

"Wow! So many people are here tonight!" Maya says as we take our seats. "Princess, I've got a really good feeling about this song."

"Me too! I can't stop listening to it," Jessie adds. "Everyone from home is talking about it too."

I'm giddy as I take in the packed room. It's so nice that all these friends showed up for the event. *Friends.* Should I really call them that? To be honest, a lot of these people are more like acquaintances. I recognize faces everywhere I look, but I can't help but wonder how many of them *really* came tonight to celebrate me.

Hollywood's like a high school cafeteria, with a designated table for each little clique. Except instead of being separated into groups of jocks and preps and freshmen and nerds, there are only two tables around here: the popular group and the people outside of that group. And there's always a ringleader who decides who's in and who's out.

"Do you want a drink, babe?" Maya asks, pointing to the server as he reaches for the tequila.

"Sure, thanks." I'm mesmerized by the dancing crowd.

Tonight, *we're* sitting on the throne of popularity, and everyone in LA knows the popular group runs the show.

And I'll always stick with my girls. We're tight. We keep each other close because we know we can trust each other completely. From what

I've seen, despite all the perfectly timed paparazzi shots of coffee dates and shopping trips, a lot of celebrity "BFFs" are just as fake as most of the boobs in this room tonight. But with Jessie, Val, and Maya, I never have to worry about drama or gossip. Kimi may try to warn me otherwise, but I love my girls and trust them with my life.

As the girls chat loudly and laugh around me and the club lights flash *pink, purple, blue, red,* my phone vibrates with another message. Hundreds of notifications crowd the screen already, but this one steals my attention. Call it intuition, but I grab my phone instantly.

Win: Hey

Before I can type a reply, another message pops up.

Win: You look good tonight

3

Me: Where are you?

I crane my neck to look around at the other tables, knowing Win won't be on the dance floor. He's too cool for that. Like, *way* too cool.

Win: I'm in the back

There's a set of double doors in the far corner of the club, guarded by security and kind of hidden behind the swarm of dancing bodies. Of course he's in the back. I take a sip of tequila before sending my reply.

Me: I'll come say hi

Win: No rush

Win: I'll send security to escort you

Me: In a minute . . . I'll find my way

"Girl." Maya's hand lands on my shoulder. "Who are you texting?" She narrows her eyes. "Don't tell me it's John."

"Nah." I smile as I put the phone down. "It's Win."

She's clearly impressed, as her red lips form a little circle as she says, "Oh . . ."

He doesn't need any more introduction. People have deep respect for Win around here. Win's *untouchable*. A successful investor, he always looks smart and sharp. I love being out with him and seeing the way the room clings to his every word. In the time I've known him, Win's helped generate so much business for me. I think of him as a friend, but there's always an air of mystery around him too. My curiosity makes me really want to solve it.

Anyway, everyone here knows that when Win speaks, you stop and listen.

Or, if you're into suave guys in their late twenties, you stop and *drool*. And even if you're not, I've never come across anyone who's immune to his charm.

"I wanna dance!" Valerie stands and smooths down her tight white dress. "Come on! I didn't come out looking this hot just to sit at a table all night. Let's celebrate!"

"Amen, sister." Maya jumps up, too, and I laugh with Jessie as we join them.

The thump of the bass vibrates up from the dance floor and straight through my sparkly heels. With security standing close by, we party with everyone else, throwing our hands up in time with the music and singing extra loud when Maya requests our favorite song. We dance with old friends and greet new faces under the flash of the club lights, grinding and swaying, the haze of stage smoke pouring over us before the DJ releases a stream of glittering confetti into the air.

After a few songs, one of the black-suited security guys taps me on the shoulder and directs me over to the double doors at the back of the club.

"Where are you going?" Val shouts above the music.

I point to the doors. "I'll be back—I'm gonna say hi to Win!"

The guys escort me through the crowd to another set of doors guarded by more security. They push them open onto a whole other party in an almost identical back room. The dance floor vibrates with music too.

"Oh, look! Is that Princess?" someone asks as we walk by.

In the center of the room, Win, dressed in an immaculately tailored suit, lounges at his regular table. His brown hair is pristine as always, his skin glowing, and his jawline sharp. Just looking at him makes my knees shake a bit, but I straighten my back and smile. Bottles of expensive alcohol surround him and his friends, and he's deep in conversation with another important-looking guy when we approach. His eyes drift, and when he sees me, Win stops his sentence short and stands up, a smile breaking as he pushes off of the booth and walks over.

"Princess! Happy release day, superstar. You're shining tonight. I saw all the press coverage online."

I don't miss the way everyone's eyes follow us. The girls hanging around Win try to look casual as they move to stay in his orbit but he's too much of a gentleman to react, which only makes them want him more. Or maybe he's already taken . . . I don't actually know if he's dating anyone. If he is, she must match his energy—probably comes from the same kind of successful family, the same kind of lifestyle. When it comes to a life partner he wouldn't have it any other way, I'm sure. I wonder for a brief moment if I match his energy . . .

"Thank you, Win." He leans in for a hug. He's so tall, and his broad shoulders are huge inside the suit jacket, so I'm swamped by his big arms until he pulls back. "Are you having a good night?"

Win looks down at my dress, approval in his dark eyes as he says, "Yeah, it's going great. I invited a few friends, hope you don't mind. They're all people you should get to know." I made sure Kimi and Wayne would have Win situated tonight. I was so happy when he said he'd come; I wanted to make sure he was impressed. He reaches out to lift a shot of what looks like tequila from a tray one of the bottle servers is holding and hands the glass to me, his Rolex glinting gold against his tanned arm where his sleeve pulls up a little.

"Of course." I glance at his busy table, at the people standing around it. I know he could tell me the name of each and every person in here if I asked.

"Actually, I'm glad you came to see me." He places a huge hand on my shoulder and guides me forward, over to the guy he was talking to before. "Last time we spoke, I told you about Zack, an old friend of mine?"

"Yeah! I didn't realize he'd be here tonight."

"Well, let me introduce you. He's a great guy. We'll set a meeting to discuss venture ideas, see where it leads."

As he introduces us, I'm amazed at how fast he works. It was only yesterday, while we were facetiming before the midnight release, that Win mentioned he wanted to connect me with Zack for potential future opportunities.

If only more people in this industry were like Win.

While Zack and I exchange details, Win sends a group of glamorous women on their way, acknowledging each with a flattering compliment or a dazzling smile. He knows how to make women swoon but manages to keep a polite boundary at the same time.

"I need to head back now," I say. "But thank you so much for coming, guys. Hit me up tomorrow."

"Anytime, Princess." Win shrugs as if it's no big deal. We hug again before I leave, and he says with a handsome grin, "Go enjoy your big night. You earned it."

Sure did.

Jessie and Val are still on the dance floor when I get back, and they pull me in to party hard for another half hour. The place is packed with more bodies now, and the music is much faster. I recognize a lot of faces amid the flashing lights. My glam team, who promised they'd show up, are partying, enjoying the bottles of champagne and tequila too. Angel waves at me when I meet his eye.

"Great party, Princess!" a voice calls from behind me.

"Congratulations on the release!" another shouts as we dance, but they don't come over.

Mostly, everyone sticks by the people they came with, having a great time in their own little bubbles. I've gotten used to it. That's Hollywood. It's one of the reasons your team becomes your closest friends, your own little bubble to float through it all with.

"Hey!" Jessie grips my arm while we dance and points to a darkened corner of the dance floor. "Check it out."

I follow her gaze and glimpse a couple making out against the wall, a blond head of hair buried deep in the neck of a girl with long auburn curls. A girl whose leg lifts off the ground when the guy grips the top of her thigh so I see a flash of red-soled heels as the strobe lights pass over them. A girl who digs her red-painted stiletto nails into the guy's hair as she pulls his mouth back to hers.

A girl I'd recognize anywhere, even when she's trying not to be seen.

"Maya's getting laid tonight," Valerie shouts across the dance floor at me, pointing in their direction with a giggle.

"Scandalous." I laugh back, words arriving breathlessly.

I kind of wish I had someone special to share tonight with, and I can't help but wonder if John hadn't shown up with that other girl would something have happened between us? I know we broke up for good reasons, but I can't help feeling like there's a part of me missing without him. Our chemistry is still undeniable and even through the tension my mind and body always gravitate toward him. My stream of thoughts breaks as Maxi—a basketball player who took me on a date forever ago—comes up to say hi. He's tall and cute in a lanky kind of way, and not cocky like most athletes. *Long and hot like a summer's day, I'll bet*, Maya said at the time. Maxi is gorgeous and sweet and all, but . . . I don't know. It just wasn't the right time, or maybe it was too hard to align our schedules, but we kind of fizzled. That seems to happen with everyone—except John. And although maybe we're better apart, I miss him so much.

"We should grab dinner sometime to celebrate and catch up. It's been too long," Maxi says over the music.

Part of me hopes John can see us. I almost lean in just to put on a show in case he's watching, but that wouldn't be fair to Maxi.

"I'd love to catch up—" I hesitate, knowing deep down I have no interest in going out with anyone right now. My wounds from John haven't healed yet. "But I don't want to give you the wrong impression, Maxi. I'm not looking to see anyone right now. You're great, and I'm sure you could have your pick of any girl in here tonight," I tell him, meaning it.

He seems surprised and impressed by my response. "Thank you for being honest. If only more people were like you." His smile and sincerity make me feel a little more guilty, but proud of myself. I'm going to stay true to who I am, no matter what.

With a slightly awkward good-bye, Maxi leaves us to dance and makes his way to a sexy brunette who had been staring at him during our conversation.

I glide my attention over face after face as I move to the music, but there's too much alcohol swimming in my brain for me to give a damn about anything other than dancing, swaying, and moving with my best friends.

I don't know how much time passes but we eventually return to the table a little more than tipsy. There's so much happening around us, so many people pushing to get in, that Wayne and Kimi are having to approve guests and kick out any randoms. I know everyone sitting at our table, but not very well. Most of them are only acquaintances who conveniently like to hang out whenever my career is considered "hot." Skimming over them as we approach, I'm trying to remind myself of their names and how we met, when my heart stops dead in my chest.

What?

I notice the pretty brunette first, and I recognize her from some-where, but . . . *where*? I'm searching for the answer when it appears right next to her, in the set of blue eyes already staring back.

Brown hair.

Lazy yet intoxicating smile.

Short stubble on the jaw I've kissed maybe a thousand times.

My pulse comes alive again, and beneath my rib cage, it's *thumping*.

"What the hell is he doing at our table?" Val hisses.

"Oh man." Jessie groans under her breath when she sees him.

I pull myself together and form my expression into a perfect, happy mask. My girls are protective of me when it comes to anyone, but espe-cially John. They don't want to see me in such a low place again, and I can't blame them, but I can't help it. My self-preservation disappears when he's around.

"Hey." I try my hardest to stay unfazed as I slide into my seat beside them.

I invited him, but with everything that's happened between us and after not seeing him for nearly a month, I didn't think he'd actually come.

"Hi, Princess! Love the party!" The girl beams at me.

John's staring at his drink as if it's the most interesting thing in the world. I know him so well—tension so obvious in his shoulders, the vein in his neck that's highlighted by the bright moving lights. His fingers grip the glass but he's trying to seem detached.

"Hey," I say a little louder, and his eyes shine electric as he lifts his chin in greeting beside me. "Thanks for coming, John."

This pulls him out of his thoughts. "Great to see you, Princess. Congratulations on the release. I'm so happy for you."

Is it just me or does he sound a little sad? But that doesn't make sense.

I'm over it.

We're over it.

Princess, you liar.

"Thanks." I hold my smile so he won't see the questions forming behind my eyes. So many freaking questions. Like how's he been? Has he been happy? Does he miss me at all? Is this his new girlfriend?

The brunette smiles up at him, a twinkle in her dark eyes, and it's like a pinch straight to my heart. John's classic cute, like the guy everyone crushes on in high school, but he's so chill and in his own zone he probably isn't even aware of her puppy-dog stare, lovestruck and smitten, beside him. I wonder if that's how I used to look around him.

God, I hope not.

"Sorry," I say quickly, reaching across to place a hand on her arm. "I should've asked your name. Princess."

"Emma." She seems to relax. "It's great to meet you. I love your new song, I've been playing it on repeat. It's so cool to be here. Seriously, *amazing* party."

"Thanks. I *love* your hair. Is it all natural?"

She nods, her eyes brightening even more from my compliment. I feel a little sorry for her. She seems too naïve for this kind of place. As much as I hate that she's with him, I never want to be the type of girl who's mean to other girls over a boy, not even the love of my life.

"Hey, if you pull this piece back"—I reach to move the loose curl covering her brow—"it really makes your eyes pop."

Emma catches the strand when I let go and tests it out for herself, checking her hair out in the front camera of her cell phone. The whole time I'm aware of John's warm breath on my cheek, the heat of his chest radiating from his shirt where I lean across his body.

"Oh my god! It looks so good, thank you!" She's giddy and it makes me feel bad for the way I want her to move away from John. Nothing against her; I can't help it.

I move my attention back to John, sensing his hesitation as I straighten up. "She's so pretty," I say only loud enough for him to hear.

He scrubs a hand across his jaw. "Um, yeah. Right," he says quietly, clearly not comfortable. I'm not exactly comfortable, either, so I can't find it within myself to sympathize with him. He brought her here, not me.

"Emma and I are just friends," John says, making sure she and everyone around us can hear him. Emma looks a little disappointed, but I'd be lying if I said it didn't make me feel good to have him publicly declare it like that.

"I didn't ask," I say as casually as I can manage. Our playful sarcastic banter has always been something I loved about our dynamic.

"I know, but I wanted to make sure you knew before you got the wrong idea," he practically whispers in my ear, sending a wave of electricity through me.

I lean back, pushing at his shoulder, hoping he can't read my face and see how affected I am. It's way, way too early in the night to get distracted by him.

I meet Val's eye across the table. She smirks into her glass of tequila, living for the drama but ready to pounce on him if he makes one wrong move.

Thankfully, Jessie saves us from any painful small talk as she dives into a story about her week and the nightmare she had studying for her finals. It's a relief to have the distraction of something I actually care about. Val joins in, too, and pretty soon we're sucked into conversation about flying first class and Val's dad's obsession with private jets. I know Jessie can't relate—most people can't—but she gives it her best shot anyway, asking all the right questions the way she always knows how to. If comfort was a person, it would be Jessie.

I'm lost, trying so hard to concentrate on Val's story above the music, when I feel the touch of cold glass against my fingers. I look up to find John handing me a drink. He pauses for a moment after I take it, his thumb pressed against the pulse point of my wrist. He knows exactly what he's doing. He doesn't say anything, just keeps on refilling the others' glasses.

But he gave me *mine* first . . .

He leans in close a few minutes later, while I'm busy taking a sip, attempting to let the sweet burn of the drink take over and trying not to get too deep into thinking about our history.

"I would never bring another girl to your release party, Princess. I hope you know that," he murmurs. "And you know how it is. She knows someone I know, and she's really a fan of yours so I said I'd bring her. She has a lot of followers, too, so her posting will be good for the song."

I swallow and nod. *Is he wearing the cologne I bought him?* Those piercing blue eyes watch me as if he's waiting for some sort of signal— the slightest reaction.

"She seems nice, and it's none of my business who you date, but thanks for the info," I shoot back, fighting an internal battle to move away so I don't breathe in the familiar scent or move closer to get more of it.

He holds my stare for a second too long before he downs the rest of his tequila. The urge to tell him to slow down on the drinks so early in the night is strong but my will is stronger, for once.

I turn to Jessie.

"So, where'd you get this dress again?" I ask, admiring the blue chiffon.

Although Jessie answers, all I can focus on is my pulse *thump, thump, thumpi*ng again inside my chest. Because John's fingertips drift lightly across my shoulder as he moves his hand away.

And I know for damned sure he didn't do it accidentally.

What does this mean?

4

For the rest of the night I feel John's gaze on me everywhere I go. On the dance floor his eyes slide like warm hands over my body. At the table he's a dark shadow in the corner of my eye. In conversation with other people I overhear his one-word answers and know without even having to look that he's watching me.

But we barely speak, and I busy myself enjoying my time with my girls. "Why's that Emma girl waiting in line for the bathroom?" Val says with a short laugh as we approach the restrooms later on.

I'm giddy on my high heels, the bass thumping through my bones.

"Emma?" I tug her out of the long line of girls waiting to get in and pull her with us to the bathroom door. "We don't wait in line. Not tonight, come with me." Inside, the bathroom's crowded, chaos and commotion everywhere as girls wait around to use the stalls and stand in groups at the sinks reapplying their makeup. A couple of pretty blondes I don't recognize are gossiping by the hand dryers, and they gasp, their eyes going wide, when we walk in. "I fucking love your new song, Princess!" one of them slurs, clearly drunk. Her eyes are distant and bloodshot.

"Thanks!" I press my lips together in a polite smile as we push through.

"We should get the big stall." Val directs Jessie to the end of the row and reaches out to hold my hand.

"There's someone in there, Val," Jessie says.

"Hurry it up!" Valerie calls through the door and pounds her fists on the wood, making another girl dart away as if she just remembered she didn't need to use the bathroom after all. "Period and a white dress out here—there are, like, eight more seconds until you're responsible for a crime against my dignity!"

I laugh out loud. Val's unhinged when she's drunk. And it's a bit worrying how frequently it's happening these days. But tonight isn't the time.

"Emma!"

We all turn around at the sound of her name. When Emma sees the tall girl standing behind us, her eyes light up over a smile.

"Hey! I was looking for you!" Emma says.

"This is such a sick party, Princess." The stranger compliments me as she throws her arms around Emma in a tight hug, beaming at me over Emma's shoulder. Her eyes are dark, her pupils as wide as saucers beneath her glittery gold eyeshadow. I don't know who she is or how she got on the guest list, but Emma dives into excited gossip with her, as club girls usually do, talking shit about some promoter dinner she went to at Tao, while beside us, the door to the big stall opens.

"Finally!" Val grabs Jessie's hand, and Jessie grabs mine. "Come on, Emma!" she calls over her shoulder as we step in, heels *click-clack*ing on the shiny tile.

Emma and her friend follow us inside, locking the door behind them. While Jessie helps Val out on the other side of the stall, I touch up my makeup in the mirror, adding another layer of glistening coconut-flavored lip gloss. In the reflection, I see the tall girl reach into her bra and pull out a small plastic baggie containing what looks like white powder.

"My treat." She giggles and leans on the door to steady herself as she sways on her stilettos. "Take as much as you want, Em."

"You're the best." Emma takes the baggie from her.

Capping my lip gloss, I watch in the mirror as she pours some of the powder onto the back of her hand.

Everyone has a vice and sweet Emma is no exception.

Emma lifts her hand, one finger from the other hand pushed against one nostril, wincing as she sniffs in the powder. Behind her, the other girl moves over to Jessie and Val, her voice way too loud for the enclosed space. Emma's messy, that much I can already tell. Maybe I shouldn't have been so gracious to her after all, and the idea of the potential influence she could have on John makes my stomach twist.

"Oh fuck! I just realized, you're Valerie Sinclair! *Valerie Sinclair!*" The tall girl wipes her nose with her thumb a couple of times, making sure there's no trace of anything, shaking her head in wide-eyed disbelief. "Your family owns, like, half the hotels in the world!"

"Do we know each other?" Val asks, one eyebrow raised.

Instead of replying, the girl moves to the sink, bumping Jessie's shoulder and almost knocking her off balance in the process.

"Hey, watch it!" Val shouts.

Instead of apologizing, Emma's friend simply shrugs and changes direction, heading straight toward me and stopping when her face is inches from mine.

"Babe, seriously, you gotta get it together," Val warns her.

She's so high she barely notices.

"Hey," Emma says. "Sure you don't want some?" She holds up a bump of powder in the dip of her long pinkie fingernail.

"Ooh! Good idea, Em, share it with the girls! Plenty more where that came from." Her friend trips over, and before I can reply, they're both dancing in the damn bathroom stall.

Val, Jessie, and I share a look with each other. It's normal to see shit like this, so I'm used to minding my business.

"Princess?" Emma asks again.

"No thanks, I'm cool," I say with a shake of my head.

"Girls? Valerie, you sure?" Her friend offers the baggie to us, but Val and Jessie turn it down too. I don't miss the way she keeps pressing Val—it's kind of weird.

Val glances at me before replying, "No thanks."

"Okay, then. I'm a little surprised, but whatever." She shrugs and looks at Emma. "More for you and me."

"Enjoy," Val mutters.

The pair keep dancing together, and without warning, a memory I tried to forget springs to the surface: the last time I danced with John. I wasn't high on coke obviously, but tipsy on alcohol after a night of partying. It was just the two of us, in a different club, a different world almost, out on a date, back when things were so different. Throughout the night, we stole kisses in the dark under the flashing lights.

Dancing close, almost every inch of our bodies touching. I turned around, feeling a little wild, and pushed my ass to the front of his trousers, placing his hands on my hips, knowing exactly how to tease him. Then, in time with the fast beat, I ground into him in the way I knew he loved, the way that would drive him crazy.

John's grip on my waist tightened. He groaned against my ear, his breath hot on my skin. His warm, slick tongue made a line down my neck and my knees nearly buckled. I didn't stop moving, feeling his desire growing. It ignited a fire inside me and made me burn for him. When the music changed and the DJ dropped a harder beat, I danced faster until John spun me around and placed his hand under my chin so I could look into his eyes. Bending close, he whispered, "Tonight, I'll pay you back for all this teasing."

"Yeah?" I groaned, my breath lost in my throat.

In response, his hand traced a path through the slit of my dress, sending delicious shivers down my spine.

"I'm going to kiss every inch of this," he said.

My pulse ramped higher and higher as he moved his hand up, this time tracing a path from my neck to my supple cleavage, ending where the dress began. "And this," he added.

"What else?" I continued to tease him, feeling the pull in the bottom of my belly, the wetness gathering in my panties.

Tilting his head, he placed a kiss in the crease of my neck. It was a light brush of his lips, but it held so much promise for what was to come. I shivered.

"God, you turn me on so much. It drives me fucking crazy." He rubbed the evidence of his arousal against me, and my breath hitched. Inside, pressure climbed. He drove me wild too. In bed with him, pleasure was all I knew; the rest of the world just melted away.

I squeezed my thighs to relieve some of the pressure. I was so wet for him, and I wished we weren't in a public place.

John chuckled when he saw me stop dancing. "Want this?" he teased.

Oh boy, this man can move . . .

"Yes," I gasped. "Yes."

He tugged on my hand and pulled me toward the club's exit. We'd barely made it to the door when he stopped suddenly, but before I could ask what was going on, he dragged me into a dark corner. There, his head dipped and his lips found mine.

Finally.

I tasted the tequila on his tongue as he claimed my mouth in a kiss so hungry and intense my knees almost gave way, especially when his hand curled around the back of my head in a dominant move, bringing me even closer to him. In response, I lifted my hands and ran my fingers through his hair, pulling a little, just the way he liked. When I moaned against his lips, John pulled away with a groan.

"Let's get the fuck home," he said.

"Hello?" A hand waves in front of my face. "Earth to Princess!" Val shouts.

I try to breathe through the flashback, which glows like fire in my blood. The memory of passion is tainted by the bitterness of our breakup, and I search for something, anything, else to focus on.

Whether I like it or not, there's a possibility that I'll spend the rest of my life distracted by thoughts of him. But I'm slowly getting over it. Every fire takes time to die, I remind myself. Embers of memories are just part of the process—a necessary transition. They'll fade eventually. I've got to deprive them of oxygen, that's all.

We're moving on.

"Let's get out of here," I say, unlocking the door and gesturing for Val and Jessie to follow. "I don't want to waste all night locked in a bathroom stall."

Or locked in a memory.

"See you later, Emma!" Jessie waves as we leave.

"I'll find you at the table!" she calls back.

Please don't.

Out on the dance floor, with the DJ hyping me up from the booth, spraying more pink confetti into the air and playing all my favorite songs, I don't have time to think too deeply about the past anyway, and I refuse to even give John one more glance.

Fuck white lines and blue eyes. All I can see is pink, gold, and glam.

The Next Morning

"Ugh, I feel dead."

Jessie's groan drags me out of a deep sleep. Her voice sounds croaky in my ear, and when my eyes flutter open onto a stream of bright morning sunlight—made only brighter by the white walls and bedsheets—I groan, too, and roll back under the covers.

"It's too early," I try to say, but my tongue feels rough like sandpaper, and with one blink of my eyes, I'm sinking underwater again into a wavy, head-thumping sleep.

It's the buzz of my cell phone that wakes me up next. It pulses on the table beside the bed, an irritating vibration in the back of my mind. I pull myself up and pat my hands over my face just to feel something that isn't *numb*.

"Who is it?" Valerie mumbles into the pillow on my other side, her voice groggy, while Jessie rubs her eyes awake and practically crawls out of bed.

I roll over and flip my phone, answering right away when I see the FaceTime request. "Maya? Where the fuck did you end up?" *Wow*, my voice sounds rough. But she looks rougher. Her hair's a mess and her makeup's smudged.

"What's the code for the gate?" she asks. "Come *on*, Princess, I'm standing out here on show for the entire fucking *street*."

"Code? Huh?"

"Why's the screen black?" Maya grumbles.

It's instinct. If someone calls when I'm just waking up or not ready to be seen yet, one finger automatically covers the camera.

"Because you really don't want to see me this early in the morning," I tell her as my mind catches up. Getting my thoughts more in order, I remember Wayne mentioned something about a code to get into the beach house. Apparently, it's in the guest book on the kitchen island.

"And all of fucking Malibu doesn't want to see me this early in the morning, either, babe! The code, Princess. What is it?"

"Ugh." I press my hand to my forehead to rub away the ache. "Give me a sec. I'll go find it."

"Thanks for the wake-up call, Maya," Val complains loud enough for Maya to hear as she gets out of bed too. "Some of us actually *need* our beauty sleep." But she's only joking.

Really, Val slept like a baby last night—literally asked me to sing her to sleep. It's her request at every sleepover we have. She loves listening to my voice and says it soothes her, which is cool because I'm used to people telling me to shut up. People used to make fun of me for singing around them when I was a kid. It made me so shy I only ever used to sing in the studio or when I was at work, and even then insecurity still occasionally plagued me.

Bodies aching, we all head into the kitchen together. I find the code for Maya and then hang up before stepping over to the refrigerator and pulling it open.

"Lord, save me if they don't have orange juice . . ." I cross my fingers but my prayers are answered. A huge glass bottle of orange juice sits inside, and I pull it out along with four bottles of sparkling water—one for each of us.

"I've got such a bad fucking hangover," Valerie groans, wrapping her robe around her body as she sinks, grumpy, onto the couch.

"Same here," Jessie agrees, dropping next to her.

"Don't even." I sigh.

We forgot step one of our hangover cure, which hasn't happened in forever. I guess we were too distracted last night by the excitement of the release and having the beach house.

I only have two golden rules for when I go out drinking:

Step 1: Chug a bottle of grape-flavored Pedialyte before going to sleep until I can't chug any more.

Step 2: The morning after, sip a bottle of sparkling water mixed with fresh orange juice until I start to feel my body lift back to life.

Let's just say we're going to need a *lot* of sparkling water and OJ this morning.

"Oh my god, I'm so embarrassed." Maya dives into the kitchen with her heels in her hands, red in the face, just as I'm taking my first sip of water.

"My driver totally knew what was up." She gestures to her short black dress and then wafts a hand in front of last night's makeup smeared around her eyes. It's kind of patchy where she must've tried to wipe it off with water or something.

"Don't tell me you had to call your own car—" I grimace.

Maya drops her heels and reaches for a bottle of water. "I did! Ugh. Men. Chivalry is dead."

"How was it, baby girl?" Val teases, twisting around on the couch to look. "*Shiiiit*, you went hard."

Maya chugs three big gulps of water before wiping her mouth and grinning. "Oh, you have no idea."

I pinch her side playfully as I walk past. "Kiss and tell, bitch. Can't believe you ditched on my big night."

"I didn't mean to, I promise. It's just, he was *so* into me, and honey, I haven't felt that fire since the last guy . . . or the last guy . . . or the guy before that." She grins.

"Quit bragging." I laugh. "Tell us exactly what happened."

"We want *all* the gory details," Jessie adds, kneeling on the sofa. "He was *hot*, Maya."

Maya walks into the lounge and sinks down on the huge couch with us.

"Okay, underwear model first of all," she says, matter-of-factly. "And when I say he was packing, I mean, *goddamn*. They say underwear models wear padding, but nope. Not this one. And that wasn't even the main course." She rolls her eyes and drags a groan. "Seriously, I can't even *describe* the things that man did with his tongue—"

"So, you got his number, right?" Val presses, suddenly wide awake. "And you're gonna hook me up with his underwear model friends, *right?*"

"Girl." Maya fans her face and drops back against the seat. "If he's got friends, I think I'll need to test-ride them for you first."

Valerie throws a pillow at her.

"What?" Maya laughs. "I just wanna make sure you'll get what I advertised!"

We hang around in the lounge listening to Maya's stories until my headache eases and the sun rises a little higher in the sky. Then, Jessie, Val, and I change into our bikinis and head down to the beach like we love to do in the mornings when we can—although usually we don't have a house that's literally right on the sand. Maya stays behind to scrub away last night's evidence in the rain shower, promising she'll join us soon.

I take my journal down to the beach, and while we sunbathe under the morning rays, I open it to a fresh page. Beside me, Val's preoccupied on her phone and Jessie's lost inside a heavy book. I breathe in the familiar ocean air and stare at the rolling waves as I think about what to write.

I've just put my pen to the paper when a shadow blocks the sun from behind.

"Guess what just arrived?" Maya says. She's holding a tall white box with *Princess* written in gold lettering across the front, a thick velvet ribbon tied in a bow underneath.

"For me?" I ask, confused, as she hands the box down.

"Unless any other princesses are staying at this address . . ." Maya shrugs.

I set the box on the sand and carefully pull off the bow and the lid to reveal an arrangement of flawless long-stemmed red roses, each silky petal immaculate, as if they've been handpicked fresh from a fairy-tale garden. They look almost too perfect to be real, but I know with one gentle touch that they are.

"Oh wow." Stunned, I pull out the note card and slide my finger under the lip of the envelope, opening it to read the handwritten words slowly. My heartbeat kicks faster with each unexpected line.

> *Princess,*
> *Congratulations, honey baby.*
> *You stole the spotlight.*
> *Couldn't take my eyes off you.*
> *—John*

A familiar flare of heat ripples across my skin. I can already feel it, my insides melting to mush, sinking deep into those dark, dangerous blue waters I lose myself in every time our eyes meet or our shoulders bump or he whispers words like those into the shell of my ear.

I swallow the feeling as I close the card to get a better look at the flowers.

What game is he playing here?

Is he trying to get back together?

Does he still love me?

My thoughts are cut off when my phone buzzes on the beach towel. I know without looking it's him.

Maybe it's fate.

Maybe we're meant to be.

Maybe I wouldn't mind sinking deep with him one more time . . . just to see.

5

As I make my way offstage to a roar of applause, I catch John's eye and smile wide. He's holding a cocktail, walking toward me through the dark of the venue Win booked for tonight's fundraiser, and he looks hot as hell. His all-black outfit matches the sleek décor. His eyes smolder with a heat that's all for *me*. My belly flips just looking at him.

"You did amazing, babe," he says directly into my ear, leaning in close as he hands the cocktail over. "Fucking incredible."

I throw my free arm around him and land a kiss on his cheek. "Thanks, babe. Win really never cuts corners. That setup was better than I had on tour."

"No way," Maya scoffs as she walks over from her spot backstage. "You killed it up there, Princess, but nothing's ever gonna top those shows last year."

I disagree with her but it's not worth saying it again.

"You looked so fucking intoxicating. You mesmerized everyone in the room, P. I'm so proud of you." John kisses my cheek and glances around at the crowd of people in the club, all psyched up from my set—multimillionaires and the Hollywood A-list, mostly. I can feel how happy he is for me; he's always been my biggest hype man. "And Win doesn't skimp. No surprise his events are gonna be next-level."

I take a sip of the cocktail, a special secret recipe the bartender came up with for the fundraiser, decorated with edible gold flakes and black cherries to match the theme. The ice-cold concoction feels like heaven as it coats my throat, much needed after singing for a half hour.

"Did you get a video for the girls?" I ask excitedly.

John holds up his phone. "Yup, of course."

"But you didn't get me a drink?" Maya pouts jokingly.

"My bad." He shrugs playfully.

"Take mine." I offer the cocktail to Maya, and grab John's phone so I can AirDrop the video to my own. Val flew out to NYC for some mysterious business thing with her dad and Jessie rarely makes it to these events unless she can take time off school, so I promised I'd send them a video after the show. Even when they're not here physically, they still find a way to hype me up.

I'm about to hit Send when an amp buzzes with static on the stage behind me and Win's deep voice rumbles out of the speakers. "What a phenomenal performance! Can we get another round of applause for the one and only Princess?" Win beams out at the crowd as they follow his lead, and an eruption of shouts and whistles fills the air.

"See, babe? They loved you." John drapes his arm around me and pulls me in for a kiss. His lips are warm against my already flushed neck. The way my body reacts to him never changes, no matter where we are or who's around.

"Holy shit, these cocktails are to die for." Maya groans orgasmically, eyes rolling, totally unfazed by all the attention. She doesn't give a shit what people think, and I love her for it.

Laughing in response, I tune back into Win's speech. He sure knows how to command a crowd.

"Well, you're an incredibly lucky crowd here," Win continues onstage, "because the show isn't over yet—we have another VIP guest for you tonight."

"Wait, what?" I whisper to John, pulling a face in confusion. No one told me there'd be other performances tonight. Not that I really care about that, but—

"John!" a sickly sweet voice interrupts from behind. "Oh my god, I didn't know you were here!"

Okay, *now* I care.

I turn to find my tall, shiny black-haired arch-fucking-nemesis dressed in a black catsuit, hooked up to her mic, ready for the show. My stomach drops. Riley Vega. Of all the musical artists in Hollywood, it *had* to be her. And she looks like a superstar. Insecurities immediately flood over me. I hate the power she has over me. I went from feeling on top of the world to feeling so small. I straighten my spine and try to seem unfazed, but she towers over me, in more ways than one. Even my hands are uncontrollable as I mess with my hair.

"What's up, Riley?" John greets her as Riley throws her arms around him in a hug, patting her back kind of awkwardly, avoiding looking at me. A hug that's a little too familiar, a little too intimate. I hate it.

What the fuck?

"Hey, Riley, honey," Maya says loudly, matching Riley's squeaky-clean tone with an equally fake smile. "Who's the handsome new man?"

Riley's attention turns to the guy beside her. I vaguely recognize him from a billboard somewhere—or a perfume commercial maybe, some ad that got plastered all over the city last month. Anyway, Riley looks uncomfortable as Maya rests a hand on the blond guy's arm and flashes him a sultry smile, which he returns without hesitation. Maya is to men like honey is to bees, sex appeal in spades, and I love when it works in my favor to put people like Riley Vega in their place.

"We're just friends," she answers, her eyes flitting to John's for a second. "This is Cal."

"Pleasure to meet you," Maya drawls.

Riley turns to John. "I'm so glad you're here. I have so many ideas to run past you about that song we talked about."

"You're working on music together?" I ask politely, feeling my blood start to boil. "And hi, Riley, it's great to see you."

She presses her lips together in a thin smile, as if I'm an annoyance.

"Yeah, we'll figure it out in the studio or something, Rye. I'll call you, okay?" John says easily. It's obvious that he's trying to get her away from us before I explode.

"You guys are working together?" I ask again.

"It's cool, Princess," John reassures me, but something about the way he's acting doesn't sit right. He knows this would bother me, and he's brushing it off. I suddenly feel like the third wheel in my own relationship.

"It's totally cool," Riley adds with a shit-eating grin. A grin that takes me right back to our messy, painful history. "I'll text you, John. I gotta get onstage—this is my cue."

With a flick of her hair she steps away from Cal, who's having some sort of moment with Maya, eyeing her up as if he can't wait to run off with her. He's probably already forgotten he's with Riley. Petty or not, after what Riley has taken from me, I welcome the fact that Maya is taking her arm candy for the night.

"Break a leg," I offer, trying my best to be genuine no matter how she treats me, but Riley just gives a little laugh as she hops onstage.

"Thanks, but I don't need it. Win always saves the best for last, you know."

Maya's the first to voice my thoughts once Riley's out of earshot. "What a bitch."

"Don't." I take the cocktail back from Maya and swallow the last of it. I turn my attention to John. "I can't believe you talked to her about working on a song."

"What's the issue?" John asks.

Maya interjects. "Uh, hello? Do you even remember what she did to Princess? The dress? Every time Princess gives her the benefit of the doubt, Riley screws her over." Maya widens her eyes as if she can't believe John doesn't get it.

"It's shady as fuck," I say matter-of-factly when John looks to me for an explanation. "And if it wasn't, you would have told me you're working with her."

For Cal's benefit, Maya elaborates. "Riley purposefully fucked up a big opportunity for Princess."

Humiliation crawls up my throat as I think about what happened, and I swallow it with difficulty.

"I don't even get it. We used to be good friends. I swear the Riley I met and knew is not the same girl we are seeing now," I begin, but John rolls his eyes and slides a hand around the nape of my neck to pull me close for a kiss before I can say any more. The smell of liquor on his breath overpowers the cologne I love so much.

"I'm gonna get some fresh air on the balcony," he tells me. "Don't overthink it, babe. You're above that."

I'm stunned. Has he really forgotten? Or is he too drunk now to recall? My temper flares. It feels like he's taking her side, again. "Are you kidding?"

"John, she's not overthinking anything. This shit isn't okay, and Riley's got some serious issues she needs to work on. You should stay away from her and defend your girl. You know what Riley did." Maya is clearly annoyed with John, but for my sake she lets him off easier than she usually would.

Cal says softly, "I won't tell anyone. I want to know what she's like, for my own sake—before I get too wrapped up with her." His eyes are sympathetic, and my anger at John's casual reaction gives me the freedom to talk about the long list of ways Riley has betrayed me.

I really don't want to talk about it too much, and it's not like anyone will believe me over her. When it all went down, I took the higher road and never spoke out publicly. People always asked but never got the answer as to why our friendship faded, but I guess I'll shed some light for him. "She did something unforgiveable that I'm not going to get into right now. But aside from the major issue, she's also done so many other, smaller things, so immature—like invite me out and then purposely not include me, have her stylist put me on her inspo board to rip my look but then gaslight me as if it was the other way around. Purposely post photos where I look awful, and she looks amazing. Petty and dumb stuff, I know, but real friends don't do that shit.

"There was one time I was holding her phone and all these notifications came in on the lock screen clearly talking shit about me with the guy she was dating at the time. I could tell from the message previews she wasn't defending me in the conversation, she was leading it. I never told her I saw the texts. It was so hurtful because I thought we had a real friendship and shit like this would happen.

"Yet every time her life was melting down, I'm the one she called to help pick up the pieces. And somehow she always made it seem like it's nothing, or not a big enough deal to be upset about. Even though her life seems so perfect, I always felt bad for her because of how lonely she is deep down, so I kept letting her hurt me over and over. And not because she's Riley Vega but because she was someone I cared about, and my heart is bigger than my head."

"That's so messed up," Cal says. "I've heard rumors of her basically exiling anyone who crosses her or who she decides is a threat or doesn't fit the vibe of her group."

John's eyes are steady on me, serious and unwavering. "You didn't tell me all of that."

"I told you the parts that mattered."

He glances at the stage where Riley is performing, conflict clear in his ocean-blue eyes. He takes another drink, and the change in his mood is subtle, but I know him so well I can feel it.

"The best thing to do is move on and not give her the power to fuck with you anymore. You're the fucking Princess. The past is the past. Let's go outside?"

"Okay," I agree quietly, looping my arm through his, ignoring the massive red flags screaming in my head.

I'm aware of them, but I don't want to fight tonight. He does care about me, I know that. But if someone hurts me, it should matter to him. If someone hurt him, I would always have his back. I know he doesn't handle conflict well—especially when alcohol is involved—and the way he was raised here in Hollywood, in the industry, wasn't exactly the model for healthy communication. He's trying, but he's just not there yet.

I can tell by the look on Maya's face that she wishes I would stand up to him, but thankfully she doesn't call me out.

"Maya, you wanna join?" I ask, already knowing the answer.

She glances at Cal. "Oh, I think we were gonna go grab a drink," she says. "But you have fun—and text me if you need me."

John and I grab more drinks and head to the outdoor balcony, where the view of Los Angeles stretches out for miles around us. Lights twinkle from every angle. The city can be so magical. Especially at a distance.

Most of the crowd is inside watching Riley's performance, so we have the balcony almost to ourselves.

"It's quiet out here." We stand together by the railing overlooking the city, though I can faintly hear her catchy song thumping through the air.

"With artists like you two onstage, I'm not surprised that everyone is inside."

I try to ignore the skin-crawling sensation that comes from hearing him lump me together with Riley.

"You're not watching the show," I say.

John takes a sip of his drink and sets it on top of a post. "I watched the only set that matters."

"Doesn't seem like you think that since you took her side in front of my friends just now."

"I didn't mean to take her side, P. I wasn't trying to brush off the shit with Riley, I'm just tired of you giving her what she wants, which is your energy. You're too good for that."

"She's already made me feel crazy enough, John. You know how isolated she made me feel, and I need you to have my back."

"I do have your back." He pulls me closer to him. "I will always have your back. I've known since the moment we met that you were different. Special. You're a good person and you can hold your own in this industry, very few people can say that. I'm not surprised Riley feels threatened. You're on a whole other level and I've always known that—now the world is catching up with me."

I glance down at his black suit. He really does look so goddamn hot. It makes me want to forget everything bad about tonight and not bring up what Riley said, but I can't ignore it like I usually would. That's one of the problems when it comes to him; I tend to ignore the rational part of my brain when he's close.

"John, what did Riley mean back there? You haven't mentioned anything about working with her."

John's jaw flexes as he leans against the railing. He doesn't want this conversation either. "I'm working with her, but it's not a big deal. I should have mentioned it, but you know how it is. My team set it up and was really pressing me about it. It's just business," he says, twisting to face me when I don't answer right away.

"You could have at least warned me so I wasn't blindsided like that."

"I knew you wouldn't like it."

I grip the railing, trying to keep my voice steady. "Yeah, but we're together. You should be able to tell me things even if you know I won't like them. And if you know I wouldn't be comfortable with it, you probably shouldn't do it and hide it. We have to be able to communicate."

"See how you're acting?" he says. "This is why I didn't tell you."

"Oh my god." He really doesn't get it, or just doesn't care to.

He shrugs. "What?"

"Are you being for real right now? 'See how you're acting'? As if I don't have a reason to be upset? I never have and never would work with your rivals even if they hit me up and my team was pushing for it."

"Look, I don't know what you want me to say, Princess. We're working on one song together. No big deal. It's work, I produce for tons of artists, and you never have a problem. This has nothing to do with you, and this shouldn't be an issue."

"John! I'm your *girlfriend*."

He looks away.

"You don't get to decide if it has nothing to do with me. I just found out you've been hanging out with her in the studio even though you know she has it out for me. It doesn't add up. She probably wants to take our sound and claim it as hers," I say. "I wouldn't put it past her. And you lying about this, like, what else is there I don't know about?"

"You're saying I can't work or hang with other artists now if they're women?"

My voice wobbles with frustration as I say, "*No*, John, that's not what I'm saying at all. But outside of work, why would you? Would you be okay with me hanging out with other guys?"

"Yeah, and you do." He downs his drink in one gulp. "You think I don't see the way Win and every guy in here looks at you? And your Instagram is full of guys commenting how sexy you are, and I never say shit. I'm producing one song with an artist who's on top of the charts right now and you expect me to turn it down because she was a shitty friend to you?"

He can't mean what he's saying and both of our tempers are getting the best of us, but I can't stop myself from reacting.

"Yes, John! I do. Anyone would. You should care how she treats me and how I feel about it. If the tables were turned, I'd be on your side, hands down." I'm so close to tears it's embarrassing, but I literally can't believe what I'm hearing. The thought of him spending time with Riley makes me sick. It makes me want to scream. I still don't even know what I did to make her act like this, and it feels unfair. I don't want to have a rivalry with her, or with any woman.

I stare at him, waiting for some kind of response. Waiting for him to explain why the hell he's defending her so strongly. I must be missing something because my kind, sweet, wonderful John wouldn't choose Riley over me.

"You're overreacting," he says after a while, staring back out over the city and not even bothering to look at me. "Relax and understand this is about work and not personal."

"It absolutely is personal, John!" I try to laugh but tears spill over instead. Stupid fucking tears, and people are starting to wander outside now. *Oh my god.* "This is about you not *getting* it."

As I say the words, I instantly realize how true they are. He doesn't get it. All our fights stem from the same root issue, that he listens but doesn't fully take my side when it comes to anything to do with his career. It's like he has blinders on. How can someone know me so well but be so dismissive of the way I feel sometimes? My relationship with him always feels so high or so low. There's never an in-between, and it's exhausting.

Without needing to think, more harsh truths spill out. "I'm just so tired, John."

He glances at me out of the corner of his eye but doesn't move.

"Can you just make the right decision and tell me you'll stop working with her? It doesn't have to be a big deal—just say something else came up. I really, really don't feel comfortable with you spending time with her. Can't you respect that?"

"It's not that easy, P. My management, everyone will lose it if I pull out because you told me to—"

"For *me*, John," I cut in, my voice rising in pitch. "I'm asking you to do this for me, for my feelings. Because I'm your girl and it's making me unhappy. It's not just a song to me."

Pushing himself upright, John finishes the last of his drink in one gulp and moves to walk away. "You know what, I think I'm going to head home."

"Wait—you're going without me?" I reach for his arm but he shrugs me off. "It's literally impossible to get through to you when you're like this. I'm just telling you how I feel and you're not even listening. All you care about is some song—"

"You're making a scene, Princess," he accuses me, moving closer. His voice is a low murmur as he tells me coldly, "I'm saying this for your sake, you don't want anyone to see you arguing with me in public. It's a bad look, and you'll be over it in the morning."

Tears momentarily blind my eyes. Deep down, I need him to validate my feelings, to offer to do the right thing for our relationship and not leave me hanging like some emotional wreck. It's manipulative and I hate it. He's not like this deep down—I know him. But as hard as I will the ice in his eyes to melt, he stays cool and unfazed, and I grow hotter with anger.

And also, what kind of disrespectful bullshit was that? *I'll be over it in the morning?* Who does he think he is? I hate how messy he makes me feel.

"Why are you being so cold? This isn't you." I try to meet his eyes again, to find a glimpse of the soft, thoughtful man I love.

"It is me." He sighs. "You're the one changing, Princess. You know how much I value my job, and working with Riley is a huge opportunity for me professionally. She's the hottest artist out there right now—" He stops midsentence, realizing what he just said.

My stomach drops and my heart feels like it's breaking into pieces as I try to compose myself.

"What?" I try to catch my breath.

"I didn't mean it like that, but . . ."

"I'm done, John," I snap, and there's a second of silence when the whole world seems to black out. "I'm so fucking done." It's hard to think straight beyond my feelings and ego being crushed by him on such an important night for me.

"You're overreacting—"

"No, I'm not. You lied to me by not telling me you're working with Riley. You're choosing *one* song and her over me, and I can't handle it. I don't have the time or energy to deal with this. I'm done."

"Princess, don't do this. Not like this. Emotions are high, we both said shit we didn't mean. Sleep on it." He shakes his head, glancing around at the other people spilling onto the balcony. He seems to care more about people hearing us than comforting me, which pushes me further over the edge.

"I'm serious. Don't call me, don't text me. We're done, John. Have fun with your new *hottest* artist's project."

Before he can say any more, I stride away as fast as I can, my high heels pinching my toes as I make my way back into the party and try to find Maya. The lighting's dark enough that no one can see my tears, which is my only saving grace. The more I try to brush them away, the heavier they fall.

I'm twenty minutes into searching for Maya or Cal in every dark corner when a hand lands on my shoulder from behind. A big hand, warm and reassuring, with a grip firm enough that I halt immediately and turn around, half expecting John.

"Win!" I try to pull myself together and hope he can't tell through the chaos that I'm crying. "Hey, have you seen Maya?"

"Not since earlier," Win says, separating from the glamorous girl he was dancing with to move off to one side of the floor with me. "Hey, everything okay?" He leans back to study my face. His hands reach up, wiping under my eyes and across my cheeks. The gesture makes me want to cry even harder. "Princess, what's going on?"

"It's nothing, Win, really," I explain, but he places his free hand on my other shoulder and grounds me with his concern. Instantly, all the adrenaline in my blood seems to settle, and I want to melt into him, to tell him everything.

"Where's John?" He looks around.

Staring at the floor, I shake my head, and he seems to get it without explanation.

"And you lost Maya too?"

"I guess she went home with that Cal guy." Unlike me, who's a crying mess and clearly going home alone, like the sad, tragic—*Oh, wait, shit. John was my ride home.*

"Do you need me to do anything?" Win asks. "I can kick him out if he's being a problem."

"Thank you but it's just—" I say quickly, shaking my head. "No, Win, I just . . . I just want to go home."

Win slides an arm around my shoulder and guides me out of the main room into a private hallway, abandoning the girl he was with as if he's forgotten about her already. Without another word he slides his phone out of his pocket and makes a call. His touch and presence feel so comforting and safe that my body releases what feels like a lifetime of tension.

"Tell my security to pull the car up front—I need him to drive Princess home and escort her to the door to make sure she's safe. Great, thanks." He ends the call and turns his attention back to me, wiping my fresh tears away with the thick pad of his thumb. "Do you want to talk about it?"

Embarrassment flushes my cheeks. "No, honestly."

He watches me contemplatively for a few long seconds. "I had no clue about Riley," he murmurs.

I look up into his brown eyes. "Riley?" *How does he know?* I try to play it cool, like I don't know what he's talking about.

Win smiles, sympathy in his kind eyes. "I wasn't eavesdropping, but I was walking by and overheard your conversation with Maya and the group. I had no idea that she did all that to you. She won't be performing at any of my events again, Princess. Trust me." When I open my mouth to protest, he places a hand in the small of my back to steer me down the hallway. "Come on, superstar. Let's get you home."

My mind reels with a thousand possibilities while Win leads me out of the party through the back exit. We step into the hot LA night air. As he helps me into his Maybach, I wonder if he thinks less of me knowing that Riley has the power to ruin my nights, big and small. Does he know something that I don't? Did Riley try to talk shit about me to Win too? I don't even know. The only thing on my mind above all the bullshit with John is one glaring fact that actually hurts to think about: If Win can dismiss Riley so easily, why the hell does my own *boyfriend* struggle so much?

6

Present day

It's Maya who snaps me out of my thoughts first, bringing me back to the sunny beach. "So, who's the secret admirer?"

"No secret," I say with a sigh, opening up the note card to give them all a look at the message inside. "They're from John."

A unanimous groan fills the air as Maya, Val, and Jessie tip their heads back at once. I guess I can't blame them. They're more protective of me than I am of myself when it comes to John. They were the ones who picked up the pieces after that night on the balcony, when I realized once and forever that he had a cold, calculating streak about him that would never consider me. Or my feelings. Still, this is a message I can't ignore—maybe he regrets that night as much as I do.

"You've got to be kidding me," Val says, exasperated, snatching the note card and reading it out loud. "'Princess. Congratulations, honey baby. You stole the spotlight. Couldn't take my eyes off you. John.' It's not exactly Shakespeare, is it? Fuck, how long did it take him to come up with that?"

"It's kind of sweet," Maya tries, picking up one of the roses and twirling it around.

"Wasn't he with Emma last night, though?" Jessie asks. "When did he even buy these? And how did he know where to send them?"

"Maybe while Riley was sleeping next to him," Val sarcastically tells her. When she sees the look on my face, she grimaces. "I'm sorry, Princess. That was uncalled for. I'm just so pissed at him."

"It is what it is. It's none of my business anymore anyway," I tell her, though this back-and-forth is starting to feel like a carnival ride. It's been a month of misery wondering if I made a rash decision at the party—if we both damaged what we had beyond repair—and not a day's gone by where I haven't convinced myself I made a mistake. He has such a grip on me, and I'd like to think he's been just as miserable as I've been. I try not to let the flowers drag me back into his orbit, though that's easier said than done. Because, at the end of the day, I still can't trust him.

"Princess, I really don't want to break your heart some more, babe," Maya says, sitting down in the sand beside me and squeezing my arm, "but she has a point, harsh or not. We didn't want to tell you because we knew it'd hurt, but since he's trying to work his way back into your life, I guess you'd better know about—"

"Know about what?" I don't like where this is going, nor the way Maya and Val exchange glances as if they're about to drop a bomb onto my world.

"Riley was in the studio with John the other day, and they went to lunch after," Val says carefully, watching closely for my reaction.

I keep a straight face, trying not to let it show that this affects me. "How do you know?" I hesitate to ask, but I need details.

"Her IG. She posted the two of them in the studio and then tagged him in a pic of her lunch at Great White."

I can taste the bile rising in my throat. Working together is one thing, and that already fucking sucked, but going to lunch together is a whole other thing.

"You'd think if he was so set on winning you back he'd be a *little* more cautious about getting caught doing the one thing that made him lose you, right?" Maya shakes her head.

"Riley knew exactly what she was doing, posting him like that. She's so damn petty." Jessie sighs. "You can do so much better, Princess," she adds, offering a smile, as if she knows I'm spiraling inside.

I don't want to do better. As much as I hate to admit it, I still want John. Part of me feels guilty for making him choose between his work and me—and for having the girls go so hard on him. I know that's not fair, but neither is this fucked-up situation. If we were really a team the way he'd always claimed we were, then my being disrespected by Riley should be equally a problem to John and intolerable in his eyes. Her unpredictable backstabbing and how low she's willing to go should be a warning to John too. Imagine what would happen if she turned on him? I've seen it happen to other people, and John could be next if he doesn't do everything she asks him to do. People are disposable to her—why would he be any different?

"They're only flowers at the end of the day. I'll text him to say thank—"

"No!" Val and Maya blurt at once.

"Don't give him what he wants," Val continues, shaking her head firmly. "He hasn't even apologized, let alone changed."

"Seriously, he needs to do a lot more than send flowers." Maya pulls a face in disgust. "You don't need that energy in your life. You're on some new shit now—I mean, look at you, Princess! You just had a huge release party, your music is streaming like crazy. Babe, you need to focus on yourself and not let him distract you."

"Agreed," Jessie says. She knows how conflicted I am about all this. We've spent hours on FaceTime going through everything together. "Focus on you and let the John drama go. If he proves himself worthy of you, that's a different story, but for now, they're just flowers."

With a sigh, I close the lid on the box of roses and lie back on the beach towel. "You're right. I need to worry about myself." But even as I say it, the words feel empty. Honestly, I don't know if I'll ever want anyone else. I just wish he'd stop acting so clueless and make things right between us.

Whatever. For now, I've got the sun, sand, and my girls. I'm good. Right?

After another hour on the beach we head back to the house, planning to make use of the home movie theater with some of our old favorite movies and all the softest Barefoot Dreams blankets we can find.

But when we step inside the walled driveway, that plan fizzles out instantly.

"You have got to be kidding me. We have a girls' day planned." Maya growls under her breath, gripping my arm and striding forward with me as if we're about to bypass him altogether.

"I repeat, how'd he even get this address?" Jessie whispers.

John leans against the wall beside the fancy front doors, but when he hears Maya's voice he looks up from his phone and right at me. Those ocean-blue eyes glitter in the midday sun as he stands tall to greet us. He's dressed casually, in sweatpants, an oversized designer sweatshirt with a subtle logo, and stark white sneakers, my favorite look of his. He looks gorgeous but tired. Maybe he has missed me after all?

"Kimi gave me the codes to get in, I hope you don't mind. She said to blame her if anyone was pissed," John jokes.

"You should leave," Val warns him, pushing her shades onto her forehead. "Read the room."

"This better be good, John," Maya says.

"Guys, let me just hear him out." I pull free from Maya's grip and linger as the girls step into the house.

John clears his throat and scratches the back of his neck. "Can, uh . . . can we talk?"

I glance at the girls urging me in through the doors and then back at him. I'm still carrying the box of roses, and it's such a shock to see him here. I would be lying to myself if I said I wasn't dying to hear what he has to say. Am I about to get some big romantic apology like in the movies? Isn't it actually pretty sweet he went out of his way to find me here? Or am I just being impressed by the bare minimum again?

"Give me five minutes," I say, offering an apologetic smile as Maya rolls her eyes theatrically and Val groans her disapproval. "I'm sorry, I'll be in ASAP. And if you're voting on which movie to watch first, I say *The Proposal*."

"We're just worried you're making a mistake," Maya singsongs quietly to me, shooting John a look that makes him shift uncomfortably beside me.

"It's my mistake to make. I'll be back in five," I repeat, gesturing for John to join me on the small deck at the side of the house overlooking the smooth sand and picturesque waves of the Pacific.

"Thanks for hearing me out, Princess."

As we walk away, I keep my eyes focused on the never-ending ocean ahead and don't acknowledge him until we're seated on a set of huge beanbag chairs. All I want to do is melt into his arms and forget this whole thing happened. But I've got to get a grip, keep it together, and have some self-respect. John knows he's lucky I'm giving him a chance to talk right now. I just hope what he has to say is worth it.

"Why are you here, John?" I ask, staring out at the water.

"Seeing you at the release party last night, I was so proud of you. You're really blowing up and I hate that we aren't on good terms."

"So you came here because my career is doing well?"

He shakes his head. "No. That's not why I came." He drops his shoulders in disappointment. "Listen, I took some time to think about what happened and I understand now where you were coming from."

"Are you gonna stop working with Riley?" I ask, before I allow myself to even consider forgiving him.

"I get it, it wasn't just about the song. You felt betrayed, and I know it didn't feel good to have to share the spotlight with Riley and then to hear from her that we're working together. It wasn't cool and I should have had your back. Honestly, I drank too much, and I was only thinking about how I felt and how big a song with her would be. I didn't mean to break your trust or embarrass you."

I close my eyes for a moment, taking in what he said. His apology feels deeply genuine. Neither of us is perfect. The vulnerability in his eyes and his voice makes me weak, but I need to be strong or we'll continue this cycle.

"And," he continues, "I know I should have said all this sooner, but I wanted to give you time, and I wanted to make sure I didn't make things worse."

"You didn't answer my question. Are you still going to work with her?" I open my eyes to see he's focused on me.

He shifts nervously. "We already finished the song."

"Of course you did."

"I want you to trust me, Princess. It's just work, and she's well aware that talking about you is off-limits."

"Trust is *earned*, John. That means not going behind my back to work with the one person in the whole of fucking Hollywood I have an issue with. And you've been hanging out with her outside of the studio. Please don't even try to deny it, the girls have seen the posts."

"I'm not trying to make excuses here, but you know how the industry is—we're working together, I was just keeping everything cool."

I hate that he has a point. I've done my fair share of long uncomfortable dinners and gone to parties I didn't want to be at with people I didn't want to be around, all for the sake of making connections. It's part of the business.

"You should be careful with her, John. I've seen what she's capable of and it's not fucking pretty."

"Princess." He evens his tone. "I didn't come here today to go back through all this. I actually have something to ask you."

I shake my head. He continues to avoid accountability.

"I want us to work together again," he says.

My eyes flick to meet his, and he tries a smile. "Not just me—my publisher wants this too. I would produce your next project. I have some great co-writers on board already. It's a solid team, P. You should at least consider it, regardless of what's going on with us."

He's right; it could be amazing. It would just be so much sweeter if this whole thing wasn't lingering over us.

"Are you asking me to work with you because you want to work with me or because your publisher thinks you should? Is this about us or about your work?"

"It's about us being good together—in the studio," John says quickly, the look in his eyes telling me more than his words. "The song with Riley is finished and doesn't mean shit compared to this, compared to us. Let's create something special together and forget all the other bullshit."

There's so much passion in his voice, and I can tell he really wants this. I just don't know if it's because he cares about me or because it's good for his career. I study him while I think about it. He watches me, too, his familiar sweet smile tugging at my heartstrings.

"This is all about you. No one and nothing else. We can make the biggest song of the year. I can get you a huge feature. You could have a massive record, go on tour, so many opportunities could come from this. The possibilities are endless. We both know you level everything up. This could be huge, for both of us."

The sound of the ocean masks my silence. I'm not quite ready to respond. John doesn't push me, and I appreciate it.

"Okay. For the sake of music, let's do it." His face lights up, so I hold up a finger. "*But* I'm in this for the music only right now, nothing else. This isn't me agreeing to forgive you on a personal level. Let's just take it day by day and see what happens, okay?"

"I get it, I hear you, and honestly, P., I've been thinking a lot about our breakup, and you were right," he says.

My chest sinks. I had stupidly assumed that he came here to try to win me back, using our chemistry in the studio as a cover, but in reality, this is just about work.

"You won't regret this, Princess. We're going to make your biggest music yet."

If he's over us, so am I. And if I trust anyone to make a hit with me, it's John. Now that I'm having such a big moment, I know everyone will be asking me what's next. Always hungry for more.

That's how it always is in this town; no matter how high you are, what's next is all that matters, and for me, the next thing has to be a hit produced by John with a big feature attached.

"You better hope so." I join his smile with mine. It worries me a little how easily I succumb to him, but I know how talented a producer he is, and at the end of the day, the song will speak for itself.

"Have your people hit up Kimi or Wayne so they can discuss the details." I stand up. "I need to get back to the girls. You're kind of intruding on our time together, and you're lucky none of them threw you over the balcony," I tease him. My shoulders are lighter; the weight on my mind has lifted so much since he arrived.

"I'll leave you to it. I don't want them to jump me," he jokes. He heads back to the driveway. I follow, listening to him express how excited he is for us to work together. Excitement bubbles inside me too; there's no one I make better music with than John.

"Don't get too hyped yet, we still need to make the song," I tell him as we reach the end of the driveway.

"I know. I know." He comes to a stop and turns to look at me. His voice goes quiet and his eyes get even more intense as he says, "I won't get ahead of myself, but I know how talented you are, and I'm more than confident that the next song we make will be massive. Just wait and see, deal?"

"Deal." I can't help but agree with him.

He turns to the gates and lifts his hand in a small wave. "I'll talk to you later, P."

"Bye, John."

"Uh, Princess?"

At the confusion in John's voice, I stop walking back to the house and turn around to face him. But John isn't looking at me. Gesturing with his finger at the gate, he urges me to follow his gaze.

I do, and my heart stops.

Standing close to the iron gates with his face pushed nearly all the way between the bars, muttering something to himself that I can't hear from this distance, is a man with wild, beady eyes and disheveled hair. And he's staring right at me.

"What the fuck?" I say at the same time as John asks, "Who the hell is this creep?"

I don't know, but something's off. And from the way this guy's fixated on me, still muttering, head still through the bars, looking like he's about to shove his whole body through and come running right at me, I know this isn't safe.

"Princessssss . . ." the man's voice slithers across the space between us.

My blood runs cold.

"You know me, PrincessesKing38. Come on and open up the gate, beautiful."

"Do you know him?" John asks me. I shake my head, something going off in the back of my head, like the tiniest of a memory. It does sound a bit familiar . . .

"Princess, open the gate. I need to talk to you!" The man's voice becomes more aggressive as he grows impatient. His arms poke through the space between the bars, reaching in my direction. I'm frozen in fear, hoping the gate does its job.

"Wait." My blood runs cold. "I think I know him. Not in real life, not him, but the username. Oh my god." I pull out my phone and open my Insta. There it is. His name on my activity feed over and over. I've thought about blocking that account, but the last time I did, it gave him the attention he wanted and he came back with a new account immediately, messaging even more often and aggressively.

"Get inside," John directs me, closing in on me and shielding my body from the stranger. "Quickly, let's go." He shuffles forward, guiding me toward the house. My feet and legs feel like molasses, my mind reacting faster than my body.

"I need to call Kimi and Wayne. I should've hired security here. The neighborhood's supposed to be safe!" I say as I enter the house, peeking behind John at the strange man who's still calling out my name.

"What's going on?" Val's walking past the front door when we rush into the house, and she stares wide-eyed at John as he slams the door shut and flips all the locks into place. "What are you doing?"

"Shut and lock every window and door in this house now," John demands, already heading into the living room to check the floor-to-ceiling windows.

"Can someone tell us what's going on?" Val shrieks. "Should we call the cops?"

"The cops?" Maya bounces into the room with Jessie, but when she sees the looks on our faces her smile drops. "What happened?"

"Lock the doors and no one go outside." John pushes through the little group we've formed in the hallway, dialing a number on his cell phone as he strides into the kitchen. "This isn't a joke. And don't go near the windows!"

I peek through the window beside the front door, relieved to see the guy's still safely behind the gates—but he's still staring right at me and his mouth is moving insanely fast.

"Who the hell is that?" Jessie whispers as we back up to the stairs. There's real fear in her eyes. I grab for her hand and squeeze it.

As John runs around checking all the windows and doors, trying his best to keep us safe, a spark of hope appears beneath the surface, and it rekindles a flame inside me that I'd thought had died. The last thing I should be thinking about is my relationship with him, and I know that, but I can't seem to help it.

John stays with us until the panic of the intruder dies down. The stalker disappears as soon as he hears the cops' sirens, no harm done—thankfully. It gives me the shivers to know someone like that has me on their radar, and we have no clue who he is, how he found me, or what he wants.

Kimi and Wayne put full-time security in place to watch over me in case he comes back, and all four of us give witness statements before heading to bed for the night, too exhausted after the commotion to even think about our planned movie night.

Later, I'm lying in bed with the girls fast asleep beside me when a text pops up at exactly 11:11 p.m. As I read it, that flame of hope burns even brighter.

John: I just wanted to say good night and sweet dreams, Princess. I hope you're okay after what happened. I can't wait to see you in the studio

7

New Year's Eve, three months ago

Our music's loud, spilling through the open glass doors of my LA apartment and into the city in the distance. Fireworks have been going off against the inky clouds all night, but inside my apartment a different type of fireworks sizzle through me. John and I escaped to my room a half hour ago, and the energy's hot between us, just like it has been for weeks since he practically moved in. He hardly ever went to his place anymore, only to check the mail. We can't keep our hands, our mouths, our everything, off one another.

"Fuck, baby, you're so good at that. Keep going—Princess, no, don't stop baby, I—" he mutters as I take him into my mouth, deep in my throat. The way his body reacts to me, his fingers clawing at my hair, gives me even more confidence.

"I wanna have some fun too," I purr, crawling up his body and trailing my hands over his hard abs. I straddle his thighs, leaning forward to kiss him flush on the mouth, my body going crazy for him as he moves his hands over my hips and slips them into my lace panties.

"Always so wet for me," he rumbles in appreciation, gliding over me. "God, I fucking love you, baby."

"I love you too," I say, tipping my head back as he slides his fingers in an addicting rhythm. It feels so fucking good, like no one else has ever made me feel. "John . . . oh my—"

The moment's interrupted by a loud crash behind us: my bedroom door banging against the wall. Music and voices from outside suddenly sound clearer as a drunken body falls into my room. The party must have gotten sloppy since John and I ran off to my bedroom.

"Holy shit," John barks, his startled noise making me laugh like crazy even though I should be scrambling to cover myself. He pushes me gently off and wraps the sheets around us, eyes wide to see who the hell just walked—no, *tumbled*—in.

"Val." I laugh harder when I recognize her coral-pink dress. She's sprawled on the floor in the doorway to my room, one of her sparkly silver heels snapped right off. "What happened?"

She slurs some words I don't understand and moves to drag herself up, but when she falls back down and makes a weird sputtering noise, my laughter dies instantly. This isn't funny anymore.

"Oh shit. John, she's not okay." A chill rushes through me as I realize this isn't just another drunken episode; Val's on something. I've seen her drunk at least a hundred times but this is different. "Help me."

We snatch our clothes up fast from where they're scattered around us in the bed and pull them on, jumping out and across the room to lift Val up from where she collapsed.

"Prin . . . Princess . . . sssstop. Stop," she stutters as we pull her upright and lean her back against the open door.

"What did you take, Val?" I ask, brushing her long brown hair out of her face. "What was it this time?"

She mumbles another incoherent sentence, and I glance helplessly at John.

"She's really out of it," he says, shaking his head.

"What are we gonna do?" I look into my apartment, where the party is still going strong. I doubt anyone else knows she's in this state, and for her sake, I don't want them to. I can hear people down the hallway laughing together, carrying on with their night, not realizing one of my best friends is in trouble.

"I don't want anyone to see her like this, she'll be mortified," I tell him, my voice cracking.

When I was getting ready with the girls earlier tonight, Riley was all over Val, helping her with her makeup, hugging her, desperate to get her alone. Riley was always willing to go further than we were—walking the edge. And Val struggled with saying no, always tempted to take the fun a bit further.

Regardless, rule of thumb: I don't gossip about or judge my friends, period.

"We need to get her into a bed and try to get her to drink some water. Keep her head up," John says with concern.

"Val, how'd you end up like this? Please stay with me."

Her eyes roll back in her head and I remember the girl I know and love. The one who's always had my back, the one who has demons to fight but a heart of gold.

Valerie has been cursed with one hell of a family. It's understandable why she'd want an escape from all of her trauma and responsibility. From drug use to violence and too much disposable money, there's always a fire for Val to put out, and I wish I could take all of that away for her, but I can't. All I can do is be here for her and try to help her get it together, once she's sober.

"Val? Oh shit. Is she okay?" Tripp says from down the hallway. He's my closest guy friend, and I've known him ever since I came to LA at seventeen. Concern is etched deep in his forehead. His curly black hair bounces as he moves, and when he reaches us, he drops to his knees in front of her.

"Something is really wrong, Tripp," I tell him. "Did you see what she took?"

"No," he answers. "Everything was fine until she started getting really heavy real quick. I was trying to sit her down on the couch, make sure she was okay. I only left for a second to get her some water, and when I came back she was gone."

"I'm fine," Val says clearly, though it seems to take some effort. Her lips work overtime to pronounce the words. "Riley's a fucking . . . fuck. Rye, Rye . . . Rye."

"Where's Riley?" I ask. "Maybe she can tell us what Val took."

"She bailed an hour ago, said she was hitting another party. Said something about needing to go where she'd be seen," Tripp said.

Val's shoulders heave as she leans over and vomits all over the floor. It's nearly all liquid, meaning she hasn't eaten in god knows how long. I also feel sick, not because she's thrown up, but because of how worried I am for my friend.

"What?" I frown at Val. "What about Riley?"

I can't believe Riley would get Val this out of it and then leave her to head to some other party hoping there'll be paparazzi to document her amazing New Year's Eve. I know I promised not to judge my friends but this was a bit beyond.

"Let me sleep," Val groans, obviously confused.

"She'll be okay, she just needs to hydrate and rest," Tripp says. "I'll stay with her. I promise I won't leave her side."

He pulls the strap of her dress back onto her shoulder, righting her neckline to cover her up a little better. It's a sweet move, and my belly aches at the thought of any guy acting so tender in such a vulnerable moment. It's not enough for him, so he pulls his hoodie over his head and puts it on her.

"Yeah, I think you're right," I say with a sigh. "I can't believe she got to this point. Oh, Val." I stroke her hair as she snuggles up against me.

"Tired." She sulks into my shoulder. "Please let me sleep."

Together, we help Val into my guest room, where I tuck her into bed and leave Tripp to watch over her. He insists he has it under control and that I get back to celebrating. John and I head back to my room, just as the staff finishes cleaning up after Val, both of us pulled out of our celebratory mood, worried about Val.

"She's going to be okay. Let's find a way to get her some help when the sun comes up. There's nothing you can do right now. I know it's scary, but you need to sleep, babe. The problem will still be here when you wake up." John comforts me, wrapping his arms around my body as I cuddle up close to his.

"I'm sorry," I say, though I don't know why. I'm mostly just sorry that Val's not going to remember the start of a new year. I don't know how to help her. I'm still shocked from seeing her like that.

John says nothing for a while, both of us just lying there in bed together staring out at the glittering stretch of Los Angeles through my floor-to-ceiling windows.

"I feel so lucky to be with you." I sigh.

"Lucky eleven," John says.

"What do you mean?"

He lifts his phone to show me the time. It's 11:11 p.m. "Make a wish, baby," he whispers into my hair.

"I wish to be like this, with you, forever," I say easily, tracing a pattern over his chest. "I wish for Val to stop being haunted by the demons that she's trying to erase. I hope she and Tripp end up together. I just want her to be happy—"

"It's a one-minute thing, P.," John jokes, trying to lighten my mood. "I think you ran out of wishes already."

"Doesn't matter," I say with a little laugh. "I had to say it all."

"You really want to be with me forever?" he checks.

I nod against his chest. "Absolutely."

John kisses my head and sighs, but he doesn't say anything else. He doesn't need to. It's just so easy between us in these quiet moments alone. Easy and peaceful and all I've ever wanted.

8

Present day

The week after the release of "Princess" flashes by in a whirlwind. With the plans for my new project with John in Kimi's and Wayne's hands and my security team looking out for me, I'm free to celebrate with my friends and family—and damn, do we go hard. Mom flies in to visit from Guam, bringing my little sister with her, and together with Maya and Val we hit all the best spots. I wish my dad could come too. I miss him so much, but his work schedule is so busy and the plan is for him to come out next time. For now, I take my mom and sister all around the glamourous side of LA. Our shopping trip on Rodeo Drive starts at Celine. My sister gasps at the price tag on a bag she touches. She jerks her hand away and I hug her to my side.

"Do you want it?" I ask her.

She shakes her head. "No way. That costs way too much."

I smile, kissing her on the cheek. "We're not leaving until you pick something, baby girl."

Even though she's still shocked by the prices, she agrees, and the look on her adorable face is impossible to hide as she tries on bag after bag. My mom watches us, pride clear in her big brown eyes. My mom reacts the same at Chanel, but settles on a tweed bag, the hottest one of the season. All of us, except my sister, toast with the complimentary champagne they give us as we shop from store to store. Our afternoon results in an entire trunk full of designer goodies, from purses to dresses and shiny new stilettos. We stop for coffee at the Instagram-worthy but slightly overpriced Alfred. Mom takes cute pictures of all of us in front of all the famous walls in Beverly Hills.

Later that night we go all out at Nice Guy, ordering a table full of food: seafood and ragu pastas, their insanely delicious pizzas (three different types), almost every appetizer they have. My sister and Val devour a rib eye and we all eat more than we ever have. My sister tries the pomegranate kale salad and brussels sprouts for the first time, and instantly becomes obsessed like the rest of us. The food is incredible, and it feels so good to treat my family and friends to such a nice meal. It's pretty different from the meals we've shared at home; those were full of love and devotion, but I dreamed about the day when I could do stuff like splurge at the hottest spot in LA, and it's so fulfilling—and this is just the beginning.

As the server clears the table, my mom takes my hand in hers. "This is so surreal, P., being in this city with you, celebrating your success. I knew you would make it, but as your mom, I'm so happy the world is seeing you shine the way I always have." Her eyes brim with tears, making me watery eyed too.

"Aww, Mom." I hug her, petting the back of her head like she always did for me when I was growing up. "I could never have done any of this without you. Always being there to pick me up, helping me think clearly when I'm lost. You keep me going. If I didn't have you to lean on I would never have made it this far. I'm doing this for all of us. Our lives are different now. I'm going to take care of all of us. Hot-spot dinners, shopping on Rodeo, all of this is just going to be another normal day for us," I promised.

I love making music. I couldn't live without it, but my drive doesn't come from wanting to buy myself designer bags: I'm doing it for my family. So they never have to worry about an electricity bill being too high or how to pay for my sister's college. I will make their lives easier—I promised myself that when I first got on the plane to Los Angeles.

"Honey, we don't need to go shopping or have these luxurious dinners. We just want you to be happy." My mom is full-on crying now.

She's always been my biggest cheerleader, the smartest when it comes to strategy, scraping up the money for me to leave my island, spending hours on the road driving me to auditions, and sending me enough money to get by in the city during tough times when I couldn't pay for myself. I owe my parents everything and I want to do this for them, for my whole family, for my island.

"I am happy. My song is being played on every radio station in LA and I'm doing all these interviews at all the biggest radio stations! Spotify and Apple Music added the song to every hot playlist. My merch is selling like crazy. It's all happening, we made it, Mom." I hug her again.

"I'm so proud of you, baby." She pulls out her phone to FaceTime my dad. He's grinning from ear to ear, eyes full of pride.

"We aren't supposed to have our phones in here, Dad, but we'll call you again tonight. Promise." I blow him a kiss as we hang up.

Maya and Val both sniffle beside us; it's such a meaningful moment, one that I'll never forget.

Paparazzi wait outside as we exit. My sister hides her face, growing nervous at the crowd of mostly men calling my name. My mom wraps her arm around my sister, and I tell her to go ahead of me and Maya so the attention isn't so heavy on them. I'll never get used to people selling photos of me, but sometimes it's helpful to create buzz around my name. The photos of me and Maya go viral and get a bunch of press coverage. Maya watches her phone with bright eyes, but by the end of the day she turns all her notifications off. The outfit I wore, a white cropped tank and oversized metallic jeans, is all over the blogs. The jeans sell out and I get tagged in hundreds of posts re-creating my look.

To keep the momentum going for my song, the next day is packed with more press, this time focusing on expressing my gratitude toward my fans and my team. My music is getting all the right support, and the team around me deserves all the recognition they can get. I know so many artists have issues with their management, but I'm so fortunate to be able to trust mine.

Kimi and Wayne are like family to me, and I don't feel like a walking dollar sign to them. I'm lucky in so many ways. I've been given warnings from other artists to not get too comfortable or too close to my managers, but I couldn't imagine anything bad happening with Kimi and Wayne. To thank my team for helping me get this music out I take them and their plus-ones to Nobu and we order the finest wine, liquor, and fresh sushi and sashimi until we close out the place. I'm on a high. Being able to give back to my family, my girls, and my team is all I've ever wanted.

Soon it's back to business. I spend hours on calls with business managers now that I actually have money coming in and enough "going on" for people to want to work with me. I'm able to partner with marketing teams to develop a new cosmetic line I've been pitching for the longest time. I bring Maya in, too, so she can give her expertise and promotional value. We gush over samples of the new line, and it feels like I'm living out all of the daydreaming I've done in my bedroom over the years. We go over the looks Maya will be wearing for the campaign shoot and her genuine excitement only gets me more hyped to be doing all this with her. The publicist I hired, Jen, is one of the best in the industry, and she just so happens to have her office in one of the buildings that Win owns downtown. I know because he's taken me to it before—and today we're brainstorming ideas for a social media ad campaign in her luxuriously decorated space. She oozes class and experience, and I love being surrounded by strong women like her.

"Okay, but I *loooove* the formula for this lip gloss. It's the juiciest and most hydrating gloss I think I've ever used. Coconut flavor…of course, for my island girl. And the mint-green background for those promo shots," Maya raves, leaning across the conference room table to reach for some of the cutouts the designers have pulled together. "But the pink is so on-brand with Princess right now it just feels criminal not to use it to our advantage."

"I'm happy you like it! Princess has been extremely specific about every detail from the marketing to the formulas since the beginning. Good call on the mint green," Jen says enthusiastically. "I'll have the team come up with some more options ASAP since the first shoot is coming up quick and we need to start rolling these posters out ahead of the announcement."

"They're gonna be plastered all around LA," I tell Maya.

"Shut up! I'm so excited for you." Maya claps her hands excitedly. "An entire beauty brand owned by you advertised all over the city—with us on the posters together!"

"You know that's only the tip of the iceberg." Jen laughs, closing her binder. She shoots me a knowing look, and I nod for her to continue. "We're advertising in every major city in the country, even internationally. Ad space is booked in New York City, Miami, LA, even London and Paris. This is going to be big. We're making this thing *happen*. And, Maya, you're going to be getting calls from every major agency, just don't forget about me." Jen winks playfully.

"Aww, thank you both." Maya whistles. "This is sick. I'm so excited to see what you have planned for your next drops. I'm so proud of you, P."

My head still buzzing with excitement, I thank the team for an outstanding meeting and step out of the glass-walled office, heading for the elevator with Maya. My emotions take me by surprise, hitting me all at once, and I try not to make it obvious. But taking a wider view on my life, I can't fathom how things are really coming together. It might look like an overnight success, but truthfully most of my career has felt so suffocating, like I'm barely staying above water, constantly feeling not good enough and having to prove myself. And then somehow here I am, feeling like I'm living someone else's life, walking out of a meeting with the best publicist and marketing team for a beauty brand I've always dreamed of having. Like, what is going on?!

"You gonna grab lunch with me?" Maya asks when we step inside the elevator, snapping me out of my thoughts.

"I'd love to but it'd have to be to go," I say with an apologetic smile. "I have a session I gotta get to today and another with John tomorrow that I need to prepare for."

"Are you seriously going to record with him after what he did?" Maya doesn't look impressed.

"We have to move on from it. We're working together. I have no expectations outside of that and no room for bullshit. What he does in his free time and who he chooses to do it with is really none of my business." Although the thought of him with someone else kills me inside, I guess that's life. "Our relationship begins and ends in the session. And you know there's no one I have better creative chemistry with. I'm not going to be petty and let that go."

"Sure." Maya's applying the sample for my new lip gloss in the elevator mirror. She pops her lips and shoves the tube back into her purse. "I guess I'd be more enthusiastic if this same damn thing hadn't happened a thousand times already. I'll always support your choices when it comes to him, but that doesn't mean I agree with you. It's such a roller coaster with you two, I don't know how you do it."

The elevator dings, and I'm about to answer as I step out, except I'm silenced by the tall, dominating presence that appears as the doors slide open. He oozes sex, and my palms go clammy instantly. Of all the people to bump into . . .

"Win!" I reach my arms out for a hug. "I was just going to call you!"

"Hey, Princess." A smile to die for creases his face. "How'd the big meeting go?"

"It was great," I answer as I pull back from the hug. Shit, he smells good. "Thanks so much for putting me in touch with Jen and the team."

"Anytime, Princess." Win greets Maya, too, and then his eyes slide down briefly to glimpse my bare thighs in the short shorts I'm wearing. Like the gentleman he is, his stare doesn't linger, but the heat from his eyes leaves a lasting itch. "I wish I could hang around, take you out for lunch or something, but I'm about to be late for a meeting."

"Oh, don't worry." I wave my hand through the air. "I have to get to a session at the studio. But let's do dinner soon?"

Pushing out a hand to hold the elevator doors open, Win brushes against my arm accidentally. It surprisingly leaves a tingling trail, making my hairs stand on end.

"Perfect, I'm down for dinner anytime," he says in a tone that definitely doesn't feel professional. But that's just Win all over: suave and sexy and strictly off-limits. "I'll call you."

As the elevator doors close, big pink love hearts practically burst out of Maya's wide eyes.

"He is so hot," she says, latching onto my arm and walking with me out of the office building. "How are you still hanging around with John when there are men like *that* out there wanting to take you to dinner? It's insanity if you ask me."

"It's funny you say that, I don't recall asking," I say, poking my tongue out and laughing. "Ahh, it's just not like that with Win. He's like, I don't know, like we have this amazing mutual respect. And he's always interested and helpful, and so damn smooth, but I'm not sure if it's actually a flirty vibe. I guess it's kind of like he's my—"

"Don't say it." Maya laughs. "Don't you dare tell me you've got daddy issues."

"Oh my god." I shove into her, and Maya laughs harder as she stumbles a couple of steps in her heels. Embarrassed, but also seeing the funny side, I bite my smile away and try to stay serious. "It's not like that. Categorically no. Plus, he's not that much older than us, he just has his shit together so he seems like it."

"Whatever you say, babe," she says with a wink. "But just know I'm making my move soon if you don't get there first. Clock's ticking."

"Sure, you and all the ten thousand other women lined up to warm his bed." I don't know why it sounds like jealousy in my tone. I couldn't care less if Maya hooked up with Win . . . could I? Between me and him, it's strictly business. Isn't it?

I'd never say this to her, but lately I've been seeing him in a slightly different light. I hadn't been focused on him in that way because I'd been so wrapped up in John, but he does have something irresistible and mature about him. Not that I would ever cross that line, but he's a great guy; any woman would be lucky to have him.

Later that night, as I drift off to sleep, Win, then John, then Win, flow through my mind. As if he can feel me thinking about him, my phone vibrates with a text from John.

John: I can't wait to see you tomorrow doing what we do best. Sweet dreams, Princess

I check the time in the corner of my phone. Of course—it's 11:11.

On the way to the studio, I can feel my adrenaline. Nerves, excitement, butterflies, wasps, all buzzing inside me. I know how much magic John and I can create together, so I'm excited, but I'm also nervous about our personal drama getting in the way.

When I walk in he's already working, bent over the computer wearing a hat and gray hoodie and sweats, his eyes tired but focused. He looks hot. Ugh.

I spent more time getting ready than I normally would for a session, making sure to put just enough makeup on that I still look natural but also flawless. My outfit was designed to look effortless but also make him weak in the knees: cutoff jean shorts and a cream tank, an oversized button-down, black Dior booties, and my favorite fragrance lately: Byredo's La Tulipe. I knew he would swoon, and the look on his face when he sees me is beyond satisfying. He smiles and comes out from behind the soundboard to greet me. He hugs me, which I wasn't expecting, but instinctively my arms wrap around his shoulders as he squeezes me. It feels like home being in his arms, and the smell of his cologne, the one I bought him, takes me back in time to when things between us were simple, vibrant, and easy. I don't want to let go.

"Hey." He spins me around and puts me down when I start to laugh. "You ready to make some magic?" he asks, nodding toward my microphone.

I nod enthusiastically, genuinely happy and excited. Something about John has always inspired me, and no matter what happens between us, it seems like he always will.

Hours later when we break, the sun has set, and I'm shocked at how fast the time went. John seems so happy with what we've done so far, and he orders tons of food, all our favorites, which he hasn't forgotten. He pours us both a drink and when his eyes meet mine, I'm taken out of the present and back to the past as we clink our glasses together.

One of John's friends, Cole, comes around to say hi, and we let him hear part of what we just recorded. Cole wraps his arm around my shoulder, which is a little weird, but I just go with it instead of causing a scene. Cole has a weird vibe, eyes lingering on me a little too long, but I just smile and deal with it. John watches us, his mood changing as Cole compliments me, keeps pulling me closer. John refills his glass quickly and a little too high. I try to move away but Cole keeps coming back. Thankfully, it's time to get back to work and he leaves. I don't want to let him ruin the rest of my night, so I do what I do best and turn my creative flow back on, forgetting that he showed up in the first place. This is about me and John and our music.

Back inside the recording booth, the track cuts out and restarts again as John says, "Again."

His dry monotone hits against my last nerve. This has got to be the fifteenth time he's corrected me since I stepped back into the booth ten minutes ago, and this time I barely even opened my mouth to start singing.

"John, what's the problem?" I say directly into the mic, staring hard at him through the glass separating us. "You didn't even hear me that time!"

"Your delivery isn't as strong," he mutters, not even bothering to look up at me. "Again." And then the music restarts.

Rolling my eyes, I take a deep breath and prepare myself once again. The beat kicks in, my cue arrives, and I get three words in before the sound drops away altogether.

"You're not cutting it as good," John says, exasperated, downing another shot of whiskey or whatever the hell he's drinking out there. "From the top."

I stay silent, seething inside the booth, kicking myself internally for agreeing to work on this song with him. I should've known it wouldn't end well. His mood's been so off since Cole left the studio; one too many drinks in and coupled with the shitty atmosphere between us, this is like a living hell. He can't expect to play the hero once and get a free pass on all his other bullshit.

"It's not good enough." John cuts the track again, and this time I drag my headphones off.

"John! I'm not doing this. Either let me finish my take or I'm coming out of the booth. This is a waste of my time and yours."

John shrugs dramatically, and without sparing me a glance he exits the room, letting the door slam shut behind him.

I step out of the booth and sigh.

"Maybe we should take a break?" one of the engineers awkwardly suggests.

John and I used to have fun doing this stuff. We'd spend hours recording demos just for the hell of it, sampling different songs and vibing together. We connected through our love of music, and now it just feels like we're doing the opposite of that, even though the first half of the day went so well. This is the high and the low that I keep getting addicted to.

"What's his problem? He was fine all day," I grumble to one of the other producers, walking over to the soundboard and taking John's seat.

Offering me a sympathetic smile, he says, "I thought you sounded great. He's clearly not hearing straight."

"Thanks." I smile dejectedly and lean my elbow against the desk. "Can you play back whatever we did manage to record?"

"Sure." The computer freezes so the engineer has to reopen the session, clicking a couple of options on John's screen to recover the vocal takes John deleted. He starts to play the take, but a different song plays.

"What is that?" I ask in confusion. "That's definitely not my voice."

"Uh . . . ah shit." The guy pauses the recording quickly, but not fast enough. Realization dawns as I listen closely to the vocals.

"Is that Riley Vega?" I ask in disbelief. "Is that session from today? Was she here before me?"

"That's not really for me to answer," the engineer says uneasily, looking around as if for an escape route. "I'm sorry, Princess. I have to use the restroom."

Blood pumps fast through me and my stomach is in knots. *He's got to be fucking kidding.* Did John seriously have me come here to record the song he's been hyping me up about, fully knowing he was gonna have Riley in the studio before me? He told me their working relationship was *finished.* Anger, confusion, insecurity, frustration all swirl inside of me. I want to burst into tears. This is too much. Why is he betraying me like this again?

Why can't Riley just back off and let me have my moment for once? Why can't she go find her own people to work with? She's a bigger artist than I am, she could get in the room with anyone she wants, yet she only seems to want what I have, even if it's something she's not particularly interested in; if it's good for me, if I'm growing, she's determined to put an end to it. How does John not see this? I feel so out of control I don't know if I want to scream or disappear. I was so excited about this session. I'm singing my ass off all for John to flip on me out of nowhere and storm out of the room. I wasn't cutting the record good enough . . . of course I wasn't. Why is nothing I ever do good enough for anyone?

Now I'm too emotional, and he's too drunk, for us to even be able to talk this through. We're such a mess. I should've known better and never agreed to this.

I thought things were going to be different. He told me he'd change.

"Where are you going?" John calls as I barge out of the studio doors, on a mission to get as far away from him as possible before I do or say something I'll regret. He holds his arms out to his sides, clearly amazed I'd think to leave after he treated me just so well back there.

"Move out of my way, John," I say through gritted teeth, weaving to get past him.

"Princess," he calls louder than usual at my back. "Where are you going? We're recording the—"

"You told me you finished the song with Riley. Is this another one?" I stop and turn, glaring at him with a force that makes his expression fall instantly. "How could you do this to me? Working with Riley again after what she did to me? Seriously, you say you care about me but your actions clearly show otherwise. Such a waste of my breath trying to warn you about her out of concern for you and the damage she can do to you if she doesn't get her way, but you know what? Do whatever you want, John, it's none of my business. When you said you could change, I didn't think you meant for the worse." I shake my head. "I'm done here. Next time, stay sober."

He gawks at me. My tone seems to wake him up a little. I guess he didn't expect a reaction like that. But I'm proud of myself for standing my ground. The girls would be cheering me on, too, if they were here, I know it. I mean, he practically begged me to work with him, convincing me this would be something special, our moment to put something great out there again, and the song would be huge. I don't deserve this shit.

"Can you just come back inside?" he asks. No apology or explanation. *Again.*

"Hit Wayne to schedule another session. I'm not cutting anything else today." Trying to maintain my calm, businesslike composure, I give him one final look of disgust and exit the building.

You're not gonna regret this, my ass, I think as I slam my car door. *Already do, John. Our first session back together and I already goddamn do.*

9

The Spotify party is all over socials. New artists and big names are all going. Everyone knows labels throw tons of money and promo into the artists that Spotify shows interest in, and it's so surreal that I'm one of them. I can't stop imagining how fun and wild the party is going to be. Kimi keeps reminding me how big of a deal this is. I'm going to meet so many of the people who've been supporting behind the scenes, like the people who have added me to crucial playlists I've always dreamed of being on. These connections are very important for my next single but all I can think about is how proud my younger self would be right now. All the countless hours singing in the mirror in my bedroom, and at friends and neighbors' weddings and birthdays—all of it has built to moments like this.

To make things even better, Avery, my stylist, somehow managed to get me an archive dress from Valentino. We've done three fittings and the dress is the most beautiful thing I've ever seen. I feel so honored to be wearing it; I've never pulled an archive dress before and I'm beyond obsessed with Valentino. Things are going so well right now in my career and tonight will be the icing on the cake. My performance is going to show everyone what I'm made of. I have the skill, I've put the work in, I've paid my dues, and I'm here to stay. I have interviews lined up with *Rolling Stone*, *Billboard*, *Variety*—you name it—to talk about my music and this performance.

Angel bursts through the door, practically screaming in excitement. We go over the look: dark browns and beiges to accentuate my features, and, of course, some sparkle across my cheekbones. He gossips while he works, as always, and we keep having to take breaks from laughing so hard. Once he's finished, I feel so beautiful and so fucking powerful. It's the perfect makeup look to go with my dress.

When Maya arrives, she makes me a cup of hot tea and honey. I wish I could take all my girls, but I only got a plus-one, and Kimi thought it was a better idea to bring Maya as my date instead of John, to keep the focus on me and not my love life since this is such a big event. I don't necessarily agree with her on that. I love having John with me and getting to share these special moments with him but I decided to follow Kimi's lead this time.

Maya's makeup is stunning; she went with purple tones across her lids and the prettiest sweep of highlighter on the tops of her cheeks near her eyes. Her dress is purple, too, shimmery, and she looks so damn good.

"P., where is Avery?" she asks as Angel starts doing touch-ups on me, getting ready for my final look by adding my signature bright-red lip to make it perfect.

I check my phone, making sure I have the time right. It's three in the afternoon and we have to leave by four at the latest. It's totally unlike Avery to be late. I check my messages to see when she last texted. At noon she asked if I wanted her to bring me anything on her way.

"Um, I don't know. Let me call her." It goes straight to voice mail.

"I hope she's okay. This is so weird. She's never late." I call her again.

Same thing.

My gut tells me something is wrong. Really wrong.

I check her socials to see when the last time she posted was, but I'm blocked. What the fuck?

"Maya, give me your phone, please."

She hands me her phone and I go straight to Avery's Insta. She hasn't blocked Maya, and Avery's last story was from six hours ago: her getting coffee, then a black screen with text: *Not everything is what it seems.*

What does that even mean? And why on earth would she block me randomly? She was totally fine at our fitting a few days ago.

"What's going on, P.?" Maya asks, sounding like she's ready to go to war for me before she even has the details.

My eyes are stinging, my body numb. I try to find my voice. "I don't know. I really don't know. Avery blocked me and isn't answering my calls. She has my dress for tonight. *The* dress. She's supposed to be bringing it over now. What's going on?"

"Should I call her? Give me her number," Maya says.

I shake my head. "She probably has your number saved."

"Try mine. There's no way she'd have mine saved," Angel says, clearly pissed for me too.

I use his phone to call her, my blood thumping in my ears.

Her familiar voice sounds through the other end. I can't stop myself from snapping, "Avery, what the hell? Where are you?"

She goes silent and I pray she won't hang up. "Princess?" Her voice sounds almost sad as she says my name. How can she be sad when she's the one who's ghosting me less than an hour before I have to leave?

"Did something happen to my dress? Is that why you aren't here?"

She makes a sound between a groan and a sigh, her voice trembling a little as she talks. "Princess, I'm sorry. I got a call from someone . . . I can't say who. They told me if I don't bring them your dress to wear that they'll blackball me from the industry. The dress is gone. I'm sorry. I feel awful and I can't say anything or tell you anything. But the dress is gone. I'm sorry I didn't just tell you, but I feel awful and—"

My heart stops. "Who would do that? What do you mean the dress is gone?"

"I had to give the dress to someone else. I got the call this morning right after I went to pick it up for you. They told me I'd never work for them or anyone they know again if I didn't do this. I'm so sorry, I didn't know what to do."

I'm pissed. Devastated and pissed. "Avery, you're supposed to be part of my team and you couldn't tell me earlier? At least I would have had a chance to get another dress. Now I'm totally fucked. Do you have anything else I could wear?" My head spins, and Maya and Angel look horrified. I'm going to be sick. Tears stream down my face, and I've ruined Angel's perfect makeup.

"Princess . . . I can't dress you today." She pauses. "Or ever again. I'm really sorry, but I can't work with you anymore."

My heart breaks, not only because of the dress or the party tonight, but because this is coming out of nowhere, and I trusted Avery. How could this be happening and why wouldn't she be able to work with me anymore? None of it makes sense.

"Fuck you, Avery," is all I can manage to say before I hang up.

I'm so sick of people taking advantage of my kindness and understanding.

"She says she can't work with me anymore and there's no dress," I explain, staring blankly at myself in the mirror.

I feel pathetic. I don't have anything in my closet that could work for such a big event, and there's no way I can find something else to wear now. As shallow as it sounds, what I wear tonight will be half of the buzz; no matter how good my performance is, my appearance matters just as much, if not more. That's how it is in this industry.

"This is so fucked-up! I'm going to kill Avery." Maya seethes, walking over to my bar cart and popping open a bottle of Hennessy. She downs a huge gulp and hands it to me. I take it and do the same.

"I can try to call some of my people," Angel offers. "But you know how these things are, it's nearly impossible to get a dress this late. And if we do find one, it won't be fitted to you." He's telling me what I already know.

"I'm going to call this stylist I know, Kaitlin, she's amazing and she might have something that could work." Maya paces, putting the phone up to her ear.

I'm so hurt, so embarrassed, so fucking mad, so numb, all at once. The room feels like it's spinning, like I'm spinning out of control.

A couple minutes later she gives me the update. "Ugh, so Kaitlin is out of town and can't get a look together on such short notice and while away. But she did say she's been following you and would love to work with you when she's back."

"Thanks for trying anyway." I sigh at Maya, but she's back on her phone, her long nails tapping against the screen. "Princess . . ." She hesitates. "I can't believe this, but—"

"Show me. Show me now." I reach for her phone.

Riley Vega poses next to a black Suburban with the biggest fucking smile on her face. Wearing *my* dress. My hands shake as I scroll through the reposts of her tagging Valentino and worse—Avery. The liquor I downed rises back up my throat and I try to take slow, shallow breaths so I don't throw up. Of course this is all Riley's doing. She must have heard about the archive dress, my performance tonight, my song's strong streaming numbers. Riley can't handle the thought of me finally breaking out and solidifying my career. If anyone pays attention they'll see the dress couldn't have been meant for her; it's too short because it was tailored for *me*. Knowing how calculated this betrayal is makes it worse than all of the times in the past.

The corner of my phone says it's nearly three thirty, and even though Angel is calling everyone he knows, I know the outcome.

I won't be going to the event, I won't be performing, and I won't be able to make up a good enough excuse to appease my label, the press, or the team at Spotify on such short notice.

My first thought is to call John, but I know I need to call Kimi first. She's going to lose it. I try Wayne but he doesn't pick up. Fuck. I call Kimi and she doesn't either. I don't leave a voice mail because I don't even know what to say. Maya keeps drinking and cursing Riley, watching all of the posts of her arriving at the step and repeat for press.

Kimi calls back as I take another drink. In my reflection, I notice that my tears are leaving makeup streaks down my face.

"Princess, where are you? I've been waiting here for thirty minutes," Kimi barks into the phone.

"Kimi, Riley stole my dress. Avery never showed up and I—"

She cuts me off before I can finish. "I don't care what happened, you need to get here, and now."

"I don't have anything to wear," I explain, not wanting to mention the fact that I'm so mentally shaken up by this that it would be impossible to wear anything else, even if I had another option, and pretend nothing happened, then end up face-to-face with Riley while she's wearing my dress.

"This is the problem with amateurs," Kimi snaps through the phone in a tone I've never heard from her before. "You should have had a backup. You can't show up here looking like you threw something on either. Fuck. This is not good, Princess. Really not good." She huffs out an angry sigh. "I'll figure out what to tell the execs here, but you better lie low. Do not get photographed outside your place. At all," she warns me. "I mean it." She ends the call.

I stare at my phone, unable to even react.

Seeing this side of Kimi—who's supposed to always have my back and should be taking her anger out on Riley or Avery for allowing this to happen—having her treat me like this when I'm already wounded shakes me to my core.

She's acting like she cares way more about the event than what happened to me or how I feel. Am I that disposable to her?

Tears run down my face. My makeup is ruined.

Everything is ruined.

I scream, throwing my phone across the room. It shatters and little pieces of glass scatter across the floor. The light sparkles as it hits them and it almost looks like glitter. Too bad it's an illusion, just like everything around me.

10

"I knew it was a bad idea." Maya sighs, taking a sip of her espresso and giving me an *I told you so* look. "Don't tell me I didn't warn you."

"Maya, I know," I groan, stabbing an avocado slice with my fork a little too hard. "I believe in what we can create together, and I really need this to work out. Kimi is on me asking for my next single, then an album. She's being nice about it, but I can sense the tone and I know the game. They want more. The success has been good but it's still not great. The infamous industry line I cannot bear to hear again: *You're still not there yet*. It's constant anxiety chasing the next thing, even in the middle of a huge moment of success like this. Even at the top it feels like I still have to climb the mountain, then another, then another."

"You still might." Maya's tone has softened after my vulnerable admission. "Just stay focused, don't let emotions get in the way."

"Easier said than done."

Maya shrugs. "I highly recommend the no-strings-attached life-style, especially with him." She leans forward and speaks deliberately slowly, as if trying to get through to me. "No heartache and a fuck ton of orgasms." I know she's trying to help, but she and I are very different people with opposite approaches on life.

I press my lips into a thin smile and take another bite.

We're out for brunch at a quiet little café Val discovered a few weeks ago. It's only a few blocks away from my apartment, and even if the other patrons recognize us, they don't come up asking for photos. It's nice. I feel normal here, relaxed, and the food's really good.

"Oh, here's Val," Maya says, glancing over my shoulder as a little bell chimes above the entrance door. "Finally," she says louder, and Val slides into the seat next to me.

"Hey, Princess," she says, pulling her shades off. She glares at Maya. "Hey, early bird. Who the hell wants to have brunch the morning after a party? My head's still pounding, I literally almost pulled over to throw up on the way here." She groans.

"Coffee, Val?" I offer, smirking at Maya as I push the steaming mug toward Val. "We ordered you avocado toast."

"You're an angel." Val grabs the mug and blows on the coffee to cool it, still shooting daggers at Maya as she talks. "Carbs will help."

"You have a lot to catch up on. There's more John drama—"

"Oh god, what did he do now?" Val groans. "I'm so over his shit."

I shake my head. "Same as usual."

"Riley again?" Val asks.

"You got it."

Maya catches her up on the situation while we eat. It's only after she's finished talking that I realize the time: 11:32 a.m. The last few days, John's been sending 11:11 texts—words to brighten up my day, promises about how great the song's going to be, regret at how we ended. But actions speak louder than words, and I'm tired of fighting about Riley fucking Vega.

"Weird," I mutter under my breath, picking up my phone to scroll Instagram and see what he's up to.

"What's weird?" Maya asks, leaning forward to see my screen.

"Nothing, just—" I hesitate to explain it. Admitting John sends me 11:11 texts feels like something I should be ashamed of. It's the sort of cute little detail that could be considered cringeworthy from the outside, but it makes me feel some type of way I can't even explain. Like a comfort. "I was just expecting a message from John, I guess."

"He texts you still?" Maya asks.

"Yeah, pretty much every day," I say casually.

"That's either incredibly cute or incredibly fake," Val says.

"Fake how?" I ask.

Maya raises an eyebrow. "I guess the real question here is, is he texting or just responding?"

I don't feel like explaining the whole 11:11 thing to the girls so I let it go. But the question makes me feel queasy. I'm so tired of having to analyze every little thing. Like damn, if we're cool, just be cool; if we're not, leave me the hell alone. I hate the games in this town; they make me feel insane. If John didn't want to write me, he wouldn't. So that's what I'm leaving it at. He wants to talk, that's why he writes.

Except for today, obviously. He's gone radio silent.

"Check his profile, Val," Maya directs, trying to jog Val to join our conversation again since she's distracted by something on her phone. Frown lines crease her forehead.

"What for?" I ask, but actually, I'm pretty curious too. He hasn't failed to send an 11:11 text since that day on the beach, so whatever made his mood shift so fast yesterday really fucked with him. Or worse, he's with someone else.

My pulse kicks faster at the thought.

Suddenly, it's a mission to act the fastest. Maya grabs her phone and scrolls rapidly through Instagram stories, trying to find some clue as to where he might be—a party or a road trip or a vacation or spending time with family. Val searches through all the likes on his recent posts, noting Riley hearted most of the last few. Maya stalks his X account, and I bite the bullet and search Riley's profile.

I find my answer right away.

"She posted a BTS of last night," I half gasp, spinning my phone around to show the others. "Look! Do you think this was yesterday morning, or did she go back into the studio after I left?"

"What time did she post it?" Maya snatches the phone to get a closer look. "Five hours ago. Damn. They pulled a late one."

Heat rushes to my cheeks. "Okay, so he's probably catching up on sleep," I suggest slowly, because the more obvious answer feels way too much like betrayal.

Clearly not reading the room, Maya voices it anyway. "He better not be in bed with Riley." She scoffs and passes my phone back.

"A bit harsh, Maya." Val checks Maya. "If you were in the studio until the crack of dawn you'd still be out cold too. Don't assume the worst."

Don't assume the worst. I repeat it like a mantra in my head, willing it to sink in.

"When it comes to John," Maya corrects, "I'll always assume the worst, but of course at the end of the day, it's your choice what you do with him. I just want you to be happy."

"Thanks, Maya." I smile pointedly at her.

"It's good life advice, babe," she says with a shrug. "Anyway, I'm sorry to change the subject, but I've got some big news, the reason I gathered you all here today." She sits tall in her seat, stretching her chest out and drumming her fingers on the tabletop. "Are you ready to hear it?"

"Spill it, Maya," I prompt, placing my phone face down to avoid thinking about John. I need this distraction like I need air to breathe. "Come on, what is it?"

"Well," she says with excitement, nudging Val to get her full attention too. "Last night I got a very exciting call: I'm modeling in Miami in one of those immersive experiences for a very prestigious brand next month. One of the biggest gigs of my career so far. The shitty thing about it is it's all part of this big circus-themed event thing Riley Vega's hosting, but still, do you guys know how many millionaires—no, *billionaires*—and industry people will be in town for this? I decided to not give a damn if she's hosting." She flicks her hair and strikes a pose just for us. "But—" She looks at me. "I want to make sure you're okay with it, obviously."

I jump up in my seat. "Of course! Maya, oh my god! This is amazing!" I'm so happy for her and know what this could mean for her. I still hate that Riley's involved but I would never stand in the way of my friend's success. My only worry is the chance that Riley could take her anger toward me, or whatever her issue with me is, out on Maya. I shudder at the thought but remind myself that Maya's talent speaks for itself, and there shouldn't be any reason for Riley to feel the need to control Maya's career the way she obsessively does mine.

"Congratulations, babe," Val says with a genuine smile. "My mom and dad go every year, and yeah, the people there are very high quality and have *deep* pockets. Yeah, it sucks about Riley being involved, but that's whatever. She's just hosting—there's going to be so much going on you won't have time to waste on drama."

"You said it," I agree. "You probably won't even know she's there."

"I fucking hope so." Maya shudders. "Oh, but that's not the end of it." She beams at us again, glancing around to check no one's listening and then leaning in close and making us huddle around her to hear. "This is top secret at the moment, so don't breathe a word to anyone, but my manager was saying they're still looking for someone to perform the second set during the show. I'm gonna be out there doing my thing while the performer's floating through the sky on a trapeze or some shit. It's like one huge PR event-slash-concert. As of now the spot is still free. Princess, you should jump on that. It'd be perfect for you."

Excitement bursts through me, but so does anxiety. I try to tamp my voice down so I won't seem overly excited or overly nervous. "Who would we need to call?" Then I cringe. "No way, it's Riley's team."

"No, I don't think so." Maya gives me a look. "She is a big part of the event hosting and maybe performing a short set, but it's a separate company booking everyone and running it. The people who booked me are actually pretty nice, though. Riley may be the host but the event is so, so much bigger than her."

I hesitate for a moment, weighing the options. If people in this town only worked with their friends and people they respected, there wouldn't be an industry, and Maya's right, this event is much bigger than Riley. My sister's face as she tried on sunglasses at Dior pops into my mind. Should I allow my pride to get in the way of making my family proud? Of stifling my growth? And if I did, wouldn't that just be allowing Riley to have even more power over me?

I make a choice. "I'll ask Kimi or Wayne to call them, but I'm not totally convinced that this will go well."

"Think about it and have your team reach out. It could be great, Princess. Don't let Riley's involvement stand in the way of good promo for you." Maya beams, clutching my arm across the table.

I turn to Val to gauge her opinion on all this, but when I see the look on her face my excitement pauses. "My fucking family—" she huffs, putting her phone face down on the table and staring blankly out the window beside us, no excitement or reaction visible because she's in her own little world. For the first time since she walked in, I notice the dark circles under her eyes. She looks rough.

"Val, are you okay?" I touch her arm, which makes her jump. She tunes back into our conversation and nods quickly.

"Oh, yeah, sorry. Just thinking."

"Thinking?" Maya asks. "What about?"

"It doesn't matter." Val perks up at the interest, trying to move the topic on. "Family stuff. I won't bore you with the details."

"Well, I'm interested to hear it," I say.

Maya nods. "Me too."

Val sits up. "No, it's nothing, guys, really. It's the same old family stresses and I just didn't sleep well."

Maya delivers me a look across the table. It says she doesn't believe her one bit, and honestly, I have to agree. Val's way too quiet and spaced-out this morning. We're all tired, but this is beyond that. As I take a sip of my smoothie and watch her eat, her eyes vacant and cheeks pale, I can practically see the weight on her shoulders.

"You know I'm here for whatever you need, right, Val?" I say quietly.

"I know," Val says, her bright tone not matching her dull eyes and exhausted features.

11

Later that night I'm lounging by the pool at one of Maya's friends' parties.

From the chair next to me, Maya sighs. "So, about Val . . ."

I take a sip of my drink and look at her. "I'm worried about her, Maya."

"Me too." Maya sits forward, adjusting gently so her stiletto heels don't get caught on the seat. She glances around at a cluster of people drinking and laughing nearby, and lowers her voice. "Do you think it has to do with her dad?"

"Doesn't it always have to do with her dad?"

"Well, yeah, but I mean, like, do you think it's more than just the pressure of having to take over the hotel business?"

"What do you mean?" I ask, sitting forward on my sun lounger too. I place my drink on the little table between us and wrap my cream Chanel scarf around me.

"Like, if it was just the stress of the business, she'd tell us about it, right? It's not like we don't know she doesn't want to take over the company. But the way she's acting lately, it's like there's something more going on. Something she's either ashamed of or scared to tell us about."

I consider Maya's words as I scan the various reality stars and influencers and their friends playing a drunken game of greased watermelon in the blue pool while their friends film them for content. I don't know how Maya knows these people, but I guess she found out about the party through a friend of a friend and decided it was better to be out here with cocktails and potential hookups than in bed with takeout and FaceTime. Definitely not my scene, but Maya can't resist a party.

"I wish she'd just talk to us." I sigh.

"Honestly. Since New Year's Eve, she just hasn't been the same. I can't help but think something's going on with her and honestly, I'm worried. Whenever I ask her about it she brushes it off as nothing. It's not nothing, Princess! Tell me I'm not making this shit up in my head."

"You're not. Something's up. I want the old Val back."

"Maya?"

We're interrupted by a new voice. Maya's eyes go wide as she looks up, and when I turn around to find familiar blond hair and brown eyes smiling down at us, I realize why.

"Cal!" Maya stands up and immediately wraps him in a hug. "I didn't know you were here!"

"Yeah, baby. Wouldn't miss it."

Maya laughs. "Miss me too much to keep away, did ya?"

I smile politely as Maya flirts with Cal, but internally my stomach sinks. I don't know anyone else at this party except Maya, and now she's about to hook up with Cal and leave me stranded with all my worries about Val. I know she'd stick with me if I asked, but I'm not out to cockblock my best friend. Especially not after hearing the steamy stories Maya told us all about her night with Cal last time.

"Maya," I say, standing up and squeezing her shoulder discreetly, "I'm gonna head home."

"For real?" Maya frowns. "Stay a little longer."

I shake my head, my mind made up. "I'll text you when I'm back, okay?"

"If you're sure." She pouts, but her hands are on Cal's chest and his eyes are on her lips already. This is definitely my cue. Besides, I'm so in my head about what's happening with Val I don't think I'd enjoy much more of the party if I stayed.

"Love you, babe. Be safe!" I air-kiss her cheeks and walk off, heading inside to call a driver and change out of my bikini.

I'm halfway to the door when a burst of laughter snaps my attention to the side. A group of girls I vaguely recognize sit around a firepit with a bunch of other people I don't know. Still, all of their eyes are on me as I continue toward the house, and when I hear words like *fake* and *wannabe* floating on the air I stop dead in my tracks.

"Hi." I try my best to be polite despite how awkward it feels. "Do I know you?" I ask, locking eyes with a girl whose name I can't remember, but who was definitely with Riley when I hung out with her in the past.

"Barely, but we've met," the girl responds. She's not exactly in-my-face rude, but not sweet either.

As we stand there, I shift my weight on my heels, uncomfortable and trying my hardest not to show it. I hear the small group start to whisper about me.

"She tried to steal Riley's songs and now her producer. How pathetic," one of the guys says.

When I look at them, they all turn their heads.

"And her outfit," a female voice laughs.

Every bone in my body wants to stomp over and ask them what the hell they're talking about. I've never in my life tried to take a song from anyone—especially Riley—and if the producer they're claiming I tried to steal is John, well, that's just insane. He was one of the first producers I ever worked with, long before Riley had even met him. I wish Maya was by my side so she could correct their petty bullshit, but I don't want to cause a scene, and I sure as hell don't want to go viral having a childish argument at a party.

With a fake smile, I look the girl up and down and then walk inside, not glancing back even when they carry on with their ridiculous story.

"Assholes," I growl into the phone as I pull my shirt on. "I've never done anything to Riley or any of them. Seriously . . . what the fuck! They know how replaceable they are, that's why they have to be her little minions. Don't wanna get kicked out of the group now."

"Isn't that the point?" Jessie sighs through the phone. There's background noise—traffic and loud music—and I wonder how nice it must be to go out with her girls at college. At least that kind of drama would be so much easier to deal with than this Hollywood shit. "They're doing it because you did nothing to them. These people are wannabes who have no drive, no direction, no careers. They're either born into this lifestyle or so fame hungry they'd do anything to claw their way into being part of Riley's group, not knowing they're actually knocking on hell's door. When genuine people like you come around they don't even know how to handle it, they feel so bad about themselves. Their lives are depressing and they're desperate to fill the void by ganging up on people who are too nice to do anything about it."

"But *why*?" I drag the word out, stepping into my baggy gray sweatpants and pulling them over my bikini.

"Because they're jealous and you're not like them. You're better than them and you're a good person. Imagine still being in that circle. Everyone knows they all secretly hate each other. That would be worse, right?"

"Way worse. You're right," I mutter, scraping my damp hair back and blowing out my cheeks. "How's your night going, anyway?"

"Uh." Jessie sounds guilty. "Really good, actually. Feels like I've been glued to my dorm room studying for the past few days, so it's nice to just get out and *dance*, you know?"

"You work so hard, Jess. You deserve a night out." I glance at myself in the mirror, feeling suddenly dumb for calling her. "And here I am interrupting it with my stupid drama. I'm sorry. I'll stop now."

"No, Princess, it's fine. You know I'm always here for you."

"And I got your back too," I tell her. "Which is exactly why I'm gonna hang up now. Enjoy your night, Jessie. Love you so fucking muuuuuch—"

I cut the call before she can argue. She texts me less than ten seconds later.

Jessie: ILYSFMASLHGYD

Jessie: (That means I love you so fucking much and stop letting Hollywood get you down, but you already know that right?)

Jessie: <3 <3 <3

Laughing, I go to type my reply but am interrupted when another text pops up.

John: There's an incredible full moon tonight. Have you seen it? Took one look and wanted to share it with you

Before I've even had a chance to notice the time—11:11 p.m.—my phone vibrates in my hand with his call.

—

Call me silly, but it feels like a sign when John asks if he can come pick me up. A sign of what, I'm not sure. I accept his offer mostly because the thought of going home alone seems even worse than spending the rest of my night at the party mingling with people who clearly don't want me there.

"Everything okay?" he says as I sink into the passenger seat.

"Long day," I answer. Then, when he goes quiet, I throw him a small smile. "I don't wanna talk about it, but could use this distraction, so thanks."

"Thank you for taking my call. I really thought you were going to tell me to fuck off after what I pulled at the studio the other day. I'm sorry for that, P. You were great, I was being an idiot."

Usually, I would just brush it off and not hold John accountable, but I'm really trying to get better at saying what I need and want, so I turn to face him. "I was about to tell you it's fine and in the past, but it really wasn't fine, and we were having such a good session. What made you change like that?"

He sighs, rubbing his hand over his chin, a nervous tick I haven't seen in a while. "To be honest, it drove me fucking crazy the way Cole was all over you."

"Seriously? That's why you acted like that? I barely know the guy and he's *your* friend. You should have just said something. This is why I always say we have to communicate better, John."

The idea of him being jealous feeds the immature, obsessive part of my brain, but it bothers me that he would let his emotions get in the way of our work, especially with how much is riding on this song being big.

"I know," he groans, tapping his hands against his steering wheel. "I guess I just didn't think seeing you get hit on would bother me so much. And I should have told you about Riley, but didn't know how."

"Wow, you're apologizing. I don't even know how to react," I tease him, knowing that I deserve his apology but also proud of him because I know how hard it is for him to be open about how he feels.

"I'm trying." His smile is shy, warm, and genuine. "I really am. I've been wanting to call you every minute since, but tonight I just had to when I saw the moon. I knew you would love it."

I click in my seat belt. "It was nice that you were thinking of me."

"I can be thoughtful," John says with a faint smile, pulling onto the road.

"This whole emotional maturity thing looks good on you, John."

"You make me better, P. Only you." He rests his hand over mine, and the contact steals my breath. I find him smiling the same sweet smile I've always loved. His voice is softer when he speaks again. "Wanna go for a drive?"

"Where to?" I ask.

John shrugs. "Just a drive. Around the city, maybe through the Hills. Find somewhere we can sit and talk and forget the world for a while. How does that sound?"

I shut my eyes and lean my head back against the headrest. "Honestly, that sounds like heaven."

And it is. We drive for an hour or more, talking idly like we used to about anything and nothing, playing our favorite songs, and just enjoying each other's company. The thing about John is I can say so much to him and still feel as if we've talked a whole bunch of nothing. It's the most comfortable, familiar kind of connection, with lots of laughter and dreaming about our futures. It almost makes me forget all the shit between us lately.

Eventually, John pulls to the side of the road in a spot overlooking the city. He cuts the engine and turns to me.

"I really missed this," he says.

I want to make some sort of witty comment but the words that come out instead sound hopelessly sincere. "I've really enjoyed tonight."

"Me, too, Princess."

"John—" I stare out at the city, my thoughts reeling back to the party and Val and the awful group of friends. "Do you ever think about getting away from it all?"

He studies me carefully for a few seconds before answering. "You mean Hollywood?"

"Yeah, the industry. All the darkness and being in the spotlight and cliques and politics. Do you ever wonder what it would be like to live a normal life?"

John cracks a window and sparks up a cigarette. I watch as a tendril of smoke curls around his head and fades into the midnight sky.

"I can't see myself ever not making music, but sometimes when I look at my parents and how happy they are, it makes me wonder if it's possible to have that here," he says. "A normal life. Fell in love when they were nineteen and dirt-poor, and never laid eyes on anyone else. They just fit. Like two halves of the same whole. Always downplayed the idea of a grand love story with romantic gestures, but honestly, if you ask me what's more romantic—having what they had, virtually no money but a connection that sticks for life, or these industry romances propped up on PR plays—well, the answer's obvious. I'd take what my mom and dad have any day."

"That's really sweet and sounds wonderful," I say. "And I agree. I love roses but they don't mean a thing if there's no real commitment.

You know I'm such a romantic, I can't help it. I want it all. I want commitment, to grow and share my life with someone. To look back one day, reminiscing about all these cool experiences we're having now. The lifelong love and devotion . . . and the roses." I realize what I just said. *Shit*.

"Princess—" John shakes his head. "I'm sorry I hurt you. I didn't mean for it to go down like that. These songs with Riley, it's business, that's all. Two songs. Two creative collabs, nothing else. I didn't wanna build a wall between you and me. The reason I didn't ask you first is because they're one-offs. We aren't making a whole project, I didn't feel like it was that deep. What you and I are doing together is so much bigger than that."

"Listen, you can work with whoever you want. You know I've always wanted the best for you. I just don't like feeling like I'm on the outside or that you're hiding things from me. It's not as simple as Riley wants to make music with you, there's always a strategy. She's always got a plan, and in the end it's only in her best interest. I worry about the kind of person she is—she's ruthless and will do anything to maintain her status and stay on top. You're known for being good, John, and I don't want her to ruin that. She's not as light and fun as she pretends to be. Trust me, I know from experience. She can't be trusted."

The night air has cooled around us and it's so quiet here that it's almost like we're not in the city at all.

"I'm not going to hang with her outside of the studio alone ever again, and if I could, I'd pull the song, but it's too late," he says. "And I trust what you're saying, especially about that shit she pulled with your dress. I hate that she did that to you."

"Thanks," I tell him, hoping he means it.

Not only out of jealousy, but with her backstabbing tendencies, if Riley wants John, which I'm sure she does, and he rejects her, she will stop at nothing to take him down. I've seen her ruin the lives of men who rejected her, and she knows what John means to me, which gives her more ammo. She the type of girl who loves the satisfaction of thinking she could steal anyone's man.

"Thank you for always having my back, P."

I look at him questioningly. "I always will, you know that. I love you. Whether we're together or not," I tell him, meaning it. No matter what happens between us, John was one of the first people to believe in me; he was my best friend long before we started dating and he's been there through all the ups and down since I moved here. Our bond is deep and unwavering, regardless of our roller coaster of a relationship.

"You will?" he says, running his hands over my hair in a cute and endearing way.

I nod, not able to stop the smile that fills my face.

"Well, I'm just asking in case that means you'd give me a second chance, not right this second, but someday?" he explains, and then chuckles and looks out the window. "A guy can dream."

"You'd have to earn it," I say, and he whips his head back to look at me again. "A second chance. But you're off to a decent start."

He contemplates my words for a minute and then nods. I brace myself for his reply, but instead, he changes the subject.

"Can I take you home, P.?"

"Well, it is getting late." I glance at the time on the dash. "And I am already in your car . . ."

"Is that a yes?" he asks, the hint of a smile at the corner of his mouth.

I shrug. "If you really want it to be." I can't explain the nervous energy in the pit of my stomach, but I know why it's there. For a second, it almost felt like we were flirting. And now he's driving me home.

What are you doing, Princess? As my eyes meet John's, the answer arrives just as quickly.

I'm falling for him all over again.

12

"Is that paparazzi?" John says as we pull up to my apartment building.

Three men are standing by the entrance to the parking garage with their cameras at the ready. "We can't avoid them so try to get past as quick as you can."

"It's not like we haven't been seen together before anyway."

"Ugh." I throw my head back against the seat. "It's so late. This is definitely gonna look some type of way, us arriving at my place together."

"They'll just say we're back together. And maybe it will be good once our song is announced?" John offers as their cameras flash, the guys running up to the car as John swerves into the underground garage. I notice the content look on his face, not allowing them to get a bad picture of him.

Even though I hold my purse up in front of my face, I already know it won't matter. The paparazzi are relentless. They know I live in this building, and they'll recognize John's car. I give it two hours before these photos are circulating online with rumors we're back together.

Weirdly, that doesn't bother me as much as it should.

"I guess you're coming upstairs," I say once we're parked in the garage and out of sight of any cameras.

"Do you want me to?"

I roll my eyes playfully. "Don't pretend that wasn't your plan."

He chuckles but doesn't deny it.

We ride the elevator up to my apartment, stepping inside and tossing our keys on the kitchen island.

"Want a drink?" I ask.

"No, thanks. I've gotta drive home." There's a beat of silence where he tests me with his eyes, as if waiting for me to protest. So I play him at his own game.

"Oh, I have water. Soda. Doesn't have to be alcohol."

His face drops for a second. Immediately, I laugh.

"If you want to stay over, you can use the guest room. And I kind of wouldn't mind the company tonight. You know I hate being alone after parties."

"Almost as much as you hate parties." He smiles and I nod in agreement.

John double- then triple-checks the locks on my door. He slides an arm around my shoulder and glances at his watch. "I'll stay. Want me to run you a bath with the essential oils you like before bed?"

"You don't have to do that," I say with a yawn.

"I know," John says. "But I'm going to."

He doesn't wait for me to protest and walks into my bedroom, making the decision for me. I love that about him, how he takes control of situations when he knows I want something but I won't say it. Even though it's only been one night, every minute I spend with him like this, it becomes easier to slip right back into our old ways.

Feeling exhausted now that we're back in my safe space, I drink a tall glass of cold water before heading into my room. Through the bathroom door I can see John's lit my candles, and the water running into the tub creates a floral-scented steam that mists into my room.

Why can't it be like this all the time?

"It's ready for you," he says gently. I'm wrapped in a fluffy white towel and ready for a half hour of relaxation. Maybe a whole night.

"Thanks, John."

His fingers move to my hair, gently twisting the strands, instantly making any tension fade. He knows me so well.

"It's the least I can do," he says, and I get the feeling he's hinting at all the shit with Riley and his tantrum in the studio without wanting to say it outright. He apologized earlier, so I'm not going to bring it up right now.

I reach for my makeup wipes on the counter and swipe one across my eyelid. I don't have much on but want a clean face before I get into the tub. I yawn again, exhausted. John leans over and plucks another wipe out of the pack, and I laugh.

"Do you even know what to do with that?" I look at him in the mirror as I lift myself to sit on the countertop, both of us laughing now.

He looks at it like it's from another planet, but nods. "I'm guessing you just, like, wipe it on your face? I've seen you do it a million times, P. Trust me, I'm a fast learner," he playfully says.

He does a decent job and my stomach hurts from laughing at his sweet attempt. I stand up and stretch; even my body is exhausted. Our stares linger for a beat too long, but instead of striking the match, I let it all go and step past him.

"Let me know if you need anything," he says, dusting his hand across my waist when we meet in the doorway. It sets something tingling inside me. Something impossible to ignore. "I'll just be out here, okay? To give you some space."

"John . . ." I go to say, but the words get lost on their way out.

"Yeah, P.?" he asks, eyes lit up with a spark of hope. I feel that same hope deep inside of me.

I guess it's been hot and cold with us lately. Maybe that's the way we are now. Not every relationship's smooth sailing and consistent. And so what; maybe we hit a rough patch—all couples go through that. Maybe these problems are helping us learn each other better, and sticking through the ups and downs is our way of igniting the spark between us over and over again. Maybe we shouldn't call it quits just yet. I know him better than anyone; I know that under his casual and sometimes cold façade, there's a caring, soft man who loves me.

"I want you to stay," I croak, but that's all I say. "In here, I mean."

As I slide the towel off and step into the tub, I hear his breath hitch behind me, and then his footsteps cross the tile as he comes to sit on the edge of the bath.

"Want me to wash your hair?" he murmurs, already reaching out to run his fingers through each soft strand.

"Mmm, please," I say, tilting my head back, relaxing my body in the water.

Gently, using my sandalwood shampoo, John works a lather into my hair with his strong hands, massaging my head and moving down to my neck and shoulders. Every touch feels like heaven. It makes me crave him even more. I try to push the feeling aside and just enjoy the sensation, but the longer I spend in the tub, the hotter the energy grows.

"That's so nice."

John doesn't speak, just lets me relax in total bliss. His hands continue their massage even after he's done with washing my hair. I reach up to his wrist, intertwining my fingers with his. The water sways, and John's eyes roam my body under the water lustily, but he doesn't make a move. There's just something about his restraint and the hazy look in his eyes that turns me on.

"I missed you, baby," he whispers as his other hand kneads my shoulders, then lower. I hold my breath as his palms slide over the center of my chest, and he repositions himself on the edge of the tub so he can reach better.

"I missed you too," I breathe as his hand slides under the water, fingers running a smooth path along my belly, getting closer to the one place that aches for his touch. "John . . ." His name comes out as a moan when he finally finds me as my thighs part. "Fuck."

"I missed you so much," he murmurs, voice hot and husky in my ear as he leans forward to pull my earlobe between his teeth. The sensation makes every hair stand on end, increasing the feeling between my legs as his fingers dip inside. I don't really hear his words, I'm so overcome by his actions.

"Does that feel good, baby?" he rumbles in my ear, eyes on me and nowhere else as he moves faster and faster, taking me to the edge.

I grip his arm, throwing my head back, begging him not to stop. John kisses my neck, whispering magic in my ear—all my favorite things, which he's done to me so many times before. He *knows* me. It's like my body was made for him. And after he brings me to climax and makes me see glittering stars, I can focus on only one thing: him.

In a frenzy, lips and bodies glued together, we trip backward into the bedroom, removing John's clothes as we go. He yanks his shirt over his head and I help unbuckle his belt, feeling him hard already. I need to have him closer. He pushes me onto the bed, moving above me and kissing his way from my thighs up to my mouth, knotting his tongue with mine and groaning my name as if he can't get enough of saying it.

"Tell me you need me." I gasp as he positions himself between my legs.

"Fuckin' always. I always need you. Always have and always will," he replies, burying his face in the crook of my neck and releasing a groan that makes me lose my damn mind.

It's been so long since I was last with him that I didn't realize what I was missing, but as John moves above me and the temperature builds, the sheets tangled around us and our bodies finding new angles to explore each other from, I start to remember what we are.

Each other's.

The glare of the sun streaming in through my bedroom is warm on my skin as the buzzing of my phone wakes me up. Win's name flashes on the screen and I contemplate whether or not to answer. It could be about work, but having John here, it doesn't feel right to answer, so I ignore the call and roll over in the thick blanket. John isn't in the bed, which makes me worry at first. What if last night was a fluke? A one-night stand.

As I climb out of bed to see if John dipped or not, a text comes in from Win.

Win: Morning, Princess, sorry to text so early, I wanted to talk to you about upping your security

So it is about business. Why did I think otherwise? Getting back under the sheets I return his FaceTime, feeling silly that I thought there was something wrong with answering his call just because John spent the night.

"Hey, Win."

He looks bemused to see my camera's off but doesn't question it. "Are you okay?"

I turn the volume down, shifting up a little in bed. "Yeah, I'm good," I half whisper, my voice still waking up. "So great seeing you the other day."

"Always a pleasure," Win says. "I heard you'll be at Coachella next week and wanted to talk logistics really quick if you have time."

"I have a few minutes." I listen for any noises coming from the living room or kitchen. Did John really leave? "Yes, I'll be there."

"I also heard you had an issue with a possible stalker when you had the house in Malibu. Have there been any other incidents?"

"Thankfully not," I say, shuddering as I think about my stalker still on the loose out there somewhere.

"I was calling to offer you my security team, especially for Coachella. My guys are the best."

"Thanks, Win," I say genuinely. "But Kimi and Wayne hired a couple of guys already. They're downstairs at my place now, and yeah, they'll come with us to Coachella. It's weird to have security full-time since I don't really need that normally day-to-day, but after the incident it has been making me feel better about things."

"Actually, Princess, those are my guys. I fired the others and already talked to Kimi and Wayne. I'm not taking no for an answer. Especially when it comes to you," Win says. It's barely eight o'clock but he's already in full business attire, lounging in a leather office chair in some kind of boardroom. "As long as you're safe, that's all that matters."

"Oh, don't worry about me," I say, noticing how much my voice sounds like I just woke up.

"Princess, is your camera broken?" Win sounds serious.

I laugh awkwardly, running my fingers quickly through my knotted hair to make it look less like I just had sex. "Oh, no, it's fine. Sorry, I'm looking kinda crazy right now."

There's a pause. Win looks down, chuckling as realization dawns. "You're still in bed, aren't you?"

I set the phone at an angle, revealing half my face sheepishly. "Maybe . . ."

Win stares at the screen a little too long, taking me in before shaking his head fondly and looking away. He swipes his thumb over his mouth as if trying to rub away a grin. "I don't care if you're in bed or running a marathon."

"Definitely *not* running a marathon," I tease. "But thanks for checking in on me. Seriously, I really appreciate it."

A sense of relief washes over me and a smile breaks across my face as the smell of bacon filling the air. John didn't leave.

Like always, he sighs at my thanks, shrugging as if he's trying to emphasize the fact I don't need to thank him; I should expect this sort of treatment. "What's your plan for today?" he asks. "Do you want to get lunch?"

John walks into the room, a coffee mug in his hand. "Morning, babe," he says, handing me the coffee.

Win's expression drops as he realizes it's John; with the quickest of looks, I swear his jaw ticks, but he wipes his expression back to neutral so fast that maybe I imagined it?

Caught in the middle, I don't know what to do. My face turns red as I try to decide whether to answer John or explain myself to Win. Because now it looks like I'm trying to hide the fact I spent the night with John while Win's worrying about my safety. It's awkward and I don't know why; I've never crossed a line with Win, but a little guilty pinch pangs in my stomach for some reason. It's ridiculous, so I ignore it. Win knows about my history with John, and I've never cared to shield it from him until now.

"Is that Win?" John asks, not seeming bothered at all.

I'm definitely overthinking this.

"Hey, Win." He waves at the camera and walks back to the door of my bedroom. "Breakfast is almost done, P."

"Hi, John. Princess, I'm getting another call. Sorry. I'll talk to you later." Without waiting for my reply, Win hangs up.

It's so unlike him to cut off like that, but he's a busy man so I shrug it off and wrap the blanket around my body, moving to the living room.

The kitchen smells like heaven. John pulled out all the stops making waffles, bacon, fluffy omelets full of vegetables and gooey cheese. It's so attractive seeing him get down in the kitchen.

"Eat up, baby," he tells me, tilting my chin to kiss me, and everything else fades away.

13

"You know, the dad of one of your old friends from kindergarten stopped me and your dad at the grocery store the other day," Mom tells me.

I'm chilling on my couch with my second steaming cup of coffee and a whole chunk of time while I wait for John to return with lunch. The sun reflects off the white marble floor of my apartment, but I can see the ocean glittering blue behind Mom on our FaceTime call.

There's something so much purer about the ocean in Guam compared to here in Los Angeles. Tranquil, endless, and private, it's perfectly rejuvenating after a long day. Our family home overlooks the ocean, and I miss it constantly—just like I miss my family.

"Which friend?" I ask with interest, thinking back to my island days. I haven't visited home since last Christmas, flying back in time for the New Year's Eve party, and with my busy release schedule coming up I don't think I'll be back again for a while. Which sucks. But at least I have these quiet moments to catch up.

"Liv." When I try to recall the name, Mom shakes her head. "Oh, you won't remember her—both of you were too young—but her dad's so proud of how far you've come, Princess. He said Liv still follows your career and knows the lyrics to all your songs."

"That's so sweet."

"Maybe we could send them some signed merch," Mom suggests. "What do you think?"

I scoot farther down on the couch cushions to get comfortable. "Sure, if you think she'd like that. I don't want her to think I'm self-obsessed."

"Oh, stop." Mom brushes me off with a wave of her hand. "Princess, the island loves you. Liv's a fan!"

My phone vibrates in my hand as a call from Kimi pops up. "Mom, it's Kimi," I say quickly.

"Calling you now?"

"It might be important," I say. "I'll call you back, okay?"

"Okay, hon. Love you."

"Love you, Mom. Bye." I click onto Kimi's call immediately. "Hey."

"Did you see the big news?"

I sit up swiftly and swipe onto my socials. "Big news, huh?" I tap X first, then my emails, then I skim through my texts, not knowing where to look first.

"Your song just landed at number one!" Kimi gushes excitedly. It's rare to hear her sounding anything but composed. "You're a number one charting artist, Princess!"

"What the fuck! No way!" I jump up from the couch, clutching my face. "That's insane! Are you playing with me?" My pulse jumps up and down in my throat, the excitement so palpable I don't know what to do.

"Not kidding—check the charts!"

Fingers hitting all the wrong keys, I race to select *Princess Billboard charts* from the list of autocorrect options on Google and let out a scream once I see my name right there at the top. "I'm NUMBER FUCKING ONE, KIMI! OH MY GOD!"

"Congratulations!" she says enthusiastically, but I barely hear her next words because my head's practically swimming with pride and I'm far too preoccupied with hurriedly typing a message to the girls.

"I can't believe this!" I keep saying over and over, my disbelief only interrupted by a nonstop loop of "What the fuck," "Oh my god," and "I'm fucking number one!"

"Princess." Kimi's voice eventually cuts in. "Princess, did you hear me?"

"I'm here, Kimi," I say, snapping back to reality. "What did you say? I think I lost signal or something."

"That's not the only good news." Kimi has regained her usual composure. "We got you booked on the Miami show you mentioned, same one as Maya. Billboards, stage time, a catwalk, and they want you to perform, so it's a huge opportunity for you. All of this coming right after your Coachella trip means you'll be front and center the next few weeks. Strategically, nothing could be coming together better!"

"Holy shit!" The knowledge tastes much sweeter now I know I'll be performing as a *number one charting artist.*

"I have a bunch of calls to make, catch-up with the label. Go celebrate," Kimi says as I squeal again. "I'm so proud of you. Wayne's talking to the promoters now, so be looking out for a call from him about the wardrobe fitting soon."

"Wardrobe fitting? I need time to figure out which stylist I want to use first."

"That's being handled," Kimi says. "The Image Agency is pitching us different stylists and setting up intros."

"That is perfect, Kimi! They have all the best over there."

"You deserve it all. Before we get off, do you have an idea of what your next plans are single-wise? We need to keep the momentum going and be prepared with a follow-up. People are going to be asking right away and we can't have your name die out during all this buzz. You got one shot to really break so we have to make the most of this moment."

The high of my song being number one is quickly replaced with the reality that I'm only as good or as valuable as my next thing. I can't help but feel that even though I'm number one, it's not enough. I don't want Kimi to have any doubts or feel my stress, so I keep a grin plastered on my face.

"I hear you and I'm on it. Thank you, Kimi. I can't wait to tell my mom! She's going to lose it," I gush, already hovering my thumb over the End Call button; sharing the news with my mom will hype me back up. This is the best day of my fucking life, and I won't let anything ruin it.

As morning fades into afternoon and the sun climbs higher in the sky above Los Angeles, I grow restless. I already exhausted Mom with my excitement when I called her back after hanging up on Kimi, and it's like actual torture having to hold it all in waiting for John to get back. He left around nine saying he needed to go home and change before we head to the studio for our session, but said he'd be back to pick me up later with sushi from my favorite spot just around the block. But it's past lunchtime now, and I have no clue where he is.

"Come on, answer the phone!" I mutter as another call rings through to voice mail. "It's almost two o'clock already." My stomach rumbles as if in protest as I slide my phone into my back pocket. I'm so damn hungry. At this rate, I'm more excited to eat than to tell John the news.

Just as I go to stand up and find a snack from the kitchen, my private elevator dings, signaling his arrival. I head over to the foyer, ready to greet him.

"Jeez, what took so long? It's been like eighty-four years—"

A strange noise cuts me off—a nasally whimper as the elevator doors open, then an eerie silence instead of the noise of John stepping out.

Who is *that*?

As I round the corner and stop directly in front of the elevator, my stomach drops.

"Can I help you?" I ask the strange but mildly familiar-looking guy standing in the center of the elevator. Dressed in all white from head to toe, staring right at me through beady eyes, pinning me to the spot. My heart stops. It's the man from before, the one who showed up at my Malibu rental. My head becomes fuzzy. Do I run? Try to fight him off? Scream for help? Call the police?

"With the arrow you shot at my heart, sweet dove, I'll end the man who stands in our way."

His voice takes me aback. It's robotic and creepy, and his eyes don't leave mine as he speaks, a strange, twisted smile curling the edge of his lips.

"What?" I say automatically, but it's as if he's living in his own reality. The man carries on talking without acknowledging my question at all.

"Princessssssss, my Princess, we're one and the same. My woman, my life, my heart and soul. You are my sweet one. Look at me and see who I am."

My heart pounds against my rib cage as I slowly ease my phone out of my back pocket, trying to be discreet as I activate Siri and hope like hell this guy keeps his distance.

"So lovely to meet you," he says, his tone different now, theatrical almost, as if he's switching from one character to a whole other. "So lovely, lovely, lovely." He twists his wrists in the air and steps forward with one foot, then before I can move or think prances out of the elevator onto my marble floor.

"Hey, Siri, call security!" I shout at my phone, freaking the fuck out and darting away from him, blood pounding between my ears and my legs turning to jelly behind the knees. I slam the SOS button on my intercom as I run past it, the stalker's footsteps fast on my tail.

"Ma'am, is there an emergency?" a voice asks through the intercom speaker.

"YES!" I scream, running into my bedroom and slamming the door shut behind me. "HELP!" I shout as loudly as I can, hoping it's enough for security downstairs to take action. How the fuck did this guy even get past them?

"My love, I mean you no harm," the stranger coos through the wood of my door.

I flip the lock and pace backward until I meet the wall on the other side of the room. "Get out of my house!" I scream hoarsely, voice shaking with fear. My entire body follows; I'm shivering violently from fright.

He doesn't answer. There's a sharp thud instead, and the door wobbles on its hinges with the force of whatever he just rammed against it.

He's trying to get in.

"Shit." I glance around for a weapon of some sort. There's a ceramic vase on my nightstand—that could work if I smashed it. Or maybe the razor-sharp heel of my stiletto boots. I jump to grab them, positioning myself just behind the door. It thumps again with the force of his body weight, and another small scream escapes involuntarily. *Hurry up*, I beg the security guys internally. *Come on, come on . . .*

Right on cue, the elevator dings again, and then there's shouting and heavy footsteps racing fast down the hallway. It all happens in an instant. First a huge crash, then the sound of glass splintering and a whole string of curses, followed by more shouting and the high-pitched, bone-chilling shriek of the guy as he's escorted out of my apartment. I clutch my chest as I listen to it happen, heart still hammering hard against my rib cage, nausea rolling through me at the thought of what could've happened if security wasn't downstairs.

"Princess?" The voice is on the other side of my bedroom door, breaking me out of my thoughts. "It's Hector from security. Are you in there? We've removed the intruder."

"Yes, I'm here." I don't realize I'm crying until my voice breaks on my reply. Dropping the stiletto weapon, I dab at my eyes quickly and move to open the door. "Thank you so much," I say to the bodyguard as soon as I see him. "That was way too close."

"I don't know how it happened," Hector says, shaking his head, visibly regretful. "I am right there by the elevator—I should've seen him walk in. I'm so sorry, ma'am. I'll let Kimi and Wayne know you're okay. I was watching the whole time, but my wife called me—our son is sick, or I would never have answered during work. That's when he must have got by. I'm so sorry, Princess."

"Please just make sure we get the security footage," I reply quietly, too shaken up to even begin dissecting how and why the guy ended up in here. "And get his personal information. Find out if he's with anyone, did he walk up or drive up, make sure he doesn't fucking come back—and don't let him go until the cops arrive."

"Yes, I'm on it. We're filing a report and getting a restraining order in place, this will all be handled with the police." Hector steps back, and it's only then I realize that shards of glass have rained all over my floor.

"Oh my god," I breathe.

Hector looks at the broken console table. "It smashed in the process of trying to get him out." He holds up a hand, showing off a dripping red cut in the center of his palm. "The table didn't get such a lucky escape," he jokes.

"Oh no." I step carefully forward, avoiding the glass and reaching for his arm. "You need medical attention."

"Don't worry about me." He smiles reassuringly. "I'll send house-keeping up to clean this up for you." He walks me to a nearby chair and has me sit down. "In the meantime, try and breathe in and out through your nose, it'll help calm your nervous system."

"Thank you," I murmur, not realizing I was breathing so heavily, making my chest feel like it could explode. Hands still shaking, I dial John's number, eager to get the hell out of here.

"Princess." He answers on the third ring. "What's up?"

"Where are you? Why haven't you been answering my calls?" I say, trying not to break down.

There's a short silence. "Shit, I'm sorry, babe. I didn't see them come in."

Shutting my eyes and releasing a long breath, I try to be strong but my voice breaks as I explain. "I just got attacked. In my fucking apartment. How far away are you?"

"Wait, what?" His voice instantly kicks up a notch. "What are you talking about?"

"That guy from the beach house was here. He walked right out of the elevator and came right in. He chased me down the fucking hallway. I was so scared."

"Chased you down the—" John curses under his breath. "Jesus, Princess, how the hell did he get in? Where was security? Are you okay?"

"I don't know how he got past security, but I left the front door open for *you*"—I drag the word out, wanting to get my point across with just the right amount of attitude—"I walked over thinking he was you coming back with our sushi. What's taking you so long? It's been hours. I need you here."

"Oh shit." John sighs heavily. "Traffic was brutal getting over here, and then when I got in, I had a bunch of emails I had to answer. I'm so sorry. I should have been there. Were you waiting on me?"

I'm always waiting on you, I feel like saying, but with another deep breath I reply, "Doesn't matter. Please get here, I need you. We can order something in or just figure it out when you get here. I'm too shaken up. I can't do a session right now, let's cancel."

"Yes," he replies instantly, no hesitation. "I'm coming right now."

I shudder at the thought of hanging around here alone any longer. I glance around my apartment as if expecting another creep to jump out from behind a wall. "Please hurry."

"Be there soon, P."

As soon as he hangs up, I wish he'd have stayed on the line, just in case, just to keep me company. I lean against the kitchen island with my head in my hands, massaging the stress away with my fingertips and wondering how the hell such an exciting morning turned into this kind of shit show so fast. *And how did he "forget lunch"? It was the only thing he had to do aside from go back to his place to shower and change!*

His excuse doesn't sit right with me—there's always brutal traffic in LA. John wasn't answering his calls either. *If he really did just go home, he'd have heard his phone.* I can't shake the feeling I'm missing something, but maybe I'm just overwhelmed by everything else going on.

"What a fucking roller coaster." I sigh, blowing my hair out of my face as I straighten up. Before I can think too deeply about it, my phone lights up with another call.

"Hey, Wayne," I answer, knowing security would've called him as soon as I sent out the alert.

"Princess, are you okay?"

"Honestly, I don't even know."

"Tell me what happened, from the beginning."

I lean my hip against the island and stare over at the elevator, shards of glass glinting in the sunlight on the floor all around it. "I mean, Wayne, where the fuck do I even begin?"

Before I get the chance, Win bursts into my room. His normally perfected appearance is disheveled and he's almost out of breath.

"Princess, I'm so sorry," he says.

How on earth did he get here so fast?

"My guy dropped the ball. I'm firing him. Are you okay?" he asks, studying me for my response.

"No, please don't fire anyone. I'm okay, I'm just—" My breath speeds up. Am I okay? Physically, yes, but mentally? My life was in danger, and no one was here for me. In the darkest moments, I always seem to be alone.

Win wraps his arms around me as I collapse into his chest, allowing myself to lower my guard and admit how terrified I was. He doesn't push me to talk, staying quiet until I fall asleep, and when I wake up, my apartment is empty, again.

14

One week later

"Sooooo, I saw photos of you and John arriving back here together last week. Are you two an item again?" My stylist, Kaitlin, raises her eyebrows as she thrusts a brand-new pair of thigh-high boots at me. We're in my apartment trying on outfits in preparation for Coachella later this week. Jessie flew in this morning, and she's sitting at my dining table, busy flipping through the huge catalog of clothes Kaitlin handpicked for us already. "You were coming back from a late one, huh?"

Kaitlin is my new personal stylist and she's amazing. She's got the same taste as me and an eye for new designer talent. Coincidently, she was included in the list of stylists the Image Agency provided and was also introduced to me by Maya after the whole dress incident, when somehow Riley managed to steal not just my dress but my stylist too.

"They'd been out breaking into rich people's houses," Val jokes from her spot lounging on my huge white cloud couch.

"And burying bodies in secret locations." Jessie plays along.

"Guys, the only crime committed that night was them not moving the fuck on from each other," Maya cuts in. She's helping Kaitlin dress me in an outfit they insist will make headlines. Val cackles from the couch.

"*Thank* you." I shake my head and focus on Kaitlin with a smile. "We're taking things slow, so nothing's exactly *official* yet, but yeah, I guess we're seeing each other again." I step into the boots. "It's been going well. We seem to be so in tune with each other right now."

"It's only been a week, Princess," Maya mumbles, zipping up the corset top Kaitlin picked out for me.

"And probably the best week we've ever had." I defend myself, trying my best to keep my tone even so I don't sound *too* hurt by the comment. The events with the stalker have put life into better focus. When John finally got to my place, hours late, we talked for so long. And he finally heard me—where I was coming from—and the thought of losing me made him truly scared. Since then he's been at my house every night, and our studio sessions during the day have been beyond productive. Admittedly, it sucks my friends are not as excited about this new development with John as I am.

"You make such a cute couple," Kaitlin swoons, helping Maya adjust the corset while I lace up the boots. I pretend to ignore the concerned look that floats between Jessie, Val, and Maya as I glance at myself in the mirror.

"Thanks." I appreciate Kaitlin's enthusiasm, even if my friends aren't with me one hundred percent. "This outfit is guaranteed to be on some best-dressed list. I love it."

"You look hot as hell," Jessie agrees.

"No surprise, girls." Maya chuckles. "Kaitlin's the best stylist in LA."

"I don't know about that." Kaitlin giggles bashfully, shaking her head. "But that's a real compliment coming from you, supermodel."

Maya tosses her long auburn hair, making us all laugh. "Hey, have you seen the house we got at Coachella this year? It's such a beautiful property. Huge pool, a sauna—not that we're going to need it considering it'll be a thousand degrees—cute backyard setup where we can have mimosas in the morning." She grabs her cell phone and swipes through the photos. "I mean, how gorgeous is this? Literally the biggest Jacuzzi I've ever seen!"

"Oh my—that is absolutely stunning." Kaitlin's mouth gapes wide open.

"Only the best for us, right?" I say with a wink, still in awe that this is my life now.

"Hell, yeah, Princess." Kaitlin bounces with joy, celebrating with me. "What's the deal? Did Win set it up for you?" she asks.

"Wait—how do you know Win?" I suppress a smile at the thought of Win going to Kaitlin for fashion advice. He's too slick to need a professional opinion.

"Who *doesn't* know Win?" Kaitlin grins, fanning the heat from her cheeks. "Now, there's a man I'd like to do things to." She slaps a hand over her mouth quickly.

"*Princess.*" Val and Maya accuse me instantly, both shooting pointed looks my way.

"Oh, stop." I shake my head. "You make it sound like I invite him to family dinners."

"Didn't he come to Nobu with us last time your mom and dad were in town?" Jessie throws me a butter-wouldn't-melt smile, knowing she's right.

"Ooh, you lucky thing." Kaitlin shakes her head. "So he did set you up with the house? I mean, I only know him through a friend of a friend, but this has Win written all over it."

"Actually," I say, "the house was a thank-you gift from one of my business partners."

"You got it as a gift? Exciting!"

Jessie beams with pride. "Princess is launching a new cosmetics line this year, and Maya's the face of the first collection, so the company gifted them the house as a thank-you for all the big business they're about to generate."

"Obviously confidential right now," I cut in fast, trying to signal across the room to Jessie that she shouldn't say any more.

"Top secret. Got it." Kaitlin's eyes light up. "Oh, you know I love a secret . . ."

"No, *really*." Maya swoops in, flashing me a look as she loops an arm through Kaitlin's and diverts her. "This has to be kept quiet. But you'll hear more about it soon enough."

Both of us know how fast gossip can spread with stylists. They may have never-ending lists of contacts in all the right places and be so fun to hang out with, but man can they spread word like wildfire. Kaitlin and I are still building our relationship; so far it's been great but I'd rather be cautious, especially after what happened with Avery. You never know with people.

Sorry, Jessie mouths silently across the room, looking apologetic.

I share a reassuring smile and make a mental note to brief her on being less forthcoming with new people, even though we do love Kaitlin.

In fact, there's a lot I'll need to brief Jessie about before we head to Coachella. We'll be bumping into a lot of familiar faces, some friendly but most not, and the last thing I want is to throw my lifelong bestie into the deep end without a cheat sheet on how to interact with the sort of people who show one face in the spotlight and a whole other personality behind the scenes.

"Well, all I'm gonna say is, John's about to go *insane* for that outfit on you, Princess." Kaitlin looks me up and down approvingly, satisfied with her work. She pauses. "He's going with you to Coachella, right?"

"Yeah, he's staying in the house with us."

What Kaitlin doesn't need to know is that I only made the decision to invite him yesterday afternoon, because for a second there I was set to go with just my girls, young, free, and single. But I actually like the thought of being there with him. Plus it's nice to have backup when guys get drunk and aggressively start hitting on you. Apparently, politely declining translates to *Yes, please. I'm so into this and I'd* love *for you to relentlessly hit on me because you are so sexy and I'm just dying to get with you.* With John there I can simply say, *My boyfriend's standing right here.* Easy.

Not that John's *technically* my boyfriend right now. But with the way things are going, it's only a matter of time.

"That's so cute. I'll be looking out for all the couples' photos. I read something online the other day about you two releasing a song together soon," Kaitlin subtly throws in as she heads back over to Jessie at the table, glancing at her shortlist of clothes. "Great choice," she whispers, pointing to one of Jessie's options with a wink.

Jessie practically glows with a smile. She's loving the chance to get involved in all this. It's why I specifically had her come stay with me a couple of nights before we head out to the valley.

"Yeah, we have some stuff lined up and dropping soon," I say, perking up as I think of how fast everything's moving. I always dreamed of the days I'd have a song that's working and an actual plan for other singles to drop. Even though it takes time and patience to work a song and give it enough space to develop, I feel so much more in control when I know there's a plan in place.

"Hell, yeah!" Kaitlin looks impressed. "He has something coming really soon with Riley Vega, too, right?"

"What do you mean?"

"Oh my god," Kaitlin continues, getting ahead of herself. "Is the collab the three of you! That is going to be amazing."

I glance at Maya, and I can tell she's trying desperately not to say something she'll regret. Val looks kind of awkward, avoiding eye contact, and Jessie's fumbling for her phone in her pocket. I watch as she unlocks it with a frown and starts typing rapidly. If I know her, she'll be searching for as much information about Riley and John's new song as she can find.

"Not a collab, no," I say quickly, heat rising inside. *He can't seriously be releasing our new song at the same time as his work with Riley, can he?*

"Oh, that's a shame. You guys would be great together." Kaitlin shrugs. I'm a little too caught up in my head wondering how John's even made time for Riley since we worked things out. He's been with me 24-7.

Well, except for now.

I grab my phone and shoot him a text.

Me: Hey, how's studio going? <3

"Yeah, me and John are just working on our own stuff," I say idly when Kaitlin continues singing Riley's praises. *Girl, read the room.*

"You know, last time I saw her she had so much good stuff to say about you, Val. I didn't realize you guys were so close," Kaitlin says, breaking Val's silent trance and making her head snap up.

"Huh?" Val's cheeks flush.

"Riley." Kaitlin chuckles. "Earth to Valerie . . . I was just saying, last time I spoke to her she was really into you. Kept telling me how cute you looked in that Alaïa dress on the red carpet for the premiere of that movie—oh, what was the name of it? The one with that guy from *Ozark*—"

"Riley . . . hyping *you* up?" Maya twists her neck in Val's direction, eyebrows knitted together. "After New Year's Eve—" Maya stops herself, and Kaitlin continues chattering.

"Are you two not close?" Kaitlin looks confused when Val shakes her head slowly, giving a nervous laugh.

"Not even remotely," she says.

"Hmm, that's weird. Anyway, she was being really positive about you. Maybe there's a new friend to be made there? I'm just saying . . ."

Maya pulls Kaitlin's attention away and back to the task at hand, and we finally stop talking about Riley freaking Vega not a moment too soon.

For the next fifteen minutes while we wrap up our session, and Kaitlin notes down all the clothes we want her to buy and reassures us she'll be back tomorrow with everything ready to go, I can't shake John and Riley from my mind.

"Okay, *what*?" Maya explodes as soon as the elevator dings, announcing Kaitlin's exit. Jessie's bouncing in her chair so I know she's got something she wants to say. "I swear to god, you better have found some more info about John and Riley's song while you were tapping away over there, Nancy Drew. Now, are we gonna boycott this shit, or . . . ?"

"We're not boycotting anything." I sigh, already making my way over to Jessie. "I knew John was working with Riley, I just didn't realize they were getting so close to a release date like we are."

"Prepare yourselves." Jessie holds her phone close to her chest and shoots Maya a warning look. "Don't freak out, okay?"

"Just let me see, Jess," I say, too anxious to wait any longer.

She hands me the phone, and I skim read the *Billboard* article onscreen. It's an interview with John from a couple of days ago, and in it he talks mostly about our release, no mention of Riley until the final question. The interviewer asks if John has any other exciting projects lined up, and that's when he drops Riley's name. Cherry on top of it all . . . somehow Riley was asked to comment, and she's quoted right in the middle of it all.

"Oh nice," I say dryly, my voice dripping with sarcasm. "How sweet of them to approach Riley for comment in an article about my fucking song and not once reach out to me."

"Princess, seriously, read us the damn article," Maya bosses me, grabbing for the phone.

"Hey." I snatch it back and clear my throat. "Let me do it so you can all hear. 'Riley tells us: "We're coming to the end of a really close collaborative project right now. John's been a dream to work with, so attentive and in tune with my sound. He just gets it when I'm coming at him with concepts, he'll instantly know how to put the beat together and come up with suggestions all the time for ways we can make it better. He knows me so well, which just makes this whole process so effortless. I'm really excited to share this one with you all. It's special.""' I pause to see the girls' reactions, feeling my gut hollow out with a weird, empty sensation as I continue. "'Riley and John's new song is set to be released before the end of this month, so stay tuned on their social media for more news and snippets.""

"Insanity," Maya says, stepping forward to drape an arm around my shoulders. "And just when you thought things were getting back on track with you two, ugh, babe." Her voice holds the same sympathetic note as when John and I first broke up, as if she's soothing me before I inevitably break down.

I don't get it.

"Maya, this isn't exactly a John problem," I say defensively, and Jessie and Val both straighten in their seats, their interest piqued. "I mean, yeah, it's annoying that she made it sound like they're fucking on the soundboard or something and like it's a 'project.' Babe, two songs isn't a project. But obviously she's going to make it seem like that, all important and perfect and romantic. She knows it pushes my buttons. She knows what she's doing, she probably got her PR in on it to start shaping the narrative. What I don't get is why they wouldn't ask me for a comment. It doesn't make sense."

"But then why would the article be focused on your song with John?" Jessie points out thoughtfully. "I would think they'd want all the attention to be on Riley's song. That'd piss you off more, wouldn't it? For her release to totally eclipse yours."

"That would be so obvious. Come on, you guys. She's playing a game." I shake my head with a bitter laugh. "Trust me, I know Riley."

"You really don't think it's shady John hasn't mentioned anything about their drop date clashing with yours?" Maya asks slowly, glancing at Val out of the corner of her eye.

I look at Val too. She's detached from the conversation, still sitting on the couch with her head resting in her hand, her elbow propped on the arm. Did she even hear any of what I read?

"Val, what do you think?" I ask, interrupting her daydream. "You know Riley. Do you agree this was all a setup to stir shit between me and John?"

"To be honest," Jessie cuts in before Val has a chance to speak, "it would make sense if she saw those paparazzi photos Kaitlin was talking about. She'd know you and John got back together and it might've made her jealous—which would make her do something petty like this."

"Exactly," I say with a definitive nod. "Val?"

She bites her lip. "Yeah, maybe. I don't really know."

"Very insightful, thanks for the input," I say jokingly, but Val doesn't laugh. She just pulls out her phone and starts scrolling, obviously in no mood to chat.

What's gotten into her?

Maya sighs. "All I'm saying is, it's obviously shady. You two literally just got back together and he's hiding their release date from you? It really wouldn't be such a stretch to suggest he's hiding more than that."

"Oh my god." I laugh. "Can we just give the man a break? He spent the entire interview talking about me! There's nothing suspicious about it. Maybe Riley exaggerated the release date. Maybe he doesn't know when they're gonna drop the song. Maybe he didn't want to tell me because I'm so sick of hearing about Riley Vega lately and she's already ruined too much for us."

Maya raises her eyebrows. "All right, relax. John's innocent and I'm reading too much into it." She places her hands on her hips and sighs. "I just hope you're right."

I glance down at my phone, the notification screen still empty of messages from John. Should I be worried he hasn't replied to my text? *Stop. You're spiraling when you don't need to.* I take a deep breath in to clear my head and smile.

"I'm right, Maya. Seriously. There's nothing to worry about."

Right on time, my phone buzzes with a reply.

John: Hey, babe, it's going great. Let's talk about release dates later. Try not to stress, I'm figuring it all out w my manager. Hope your fitting is going well. Can't wait to see u

I thrust my phone out in front of me so Maya can see the screen.

"See? He probably wants to talk to me about their release date tonight. It's no big deal."

Maya shows me her palms and backs away. "Famous last words, babe, that's all I'm saying."

"Wait, did he just text you about it?" Jessie asks.

"Yes, right here." I show her the phone too.

"Weird. It's like he's listening to us." She giggles and glances around dramatically. "Hidden cameras, much? Helloooooo, John, can you hear me?"

"Stop." I laugh, pushing her shoulder playfully. "I told you, we're just in tune with each other."

"You're right, Princess," Val chimes in, standing up from the couch and walking over to us. "Ignore these two haters. If you're feeling it with John, just enjoy it. Nothing in this town lasts for long anyway, but you two always seem to come back to each other."

"Thanks, Val," I say, relieved.

"Enjoy it," Val repeats with an easy shrug. "If it makes you happy, it makes you happy. You don't need to put a label on it. Or explain yourself or the situation to anyone else." She grabs her purse and slings it over her arm. "Okay, who's coming with me for lunch? I booked a table at the rooftop restaurant at the Waldorf, and I hear your favorite hot waiter's working today's shift, Maya."

15

"I love Coachella!"

These are the words that spill out of my mouth as soon as we step through the doors of our house. I knew it'd be amazing, but I literally lose my breath at the sight of the rock-pool water feature built into the entrance, water spilling into a sparkling blue pool that wraps around the floorplan, running through each bedroom's private sun terrace and onto the back patio, where we're surrounded by hills and a beautiful view of the valley.

"This is what I'm talking about, baby! Check out this place!" Maya drops her bags on the huge fluffy carpet and spins in a circle, linking our arms together and jumping with me excitedly when I do the same.

Jessie's jaw drops. "It's as big as a freaking hotel!"

"Just for us," I tell her proudly, glimpsing the twenty-seater dining table piled high with PR packages and complimentary gifts. My partner for the cosmetics company set up a cute balloon arch, a full bar cart resembling a pot of gold at the end of a rainbow, and personalized gilt-framed photos of me and Maya hang from the walls, interspersed between expensive-looking contemporary art pieces.

"Fuck, yeah," Val enthuses, kicking off her sandals and untying the white kimono she wore on the drive over. "Ugh, don't you just love a fully stocked bar?"

Shrugging the kimono onto the floor, she busies herself mixing drinks for us, laughing when Tripp walks in behind us and does a double take at Val in her bright-yellow strapless bikini. His crush on her could not be more obvious, and I would love to see Val with a great guy like him. They have undeniable natural chemistry if only either would be brave enough to just admit it and put a label on it. I make a snap decision to make sure the two of them spend as much time together as possible over the course of the festival.

"Now I know why your luggage is so damn heavy," he says with a low whistle, rolling the Louis Vuitton suitcase inside and dumping an armful of designer purses and a duffel bag beside it. "You couldn't have even worn *one* outfit for the ride out here?"

"He's saying this like he hasn't been eye-fucking you through the kimono the whole time," I joke with a wink at them both, checking to make sure our driver's all good with the rest of our luggage before heading farther into the house.

"Okay, I call dibs on the room with the waterfall shower," Maya declares. "I don't know which one it is, but I need it."

"I'll take any room," Jess says with wide eyes, strolling trancelike around the villa as she takes it all in. "Seriously, I'll happily sleep on the couch if I have to. I'm just thrilled to be here."

"Your bed better be big enough for us all to fit inside it, Princess," Val calls to me as I follow Jessie. "I still want my bedtime lullaby!"

"Lullaby?" Tripp asks, confused, but Val only dismisses him with a wave of her hand.

Once we're decided on our rooms, Val and Tripp spend some time in the pool while Jessie helps Maya take pics out in the golden-hour light. I change out of the sweatpants I traveled in and select a white couture one-piece and a pair of Oran sandals, snapping a photo in the floor-to-ceiling mirror of my en suite bathroom.

Me: You still coming? Waiting <3

I attach the photo to my text and send it to John, scrolling back through our messages to find the last one he sent me eight hours ago, while we were waiting on him to arrive at my apartment back in LA.

John: Something came up at the studio, baby. Gonna be delayed

John: Head to Coachella without me. I'll get a ride with a friend

John: Sorry, P., can't talk rn. Call you later. I'll be there, just late dw

John: <3

I let out a deep sigh. He still hasn't called me back, and I have no clue what he's caught up with. About the only thing saving me from spiraling is knowing Riley arrived in the valley yesterday—I saw her Instagram story showing off the view from her room—and John stayed at mine until late last night, not leaving until almost two in the morning.

But where the hell is he now?

As I walk to the patio in the back, I scroll through my messages, replying to everyone who's texted me since we arrived. There's a message from Kimi checking we made it to the house safely, a message from Wayne with a link to our itinerary for the festival, and a message from Win.

Win: Hope you got there safe. Check out the wine cellar when you get a chance. My treat

Wine cellar? I didn't even realize we had one. But through the kitchen, I spot a little alcove behind the breakfast bar and a door leading down a set of stone stairs. My sandals slap each step as I go down into a dimly lit room lined from floor to ceiling with wine racks, a tall mahogany table in the center with two barstools either side of it.

"Oh my god." I chuckle to myself as I lift the lid on the large wooden case sitting on the table, a pink bow and gift tag reading *Princess* beckoning me toward it. Inside are six bottles of wine with personalized labels in various shades of pink. Lifting each one out, I realize they're bespoke bottles of champagne, the first two named after my two EPs, and the others named *Princess*, *Jessie*, *Maya*, and *Val*. One for each of us.

I text Win back immediately, grinning the whole time I'm typing.

Me: You are unbelievable. How on earth did you pull this off?

I add a heart eyes emoji and hit Send, feeling an itch of heat flash through me when he replies straightaway.

Win: I know some people

Me: This is so thoughtful. Thank you so much!!

Win: Have a great time, Princess

Win: Don't drink it all at once

I laugh as I head back upstairs into the house carrying the *Princess* bottle with me. Out on the patio, Maya's teaching Jessie the choreography from an old music video of mine while Tripp and Val lounge poolside. Before I even register what's happening, my song starts playing loudly and Maya's dragging me into the dance routine.

"Are you filming this?" I shout as she grinds up on me like the guys in the video.

Instead of answering she just sings along wildly, pulling the champagne bottle out of my hands and using it like a microphone. Jessie's in hysterics as she messes up a move, and I quickly get into the rhythm with them both, laughing and dancing along.

"Oh my god, Tripp!" Maya shrieks beside me, and the next thing I see is Tripp running behind us on the patio shaking the bottle in his hands.

"You asshole!" Val laughs from the poolside as he pops the cork and the champagne sprays all over us, wrecking the dance routine as we scream and giggle, trying to leap out of the way of the spray.

"*Tripp!*" I yell, but when he starts to run away and slips in the puddle of champagne, falling flat on his ass and sliding with a dramatic "Noooo!" into the pool with a huge splash, I collapse to my knees with laughter, struggling to breathe.

"Ohmygod." Maya laughs, too, grabbing my arm as she falls to her knees beside me. "What the fuck was that! Oh. My. GOD."

"*Please* tell me you got that on camera!" Jessie can barely talk between her hysterical laughs, clutching her sides as she stumbles over to where Maya had propped her phone against a flowerpot. "That was hilarious. Oh my god. Oh yes! Yes, you got it!" She snatches the phone and hurries over to us. "Maya, you *have* to post this on TikTok. Please!"

"Please!" I beg, laughing hard as I watch it play out again onscreen. "The look on your face, Tripp!"

"What can I say? I turned your guys' little thirst trap into a full-length action movie," he jokes, swimming up to where Val's dangling her legs over the edge and wetting her with pool water as he shakes out his hair.

"Come on, Tripp!" she says, exasperated, but I catch the smirk on her lips as he bats his lashes and makes puppy-dog eyes up at her, swimming even closer to wrap an arm around her legs.

They really are so cute together. I don't know how they're not official yet.

"Okay, I posted it," Maya says, exiting out of TikTok on her phone. "Everyone's gonna love this."

"Hey, did you see the bottle Tripp stole? Personalized champagne from Win—one for each of us!"

"He did not!" Maya takes the bottle from where Tripp left it on the patio and spins it around in her hands. "Classy man!"

"Right?" I open up TikTok on my phone ready to like and comment on Maya's video. "He's the best. I also had no idea this place had a wine cellar, it's a vibe down there."

"Hello." Maya raises her eyebrows. "I saw the stocked bar cart, but a wine cellar just hits different."

"You should go check it out." I watch the video again and shake my head. "This is so good, Maya."

I scroll through the comments, full of the usual heart eyes and fire emojis and fan messages, along with laughing emojis and a dozen or so messages speculating on Tripp and Val's closeness in the pool at the start of the video. I wonder if Tripp only got out in the first place to draw attention away from him and Val. They're both so secretive about everything when it comes to their "friendship," but it's amazing how many fans still pick up on their vibe. Maybe some couples are just naturally well suited.

I wonder if people think the same about me and John.

It's as his name pops into my head that my eyes land on the top comment on Maya's video, and my face drops.

"What?" Jessie asks, noticing my expression change instantly. "Oh god, are they saying something bad?"

"Uh, Maya," I say, tapping her on the shoulder to bring her attention to the comment in question.

"What's up?" She frowns and leans in to check out what I'm showing her. "Wait, what?" She blinks and reads the comment again in total disbelief. "Um, why is she commenting on my TikTok?"

16

"'You guys are *so cute*. Save a glass for me!'" Riley's sugar-sweet tone comes across as fake as her tan.

I tilt my phone to look at the girls in amazement. "What the hell is happening right now?"

"She's trying to make it sound like you guys hang out all the time," Jessie says, equally confused.

"Yeah, but why?"

"Maybe she didn't write it," Jessie suggests.

Maya nods. "Maybe she hired a clueless social media manager or something. That's my only explanation. She wouldn't have typed that herself."

We're racking up tens of thousands of views already, and the likes and comments are popping up every minute. But the one that sticks out the most sits right there at the top of the comments section with over a thousand likes on it already. Riley Vega's.

"No, she's definitely running her own TikTok," Val says.

I look at her sitting on the other side of the pool, legs crossed beneath her and wisps of caramel brown hair dancing around her shoulders in the soft breeze. "How do you know?" I ask.

"You can just tell." Val shrugs. "She posts video responses to questions on there all the time. Same on Instagram—she's always posting on her story just doing normal shit."

"Hold up," Maya butts in, leaning forward in disbelief. "You're telling me you still watch Riley Vega's Insta stories?"

"Val, why?" I cringe.

Val laughs. "It's just a story. It's not that deep. Plus, I don't follow that many people anyway, so her shit always pops up on my feed. My life is fucking stressful right now, it's simply a distraction."

Maya's eyes widen.

"Listen, if someone repeatedly disrespects me like she does to us *all the time*, that's it, I cut them off. I don't spend any time watching their stories or keeping up with them no matter what they're doing. They don't care about me, I don't care about them. It's that simple," I say decisively.

"Too true." Maya nods, staring pointedly at Val. "You should take a note out of Princess's book."

"No, I agree," Val says, nodding too. "I just, I don't know, I get bored and go through everyone's stories sometimes. It's not like I sit around waiting for her to post. Plus, what's that saying? Who makes a better friend than your enemy? Or your friend's enemy . . ."

It makes me happy to see Val's silly, joking side come out, even for a moment.

"I do the same, Val," Jessie agrees, holding a guilty hand up and looking sheepish as she locks eyes with me. "What?" She laughs when my jaw drops in disbelief. "I just watch whatever's on my screen when I open the app. I don't think it's a big deal."

"And it's not like we can unfollow her, is it?" Val points out. "It would cause even more drama."

"I don't know." I hold up my hands. "But I don't want to talk about Riley anymore, guys. Let's enjoy our time and keep a clear boundary when it comes to her."

Val chuckles and stands up, walking around to sit next to me. "Princess, you're literally more levelheaded than my therapist. You should write a book." She drapes her arms around my shoulders and pulls me in for a hug.

Even though the conversation was about Riley, my thoughts keep going to John. He's consuming me again and I know that, but can't stop it.

"Oh please." I laugh, catching her in a hug too. If I am levelheaded, it's only because I've been bitten one too many times.

"All right, who wants another drink?" Maya sashays over to the bar cart we pulled outside earlier, grabbing a martini glass. "Anyone for another of my wicked little potions?"

A few hours later we're all sitting around the firepit by the pool, the starlit sky above looking more beautiful than ever. Tripp's out partying with his Twitch friends, and John still hasn't showed. Last I heard, he's meeting up with Tripp and heading back to the house later. But I'll believe that when I see it. Work seems to always come before me these days. I get it—to an extent—I work my ass off too. Still, there's a part of me that wanted to be his only focus this weekend. I'm not playing, there's no show for me to worry about, and my only plans were to hang out with him and my friends. And it's never fun worrying about when a guy's going to show up or if a guy's going to show up—I'm simply not that kind of girl.

"Sure, why not?" I say, knowing all too well how wild Maya gets when she's let loose with alcohol and mixers. Normally I'd refuse, but we *are* on vacation, and if John's not gonna show up, I'd rather—

My phone buzzes on the seat beside me.

John: A shining star never gets lost in the dark

It's the first text he's sent me since this morning. I type back a reply immediately, desperate for him not to leave me hanging again.

Me: Cute. Speaking of lost . . . where are you?

John: Sorry, not lost. Just took the scenic route?

Me: Not funny. Where are you, for real?

There's way too much of a delay before his reply. I take the drink Maya passes to me and gulp down a large, bitter-tasting mouthful. It scorches the back of my throat.

"Jesus, Maya!" I exclaim.

"Good, right?" She flashes me a toothy grin.

John: Sorry, P

I sigh and place my phone face down.

"Did I say something wrong?" Maya lands on the couch beside me. "Oh." She groans loudly. "My bad. I should've known. What now?"

"Don't start," I say wearily. But then I backtrack a little when I notice her expression—the one that says, *Seriously?* harder than words ever could. "Okay, fine. Maybe I'm just overthinking it all, but—" I drop my shoulders and look away.

"But?" Maya prods, gesturing for Jessie to join us on our side of the firepit.

"Did he do something shitty?" Jessie asks, scooting in beside Val.

"Like, yes . . . no . . . I don't know. Technically, he hasn't *done* anything, it's just the way he's making me feel."

"Sounds like John." Maya nods. "Princess, something's been up with him all day. He can't make it on time to Coachella? I don't think so—"

"You're turning this into something bigger than it is, Maya," Val cuts in, shooting her a warning glance. She meets my eye and smiles sympathetically. "Don't overthink it, okay? He's probably busy working. Take him at his word and don't let yourself spiral at the slightest push. If you don't have trust, what have you got?"

She's right. I know she is. But there's a part of me that feels uneasy, like my connection with John just doesn't feel like such a sure thing this time around.

"It's the little things," I say. Maya raises her eyebrows at Val's advice. "Like how he's taking forever to reply today. I'm not clingy, you know that, but when it's like seven hours between texts and he only gets back to me with a short little message, that's pretty weird."

"Damn right it's weird," Maya says.

"But what did he say?" Val asks.

I glance down at my phone, scratching my wrist, a little embarrassed to admit it. "Well, John's been sending me messages at 11:11 consistently every day, but I can tell the 11:11 message I got today wasn't the same," I mumble.

"Ignore him for now," Maya suggests.

"Hold on a sec, let's not be irrational. He took the time to stick to that schedule," Val says at the same time. "That's a *good* thing, Princess."

I offer Val a small smile, reassured by her words. "I guess."

"Val, why are you making excuses for him? He's not even here and he said he would be." Maya's voice is sharp.

"I'm not making excuses," Val counters.

"Guys, please," I say, rubbing my temples. I wish I hadn't brought this up. "Can we not turn this into a thing?"

Maya opens her mouth to say something but Val gets in first. "Sorry, I'm not trying to take sides or anything. It's this whole 'stay positive' idea my therapist's been talking about lately. I started seeing a new one, and she's really into the idea of letting people reveal themselves rather than projecting your issues onto them and ruining a good thing. Sometimes it's not worth overthinking stuff. It's probably not as bad as it seems."

"Princess," Jessie says, leaning forward to look directly at me. In true Jessie style, she just wants to cut to the chase. "Do you love him?"

My mouth's suddenly dry. It feels like sandpaper all up through my throat. I know my answer right away but somehow the word unpeels from my lips way too unconvincingly. "Yeah."

Val and Maya tilt their heads, both watching me carefully, lost in their own thoughts.

"Or is it like before," Jessie continues, "when it felt like love to you, but you were missing the reciprocation? Remember when you told me how real it felt in the moment?"

"It *does* feel real," I say quickly, thinking back on all the time John and I have been spending together lately. Morning and night we're together, the way it's supposed to be. We've been each other's sunshine at the start of the day and safe haven to fall into as the night draws in. But in between, there's just been this kind of disconnect.

That's not even the right word. Maybe I *am* overthinking this.

"Anyway," I say cheerfully, snapping out of it because I *do not* want this to ruin our night. "I think the real answer we all want is what's going on with you and Tripp now, Val?" I nudge her. "Is it official yet, or . . . ?"

She laughs out loud but her eyes don't hold any hint of real amusement. "Yeah, no. I'm pretty sure at this rate we're just gonna be in a situationship forever."

"Oh, shut up," Maya teases with a dramatic eye roll. "He's so fucking in love with you, Val."

Val rolls her eyes too as she takes a big gulp of her drink.

"Think of all the cute double dates we could go on if you two made it public," I add enthusiastically, taking another sip of my drink. "Shit, we might even inspire Maya to settle down for once."

She flips me a middle finger, and all of us laugh.

"There's simply no point," Val says when our laughter dies down. "All relationships in this town go to shit in the end anyway. Might as well not even pretend."

"Whoa, whoa, whoa," I butt in, sitting tall on the seat and holding up a hand. "Sorry, is this the same Val from, like, two seconds ago who was trying to preach positivity to me about *my* relationship?"

"Yeah, for real." Maya chuckles, pulling a face as she stirs her drink. "What's up with that?"

Val slumps in her seat and groans. "I don't wanna talk about it. It's so depressing every time I think about how much I just want to couple up and have him all to myself."

"Oh, trust me," I say, looking to the others for backup. "He's *really* not looking anywhere else."

"I know that." Val groans again, and I hate the pang of insecurity that jolts through me at how sure she sounds. *Must be nice to know you're the only one your man's got eyes for.* "But I also know the second we make it official it's like a ticking time bomb and we're headed straight for a breakup. It's how it goes. And you know that as well as I do, Maya, so don't look at me like that."

"I'm not looking at you like anything." Maya shrugs, acting nonchalant. "Just maybe like I don't see the point in being precious about it. Relationships are to build character, not hold us down for life. Next you'll be telling me you want to leave LA and buy a big plot of land out in the country, have five kids, do the family thing—"

"You mean you *don't* want that?" Val raises an eyebrow. "Shit, I *wish*."

I think about my conversation with John while we were looking out over the city and sigh quietly. Sometimes a simpler life seems so much more appealing. But would he still act the same if we didn't have the distraction of work 24-7?

Yeah, I don't wanna think about that.

While the girls chat quietly, all of us slipping into a woozy, sleepy state as the night gets darker and the stars shine brighter, my thoughts drift away. In my head I'm making music in a light and airy studio overlooking a pure white beach and azure water; I'm painting and writing poetry and reading books and singing softly. There's no pressure, no need to live up to anyone's expectations, no worries about who is or isn't commenting on my TikToks or watching my Instagram stories. I'm just chill, and it's me and him, and in my mind I can feel his presence wrapped around me like a warm embrace even though I can't see him clearly.

And I don't know why the presence I feel is Win.

I snap my eyes open, unaware I even closed them, and sit up straight in the seat.

"Princess?" Maya looks at me wide-eyed. "Everything okay?"

I swipe a hand over my face. "Yeah. Shit. Did I fall asleep?"

"You were pretty quiet," Val says.

"What time is it?"

"Time we should be at a party, if you ask me," Maya answers, but when the three of us groan and boo at her, she laughs and kicks herself up and out of her fireside chair. "All right, grandmas. Bedtime it is. Party tomorrow. I get it, we're old now."

We all get up and move into the house, talking and laughing and falling into each other, tipsy from Maya's crazy cocktails. When we reach my room, somehow everyone decides we're sleeping in my bed, and within a few minutes we're snuggled under the sheets, all of us still wearing our makeup, Jessie's and Val's heads resting on my shoulders and Maya lounging along the bottom of the huge bed.

"Sing us a lullaby, Princess?" Val asks sleepily.

"You guys better deliver my hangover cure directly to my bed in the morning," I say with a heavy sigh, pretending I'm annoyed even though they all know I love doing this as much as they enjoy listening.

"I grabbed you a bottle of Pedialyte already." Jessie chuckles, reaching over to the nightstand and passing the purple bottle to me.

"What song do you want me to sing?" I ask as I unscrew the lid.

They each make a choice, and as I sing and they fall quiet around me, the blue light of Maya's phone screen the only thing illuminating the dark room, my mind drifts back to Win. Without thinking twice, I'm building up the rest of that blissful dream world with him in my mind, John's name fading further and further away as I dream of brown eyes smiling at me across dimly lit dinner tables, the smell of cologne and Italian leather, a voice that talks with purpose and never breaks a promise, and a smile that flips my insides and sends me spiraling headfirst into the most irresistible of dangerous waters.

17

I'm woken up early the next morning by a phone call from Kimi checking in to make sure everything's good with the house. I leave the girls sleeping in my bed and head out quietly to the kitchen, where the fridge is stocked full of our favorite foods, including bottles of sparkling water and orange juice so I can complete my miracle hangover cure.

I mix the water with OJ and head outside to catch some early-morning rays. My foot skids on one of Tripp's discarded shoes as I go, so I guess the guys are sleeping off a hangover in one of the other rooms. They got back so late last night none of us heard them come in.

It's perfect outside, the sky clear and the sounds of the valley so different from the city noise of LA. I relax into a sun lounger and watch the pool water rippling in front of me, calm and serene, soothing my headache away.

"You're awake already?" a voice calls out thirty minutes later. I'm in the middle of taking a selfie, feeling much fresher and more rejuvenated, and glance up, startled, to find Jessie in her running clothes.

"Yeah, Kimi called at the crack of dawn as usual," I explain, glancing down at her sneakers and tights. "Jess, you're looking *way* too alive after last night."

Jessie shrugs. "I heeded your warning. No cocktails from Maya if I wanna be able to feel my feet when I go to bed."

I groan in response, wishing I'd taken my own advice. "Are you going for a run?" I ask.

She nods. "That's the plan. Care to join me?"

When I hang my head to look at her pointedly, she laughs and spins around. "All right, see you later."

"Be safe," I call, returning my attention to my phone. A new message pops up from Win, and my cheeks flush with the memory of last night's dream.

Win: Champagne for breakfast?

I smile. The empty personalized champagne bottle is still lying on the patio from last night. Before I have time to process what I'm doing, I attach the selfie I just took and send my reply.

Me: I think we drank it all already. . . feeling it this morning

There's a few seconds' pause before his reply pops up.

Win: I saw the TikTok

Win: Soaking up the sun? Wish I was there

Me: You couldn't get tickets? ;)

Win: Not famous enough :(

I chuckle to myself because I know for a fact if Win wanted to be at Coachella, he'd have VIP tickets rolling in from every direction in a heartbeat.

Me: Sucks to be you

Win: Sure does

Win: Enjoy X

"What are you grinning at, early bird?" Maya flicks my hair as she walks up. "That's a dirty little smile if I ever did see one."

"You're observant this morning," I say with absolutely no intention of answering her question. "Val still asleep?"

"No, she's in the kitchen chugging sparkling water and OJ and complaining she needs feeding. Girl snores like a fucking train when she's drunk—I'm not surprised you woke up early."

I laugh with her as Val shouts something indecipherable through the wide-open doors.

"Are we ordering breakfast?" I ask.

"Well, I'm sure as fuck not cooking it." Maya grabs my arm, pulling me out of my seat.

By the time Tripp's awake and with us in the kitchen, we've had enough breakfast delivered to feed all of Coachella, not just our little group. We tip the driver well and lay out everything on the huge kitchen island: a colorful spread of berries, waffles, pancakes, avocado toast, caramel coffee, croissants, yogurt, melon, oatmeal, bacon, eggs—practically every breakfast food imaginable.

"Holy shit, this is what dreams are made of," Maya groans, biting into a pastry and rolling her eyes up to the ceiling. "So *fresh*."

"You should wake John up," I say to Tripp, reaching for a slice of watermelon. "He'll be pissed if he misses out on this."

"You don't wanna wake him up with breakfast in bed?" Maya winks at me.

Tripp pauses midbite of his breakfast burrito. "John isn't here."

The watermelon slice I just bit into is suddenly flavorless. "Then where is he?" I ask, my words tight with frustration. *He didn't arrive last night? Is he fucking kidding me?*

"Here we go again," Maya says, spinning around on her seat when the front door opens and footsteps sound through the entrance hall.

"Hey," Jessie says as she rounds the corner, red in the face and a little out of breath from running.

"Hey, Jess," Val says with a smile. "We ordered breakfast—come dig in."

"Oh." Jessie's smile doesn't quite reach her eyes. It draws my attention to her face as she kicks her running shoes off and pops her AirPods back into their case. "Thanks. I'll be there in a sec."

"Everything okay, Jess?" I ask as she heads toward her room, her steps a little too fast. When she doesn't answer, I get up out of my seat. Something's off—I can feel it.

"You good?" Maya asks, reaching out for my arm. She's realized something's up, too, and this is her way of letting me know I've got her support if I need it.

"Yeah, I'll just go check on her," I say, squeezing her hand and following Jess down the hallway.

Inside her room, Jessie's stripping out of her running clothes and wrapping herself in a fluffy white towel, ready to shower. I step inside and close the door behind me, getting her attention.

"Jess, did something happen?"

"What do you mean?" She laughs nervously, the little crease in the center of her forehead letting me know she's bluffing.

I stare at her intently.

"What?" Her voice is too high-pitched, defensive. "I'm just gonna take a quick shower and I'll join you for breakfast, okay?" She doesn't meet my eye as she moves quickly over to the attached bathroom.

"You're acting weird, Jess," I say in a singsong voice, still staring hard.

"You're the one watching me step into the shower, weirdo," she says, singsong, back, grabbing the door handle and pushing it closed until only her face is visible through the crack. "I'm fine, okay? You can go eat breakfast."

"Did something happen on your run?" I persist, visions of creepy guys and harassing paparazzi flashing through my thoughts. I know she wasn't followed by security, but maybe we should change that. I don't want my friends getting hurt when they're just trying to live their lives.

"Nothing happened," she says, swallowing hard.

I scrutinize her for a little longer before eventually rolling my eyes away and backing out of the room. False alarm maybe, but it's difficult to tell with Jess being so headstrong. "You don't have to hide things from me," I say as I leave, just in case she's not telling the truth. "You know that."

"Princess," she says wearily, "I know."

Back in the kitchen I finish eating and let my thoughts glide back to John. He still hasn't texted me, which is *infuriating*, to say the least, especially when things were going so well. It takes serious effort to keep my thoughts from running in a very negative direction, and by the time Jessie returns to the kitchen and digs in, I've realized if I don't address the issue now, his silence will bug me all damn day.

I pull out my phone and shoot John a text.

Me: What's up?

I don't expect a reply. Honestly, I don't even expect him to show up at Coachella. But then I overhear Tripp telling Maya how drunk John got last night, and my eyes shoot up to meet his.

"He was at the party you went to?" I ask.

"Yeah," Tripp says, and Jessie shifts in her seat beside me, glancing between us to figure out what's going on. "He told you that, right?

Anyway, I don't know what happened to him. Last I saw, he was standing up on the table yelling some drunken shit into the room, and then I couldn't find him anywhere."

"Well, I wouldn't go filing a missing person report," Maya says dryly, and I follow her gaze through the front window to see an Uber driver pull up to the gates of the house.

John jumps out of the car and jogs quickly toward the front door.

Tripp laughs as he watches him, shaking his head. "Bro thinks he's gonna get in before we all wake up." He takes another bite out of his breakfast burrito. "Wild."

I sit tall in my seat, reeling off an inner mantra so I won't take this too far. *Don't overreact.* I don't need to confront him; I just need to know where he was. A simple question, totally calm, nothing heavy. *Don't overreact.*

"Shit," John says, jolting back when he steps in and notices us all staring at him. "Didn't know you'd all be up already." He looks sheepish as fuck and dog-tired. The dark circles under his eyes are obvious. "You ordered breakfast? Sweet."

I grind my jaw in disbelief as he saunters up to the island and helps himself to the syrupy waffles. He lands an arm around my shoulders and squeezes tight, murmuring, "Morning," into my ear as if everything's totally fine and he didn't ghost me last night. The smell of stale booze seeps out of his skin.

"You look like you haven't slept," I say, not bothering to lower my voice.

Tripp makes a low noise, chuckling at our energy until Val tells him to cut it out.

"Sorry, *Mom*." John laughs, too, turning it into a dumb joke as he pulls a face.

I feel my cheeks heat and look to the girls for support.

"Where the fuck were you, John?" Maya's quick to stop his laughter with her bitter tone. "So much for following us here yesterday."

"Chill, Maya," he says lightheartedly. "I heard about the party and figured you'd all be there too. I started drinking before I arrived and got a little carried away. Sorry." He shrugs.

Everyone goes quiet. Their eyes turn away in that universal gesture of not wanting to get involved if things get heavy. Still, I know this isn't the time or place to make a scene—sometimes John takes it too far with the drinking—but my feeling are still hurt. Irrational or not, he didn't prioritize me or this trip, and with a single text last night he would have known we didn't *actually* go to the party.

"You could've called," I say simply, meeting his eye again. He looks down. "It's basic communication, John."

"Yeah, I know." He scratches his neck as he settles into a seat. And then, like an afterthought, he adds quietly, "I'm sorry."

"Sooo," Maya says, standing up and lifting the mood, "I don't know about you guys, but I'm ready to get all dressed up and enjoy this fuckin' festival."

"Me too," I say eagerly, wanting nothing more than to be excited again, or at least pretend to be. Fake it until you make it, as they say. I know we need to have a serious conversation about the shitty communication skills, but now isn't the time. I'm at Coachella, something I've dreamed about for years; my outfits are incredible, my girls are here, and I can't wait for the chance to show them off—the outfits *and* my girls.

"Me three," Val agrees. "Jessie?"

I look over at Jessie to find her clearly still distracted by something as she watches John carefully. "The festival, Jess. Ready to get dressed up?" I prompt.

"Mm-hmm." She nods and her smile returns. "I'm a little nervous about fitting in and all but I'm excited!"

I rush to her side. "Baby, you fit in everywhere you go, look at you." I twirl a piece of her long brown hair around my fingers. "You have nothing to be nervous about. You're beautiful and about to have the time of your life." I reach up and stroke her high cheekbones.

I can relate to how she feels. Even now that everyone around me is constantly telling me how great I am, I still feel like an imposter sometimes. Like all of this could disappear in a second.

"I can't wait to show off those boots you got me," she says.

I think of the bespoke leather cowboy boots we ordered during an online shopping splurge a couple of weeks ago. Mine are decorated with pink Swarovski crystals, Jessie's matching but in blue. We're wearing supershort bodycon suits, Stetsons, and custom accessories to match—no expenses spared in the glitter-and-crystals department. Just the thought of strutting around the festival with my girls, all of us looking *that* hot, makes excitement buzz in my belly again. I'm out of my seat and heading to our rooms faster than the others can keep up.

We spend over an hour getting ready, all of us weaving in and out of each other's rooms and eventually gathering in front of Maya's huge bathroom mirror to finish up our makeup. We look amazing, and with our music blasting loud through the surround-sound system in the house, it finally feels like we're at Coachella and ready to party.

"Fuuuuck, P.," John says as he enters my room while I'm adjusting my Stetson in the mirror. We lock eyes as he walks up behind me and wraps his arms around my waist. "Look at you."

"Like it?" I ask with a grin.

"I love it." He kisses my neck, and I melt into his arms. "Let's get in bed for a minute before you head out."

I wriggle out of his grip and turn to face him. "What do you mean before I head out? Aren't you coming with us?"

He runs his tongue over his teeth, a nervous reaction, and steps over to where he dumped his bag earlier, shuffling around inside it for his charger. "I'll be there later."

"Why not now?" I watch him as he crosses the room to plug his phone in at the side of the bed. "Please tell me you're not going to spend the whole day sleeping off last night's hangover and pretending like I'm not even here?"

"I'm not pretending like you're not here," he says. "It's Coachella, Princess. You're here with Maya and Val. I'm here to make sure you're safe—"

"Obviously you're here to party. Otherwise, where were you last night?" I rest my hands on my hips. "Seriously, John. I thought you were going to go with me. I thought we were doing this together."

"Listen," he says, stepping forward to close the distance between us. "You go out and have fun, okay? While you're out at the festival I know you have security and enough people around nothing bad can happen. I'll only get in the way of you doing your thing for the photographers. I don't want people to focus on us, just on you." He leans in and kisses my forehead affectionately.

I feel my anger melt with each kiss he gives me, my forehead again, then both cheeks, nose, chin. I can't help but laugh, even though I'm still so disappointed.

"I still wish you'd *want* to spend time with me here. It kind of makes me feel bad that you'd rather just sleep."

He lifts my chin up, eyes intent on mine. "I'm going to hang out with you, Princess. I just gotta restore my energy so I'm ready to have some real fun later. This place really gets going at night anyway."

I sigh and look out the window, hoping tonight will be better.

"Princess?" Val pops her head around the door, smiling when she meets my eye. "We're ready to head out. Are you guys coming?"

"Yeah," I say, breaking away from John, but not before giving him a quick kiss on the lips. "I'm coming. John's gonna catch up on sleep."

Val eyes him carefully but she doesn't scold him like her expression tells me she wants to. "Meet you outside, okay? I'm gonna go grab Jessie."

"Sure." I check the mirror, doing a 360 to make sure everything looks right, enjoying the way John drinks me in, before saying good-bye and heading out to the car.

Outside, the midday sun heats my skin, its warmth only adding to my excitement. I say hi to the driver, and while I wait for the others to join us, I bask against the side door, pulling out my phone to check if anyone's tried to reach me.

And then my heart double-thuds.

The top notification on my home screen is from Win—not a message, but a thumbs-up reaction to the selfie I sent him earlier. I got the notification just three minutes ago.

I open the message and realize he's removed the reaction. "What the . . . ?" I mutter under my breath. I guess he did it by mistake. But there are enough messages between the selfie and the end of the screen that he would've had to scroll up to look at it—it wouldn't have just been a mistaken tap while he was swiping out of our texts.

Which means he was looking at the photo again.

The photo I sent him over two hours ago.

I try to ignore the way it makes me feel, but it's nearly impossible.

"Woo-hoo, Coachella Dream Team! Let's get this boot-scootin', hoedown-showdown cowgirl party on the road!" Maya yells, cracking up at her own corny announcement, as she bursts through the front doors of the house wearing her own Stetson and boots, making me jump and distracting me from my thoughts.

But only for a second.

Because my mind goes back to the idea of Win getting hung up on a simple selfie of me, enough so to make him scroll back and stare at it a whole two hours afterward. I have to admit to myself that it kind of does things to me. The contrast to John's behavior and lack of time spent considering me is hard not to compare. Deep down, illicit, unspeakable sensations thud low in my body and heat me all the way up. Win's time is important. He's got shit to do and people to see 24-7. And yet one little photo from me, one awkward, accidental reaction, and suddenly, the game's changed.

I wonder why he deleted it.

I wonder if he even knows I saw.

I wonder if maybe, for whatever reason, he might've meant for me to see.

18

There's something liberating about a music festival.

Deep in the crowd of people watching Tame Impala perform, we dance and sway like we're young, wild, and free, singing along at the top of our lungs until our throats are sore and we can't even hear ourselves above the noise. We're just lost in the atmosphere, three bodies among thousands more, music washing over us and letting ourselves go.

I can't even tell how long we've been out here. An hour, maybe two. All I know is after we got here we walked around for a while, bumping into people we knew and others we didn't, taking photos with fans and getting drinks from backstage and VIP bars, checking out a few of the private hangout spots for "celebs only," but we all decided eventually that the real party was out here. Well, I guess Val thought otherwise—we haven't seen her and Tripp since we headed out here to watch the show. She probably found another group of friends in one of the fancy VIP areas. The number of connections she has because of her family's business is *insane*.

"I love this song!" I shout, singing along with Maya and Jessie as we bump into people left and right, but it's no big deal. This is what I'm here for. I love immersing myself in crowds at live shows rather than barely being able to see the show from a side stage view like VIPs do a lot of the time.

Out here I can just be *real* for a change.

"Do you know who's playing next?" Maya shouts as the song finishes and Tame Impala walk offstage to a thunderous wave of applause, whistles, and screams.

"Are you kidding me?" I swig back a bottle of water and step into the line of Jessie's handheld fan. Tripp laughed when she hung it on the lanyard around her neck, but in this heat I'm nothing but grateful for the breeze, even if it does make her look—in the nicest possible way—kind of like a grandma out for a day trip. "I'm pretty sure it's SZA playing next. I can't fucking wait."

"Oh my god, remember that summer when we drove around everywhere in LA blasting 'Good Days' almost blowing the speakers out? That's our *song*, Princess!" Jessie throws her hands in the air excitedly. "Holy shit, *as if* we're finally at Coachella together!"

"Hey! Hey, Princess!"

I whip my head around at the unfamiliar voice butting in from across the crowd. Jessie and Maya's eyes follow, and as soon as I hear, "No way, she's with Maya Brown too!" I know immediately what's about to happen.

We can't go anywhere without being spotted by fans—not even in a crowd *this* alive.

"Hey!" I beam as the guy and his girlfriend push through bodies to get to us, alerting other people's attention as they do. Soon I can hear my and Maya's names on everyone's tongues, and I notice the way people elbow their friends to let them know and try to slyly angle their cell phones in our direction for a sneaky photo.

"I can't believe I'm meeting you right now!" The girlfriend freaks out, reaching for me and fumbling with her phone at the same time. "I actually can't believe it! It's really you and my phone has no battery left, oh my god!"

"It's okay, babe," her boyfriend says, "I'll get a photo for you."

"But I want you to be in it too!" the girlfriend whines.

I glance at Maya, who shrugs with a silly grin. "Here," I say, opening up my camera, "let me take the photo. I'll send it to you. You have Instagram, right?"

"Are you serious, would you do that? Really?" The girl's eyes light up as Maya pulls us all into the frame.

"Of course!" I hold my phone out in front of us, knowing my security will probably want to shut these interactions down if they keep happening.

I genuinely love meeting the people who support me. I know the way I respond to this could either make her day or ruin the entire experience, and I'm not the type to be a bitch.

"You guys are fans?" Maya asks before posing for a photo—and then another when we realize the boyfriend's eyes are closed in the first.

"Oh, she's a huge fan," he tells us proudly. "When we first met, we'd sing along to your music everywhere we went. It's still on our road trip playlist."

"And we love your work, too, of course." The girlfriend compliments Maya, smiling politely at Jessie, eyes focused, as if she's trying to figure out whether or not her face is familiar too.

"Aww, I love that!" I say to the boyfriend. "We were just saying the same thing about SZA! Love a good road trip playlist," I enthuse.

"No way!" The girl laughs excitedly. "I guess you're just like us!"

"What's your Instagram?" I ask, searching her username when she tells me and sending the photos to her in a DM. Kimi's voice warning me to keep my fans at arm's length rings through my head, but she doesn't understand my connection and love for them.

"Thank you soooo much!" She reaches out for a hug.

"Of course, girl. It was great to meet you!" I hug her back, startling when I step on another person's foot as I pull away. "Oh fuck! Sorry!"

"It's just meeeee," a voice I'd recognize anywhere drawls.

"Val!" all three of us say at once.

"Where the hell did you go?" Maya grabs her arm and drags her into our circle, discreetly guiding us all a little farther out of the crowd now people have caught wind of the fact it's us. Crowds at Coachella are usually chill about seeing industry people, but still, the last thing we want is to create a tidal wave of attention. We could be trapped in here for *hours* if that happens. I can already sense people angling themselves, ready to seize their moment and request a photo or ask me to sign their arm.

"Has the show started yet? I can't believe I missed Tame Impala. I'm so excited to watch SZA, though, aren't you excited too? Why is everyone staring at us? Princess, did you bring a new friend with you? Is that girl waving at me—ow! Fuck, Maya, you're pinching my arm! Where are we go—"

"Val." I hold her shoulders, heart drumming hard as I focus on her expression, the loose set of her jaw and the dark expanse of her ultrawide pupils. "Valerie, look at me."

"What's the matter?" She stills when I hold her firmly in place, bringing her face up close to mine to stare right back into my eyes, so close I can taste the alcohol on her breath and see how massive her pupils are. Her pulse feels erratic under her skin, her body hot to the touch and slick.

"Where did you go?" I repeat Maya's question, trying to block out the distraction of the crowd around us as I say my words slowly and calmly, clearly, talking directly to her.

"I was with Tripp hanging out, I told him how I feel about him, and then I just . . . Shit, it's really packed here, what's with all these people? Why's everyone staring at me, Princess? Why are you holding me so tight? What's going on?"

"How she feels?" Jessie says.

"Finally," Maya says. "We've been trying to get them to act on their feelings for each other for way too long."

The stage lights behind us bathe the crowd in violet all of a sudden, the huge speakers around the stage coming alive and vibrating the ground below as the music starts up, ready for the next act. Val's eyes go even wider—if that's a possibility—and she spins around on the spot like a startled rabbit, her face sheet white and horrified, as if something terrible is about to happen.

"She's freaking the fuck out," Maya mutters to me, while next to us, a few festivalgoers watching us take notice, looking concerned for Val. I'm worried they're going to come over and try to get involved. I can already see Val's mouth dropping open like a hatch, feel her trembling with the force of a horror-movie scream.

"We should get her out of here," Jessie says, the worry on her face mirroring mine as she pushes me to move forward with Val, eyeing the people beside us who've now got their cameras pointed our way.

Shit.

Behind us, SZA steps into the spotlight, and the sound as everyone roars their applause is wild. I feel it from my head to my toes, and with Val in this state, screaming out of fear, not excitement, I feel my heart clench.

"Holy shit," I just about hear Maya saying beside me as she works with me to steer a terrified Val to safety, Jessie following behind us, apologizing to everyone as security parts a way through the crowd for us. "What's causing this? Did you see where Tripp went?"

"Maybe it's a panic attack?" I ask as Val continues to scream and thrash around, making it difficult for us to pass by anyone without pissing people off.

"Hey, is she all right?" someone calls to us.

"Don't worry, dude, she's good," Maya replies over her shoulder.

"You guys need a hand?" someone else asks, but I smile politely and battle through with security and the girls.

Val in front of us clutches my arms so tight her acrylic tips pierce my skin, the glitter on her face and in her hair flying like fairy dust around us as she jerks from my grip so fast I can barely catch her in time before she falls.

"Val, relax!" I try to soothe her, reaching out to brush her mussed caramel brown hair out of her face as we help her up again. "Hey, hey, hey. Calm down, Val, it's us. It's Princess and Maya and Jessie. We're at Coachella, Val, it's a festival. You're in the crowd . . . you're safe . . . you're okay."

I keep up the steady stream of reassurance until we're in the dregs of the crowd, large open spaces between each group of people that eventually thin out entirely as we finally make it past the barrier and over to a secluded area behind some trailers. Val's no longer screaming but she's seriously not okay, her face still pasty and skin beaded with sweat.

"I hope we don't bump into any photographers," Maya says, shaking her head in disbelief as we slowly ease Val onto the ground, her back against the tire of a trailer and her shoulders slumped forward.

Maya gets down on her haunches beside Val and grasps her shoulders. "Babe, what the fuck?"

Val stares straight ahead, completely zoned out. It's like she doesn't even see Maya in front of her—or any of us, as I crouch down too and offer her some water.

"Val, drink," I say, but her head lolls and she doesn't look up.

"I'll get a medic," Jessie says, already starting off to find one.

"Is that a good idea?" I ask quickly, thinking of Val's parents and her reputation, of how many times we've found her like this and been just as scared but always gotten through it. I think of how quickly rumors spread online and how gossip can get out of hand, and how even the slightest hint that someone's taking drugs can tarnish their career forever.

But then I look at Val, the friend I've loved for years, slowly fading away, trapped inside this unfamiliar, downright scary shell of herself, and suddenly no one else's opinion and no amount of family disappointment feels important enough. *Val* is all that matters, and right now, I just want to make sure she's okay.

"Wait, forget I said anything." I shake my head to clear the racing thoughts. "Yeah, grab a medic, Jessie. Oh, Val." I collapse on my butt beside her and wrap my arm around her vacant body, hugging her into me. "You gotta talk to us about all this, okay? When you're feeling better later, you've got to tell us. I hate seeing you like this. We can *help*."

But as my arms squeeze her tight and Maya runs after Jessie to go and get help, Val just sits and stares, and I know my words are lost. She doesn't hear because she's drifting—where to, and why she's always trying to get there so bad, I don't even know.

19

"I'm not gonna lie, this feels entirely fucked-up." Maya lets out a heavy sigh as we step away from a stall selling festival-themed cocktails, two drinks each in hand. "We're all supposed to be here together, and now we have to continue the night without her. It doesn't feel right."

"The important thing is she's going to be okay," I reply, though I have to admit, leaving Val with the medics has definitely put a damper on things. They insisted there was nothing else we could do to help, and one of our security guys is staying with her and will bring her back to the house when the medics release her. I feel awful, and kind of guilty we didn't stick with her all day. Maybe she wouldn't have gotten into such a mess.

Or maybe it was unavoidable.

"How often does this kind of thing happen?" Jessie asks, biting her lip.

Maya takes a sip of one of her cocktails. "Too often, if you ask me."

"If you ask *anyone*," I correct her. "I'm scared for her, guys."

"I think you should be." Jessie glances around to check no one's looking before telling us, "People can *die* from doing what Val did tonight. This could literally ruin her life."

"We know, Jess," Maya says in the sort of way that makes it clear she doesn't need the lecture. "And getting through to her is like playing a broken record. We try to tell her, she doesn't listen, the cycle repeats. Where the fuck do we go from there?"

"Hey!"

We all spin around. Tripp jogs toward us, red in the face like he's been running around in a panic.

"Hey, do you guys know where Val is?" he calls as he approaches.

"Jesus," Maya mutters, taking another big sip of her drink.

"Tripp." I hold his hand and walk off to one side with him. "She's in the medical tent. We found her really out of it—"

"Wait, why? Which one? Is she okay?" There's genuine worry in his eyes, and even though they're bloodshot and wide, as if he might be on something himself, this news seems to sober him.

"We didn't finish our . . ."

"Security is with her and she's gonna be fine," I reassure him. "But do you know what happened? She just came out of nowhere and we couldn't make any sense of it."

"Uh, yeah." He scrubs a hand over his face, letting out a sigh. "We were together having the best time and then started making out and then—" He shakes his head. "Listen, Princess, I need to find her and make sure she's all right. Could you tell me where the medics are?"

I point in the direction we just came from. "Over there."

"Great, thanks."

He runs off.

"What did he say?" Jessie asks when I return to the girls.

"Nothing we don't already know."

"I'm sure things have gotten more serious between those two recently. Anyone else?" Maya asks.

"Oh, for sure." I nod.

"It's such a shame. This would've been the perfect place for them to go official," Jessie muses.

"That would've been so cute."

"Yeah, cute like those *Magic Mike*–looking dancers we saw onstage earlier." Maya raises her eyebrows. "Wanna go find 'em?"

Under the sun the alcohol has an even stronger effect, and surrounded by all the energy of the festival it isn't long until we're dancing around the place, posing for photos and drinking even more cocktails, more shots, more drinks. We bump into celebrities everywhere, and with every stranger who runs up asking for us to sign their arm or phone case or whatever else, reality sinks in that *I'm* one of those celebrities people look so starstruck to see. It makes the atmosphere even more electric.

"Howdy, partners!" an overenthusiastic guy calls as we pass by what looks like a mini version of a big-top circus tent. It's all red-and-white stripes with a sparkling red doorway, a smoke machine spilling smoke out from underneath. When he sees he has our attention, he breaks into character, tipping his top hat and dipping into a bow. "Roll up, roll up to the main event!"

"Isn't that what we're watching on the Coachella stage tonight?" Maya teases him.

He winks. "Ah, but this is much more exciting, cowgirl. Step inside and let me show you why."

I glance at Maya and Jessie, laughing. "Wanna check it out?"

"I do." Jessie steps right up, her steps clumsy from being so tipsy. "Let's go!"

The guy dressed as the ringmaster holds the sparkling red door open for us. It's dark in the tent, but through the smoke effect neon lights glow, and as we step farther in I see a huge popcorn cart taking center stage, a small cluster of people gathered around waiting for a box.

"What is this place?" I say, glancing around the edges of the tent. There's a guy with a python draped around his neck and various acrobats and circus performers putting on a show. Old-fashioned circus music fills the tent, interspersed with a much heavier bass note that kind of sounds like club music.

And there, behind it all, in huge lit-up letters, is the name of the event this is promoting.

"'Cirque au bord de l'eau,'" I read aloud.

"Circus by the water," the ringmaster translates for us. "It's down in Miami this summer, hosted by the one and only—"

A voiceover cuts in before he can finish his sentence, the sound blaring through the tent and making everyone's heads turn to the big screen set up behind the popcorn stand. Images of live performers, circus acts, people laughing and dancing like here at Coachella, and a drone shot of the Miami skyline and the glistening blue ocean flash across the screen. And then, looking smug with a hand on her hip, staring directly into the camera, Miami Beach in the background, is none other than . . .

"Hey, I'm Riley Vega, and I'm inviting you, Coachella party people, to come join me this summer for a beach party to remember. Cirque au bord de l'eau, right here in South Beach—it's a circus by the water, and you won't wanna miss out."

With a final wink at the camera Riley's image blinks out, and the tent resumes the old-fashioned circus music once again. The crowd goes wild as the music fades.

"Oh, Ms. Vega will be doing a meet and greet tomorrow afternoon if you'd like to come take some photos," the ringmaster butts in, clearly not recognizing us. "Prices start at fifty dollars per person, and you can book with one of our wonderful circus performers over to the left of the popcorn cart."

"Thanks," Maya says, sickly sweet, "but I think we're good."

"Well, don't forget to take away a free box of popcorn, details of the event printed on the base of the box!" The ringmaster points to the cart. "And if you're lucky, you might find a golden popcorn kernel inside. Everyone who does gets a VIP ticket for themselves and three friends."

"What is this, Willy Wonka's chocolate factory?" Jessie laughs.

"Golden popcorn kernels? Sounds more like a choking hazard." Maya plays along, but I'm already heading out of the tent, back into the sunshine.

A whole circus on Miami Beach. I can't wrap my head around it. "Who's funding this? I guess her label is really investing in her . . ."

The fact that she's the headliner and marketing is making it out to be *her* event and she's releasing her album at the same time tells me that her team knows what they're doing. This is the stuff I'm always trying to tell Kimi and Wayne. You have to stack things together to build the momentum. And for some reason we can't seem to get the timing and strategy right.

"I'm thinking it was a bad idea to agree to go, no matter how many connections I can make," I say with a sigh.

Maya scoffs. "Riley is probably banking on using you to market herself. Your fans are loyal, so they'll obviously want to come see you live, so that'll be more ticket sales for the event, and it'll be great for her PR image."

"Yeah, it's all making sense." My stomach sinks.

"What?" Maya stops still to look at me.

"That comment on our TikTok," I say. "That's why she posted it. She's trying to make it look like we're friends again so everyone will assume I'm there to support her. It helps draw attention to the event, makes her look good. It's all about her."

"You're right." Maya's jaw drops. "That bitch."

"I don't even know what's worse: fake friending me or suddenly hating me for virtually no reason."

I glance over at Jessie, wondering why she hasn't said much. And then I see why.

"Oh god, Jess, are you okay?" I wrap an arm around her shoulder, pulling her in close.

Tears stream down Jessie's face, running tracks through her highlighter, and her shoulders are hunched over as she struggles to keep herself from sobbing out loud. I rack my brain for why she'd be so upset but I can't think of anything. When I pull her into me, she cracks.

"I'm so sorry, Princess."

Over the top of her head, I meet Maya's gaze and share a look of bewilderment. "Sorry for what, Jess?

"It's just—" She rocks with more tears against me. Whatever happened must've really affected her.

"Come on, babe, you can tell us," Maya soothes, holding Jessie around the shoulders, too, and pulling us all into a tight huddle. It's what we do for privacy in a wide-open public space like this whenever one of us is going through it, forming our own little safe place built entirely of best friendship and love.

"I should've told you earlier, Princess, I'm sorry," she cries. "This morning when I went out for my run, I saw John."

"That must've been awful for you." Maya nods with fake sympathy, but she cuts the joke off when I glare at her.

"Let her speak."

"Sorry, just trying to lighten the mood."

"Well, it's not working. She's upset."

Jessie tries to laugh through her tears, but she only manages a deep sigh. "No, it's true, Princess—it was awful. I didn't want to ruin your weekend but it's driving me crazy not telling you."

Creeping dread returns with every word she speaks. "You're scaring me, Jess. What do you mean?" I ask, but I don't think I really want to know the answer.

"I saw him with Riley, Princess," she says, and my heart cracks and drops hard through my body, weighted with betrayal. "I ran past the house she rented for the weekend on my route and saw a couple hugging on the steps. I didn't realize it was him at first because they were so all over each other, but—"

"All over each other?" There's fury in Maya's tone. "You mean like making out?"

Jessie nods. "It looked pretty intimate."

"Are you sure?" Maya growls.

Jessie nods. "I guess he stayed there last night," she continues. "It's the only explanation I can think of for why he didn't come to our house until this morning. They didn't see me run past, obviously, but the more I think about it, the more I wish I'd just run right through those gates and went in on them for what they're doing to you."

I can't speak. Or move. Or feel anything except humiliation. He was supposed to be changing for me. We were supposed to be working through this. Riley was supposed to be a collab, just business, nothing more. He lied to me and, worse, is still doing it. Just this morning he tried to sleep with me. I feel sick.

"Is that why she isn't here promoting her stupid fucking circus?"

I snap, breaking out of the friendship huddle and raking my hands through my hair, pacing. "Huh? Is that why she's not here, because she's *fucking* my *boyfriend*?" I shout the last words in the direction of the circus tent, catching the ringmaster's attention, and I must look like a crazy person but I can't stop myself. He looks disturbed and turns away.

"Babe." Maya reaches for me.

"Tell me I'm dreaming," I say on autopilot, my mouth speaking angry words while inside my brain just feels numb. No feeling settles. No action seems enough. I could call him, but what if he's with her? He's going to lie anyway. The thought of him spewing his lies down the phone while Riley's all over him churns my gut. I can't believe this. And at the same time, yes, I fucking can.

"I'm sorry I didn't tell you earlier, Princess," Jessie offers meekly, her voice low but the conflict clear in her eyes. "I didn't want to ruin the weekend."

"Don't," I say, shaking my head quickly. "Don't you dare apologize for his shitty actions. I know why you didn't tell me, Jess. You don't need to apologize, this isn't your fault."

"What do you want to do, Princess?" Maya asks, running her hands through her hair while glancing between the both of us.

I look back at the circus tent and then down at my phone, the screen devoid of any messages from John. The asshole hasn't even tried to text me to check in and see if I'm having a good time or if I'm okay. Meanwhile he's back there at the house I invited him to, going behind my back . . .

But wait—of course he's not at the house.

My mind reels as I make the connection and my realization sinks deeper.

He only fucking told me that as a cover-up. He's probably with her right now.

"Come on," I say with fury, pacing forward so the girls have to jog to catch up with me.

"Where are we going?" Maya calls.

"Where do you think?" I spin around to face them, seeing red. "We're going to find John and Riley and ask them once and for all, who the *fuck* do they think I am?"

20

We run into Tripp on our way out of the festival grounds, while we're waiting for our security and our driver to come pick us up. He waves and walks over, eyeing us with confusion.

"Leaving so soon?"

"Yeah, we're off to commit murder. Or something," Maya says.

He shakes his head. "I'm not following?"

"John drama," Jessie explains, gesturing to me. "Again."

I've been staring off into space since we called for the driver, planning a thousand different scenarios in my head, but at this I turn to look at Tripp and ask him quietly, "Did you know?"

Again, Tripp eyes us all with confusion, and it seems genuine, but at this rate I don't know what to believe. "Did I know what?" he asks.

I shake my head, feeling instantly guilty for thinking the worst. It doesn't seem like Tripp has a clue what's going on. "It doesn't matter. How's Val? Did you find her?"

"She left an hour ago," he says. "The medics got her all hydrated and feeling normal again and security took her back to the house. Understandably, she didn't want me to join."

"Understandably?" Maya pries, popping her head into the conversation.

"Yeah." Tripp shuffles his feet, scuffing the sand up in a little cloud of dirt. "She said some stuff to me earlier that I don't think she was really ready to say. Maybe she's embarrassed or, I don't know, hurt. Anyway, she knows I love her, and I told her I wouldn't be here much longer." Tripp looks at the ground with a sad sigh.

My heart clenches at hearing him use the word *love* so easily. I wish it was like that with John. He's always so guarded with his feelings. I get glimpses of the man I know he can be, but that's what they are, glimpses of a man who's deathly afraid of real commitment.

"Did she tell you she wants to have your babies, by any chance?" Maya asks.

"Maya." I shake my head at her. Val's had a hard enough day as it is; it's not our business to pry into her deepest secrets when she isn't here to tell her side of the story. Even if everyone—including Tripp—already figured out her feelings for him ten million years ago.

Tripp looks at me. "Hey, you guys are headed back to the house, right?"

"No," I tell him. "We're going somewhere else."

Silence lingers while he waits for me to elaborate. I don't.

"We're off to Riley Vega's," Maya eventually says.

"You're going to Riley's party?" Tripp sounds weary with disbelief, as if he can't quite figure out why we'd want to put ourselves through such an ordeal.

"Oh, there's a party, is there?" I raise an eyebrow while inside my heart drops all over again and my stomach twists into knots, making me feel so sick I could throw up right now. Of course there's a party at Riley fucking Vega's house and of course John is there instead of with me. "How nice."

Tripp watches me carefully for a moment, an unreadable look on his face. "Uh, I don't think that's a great idea."

I look at him, my eyes narrowing a little. "Why not?"

He laughs easily, almost too quickly, staring between us all as if we can't be serious. "You all hate each other's damn guts, that's why."

"Hmm. *Hate*'s a strong word," I say, the corner of my lip twitching. "More like *dislike*. Like a very, very strong dislike." I imagine finding her in bed with John and my rage kicks up a notch. "Well, whatever. The line between hate and dislike is so thin anyway. Who needs a label?"

"You gonna do some crazy shit out there, Princess?" Tripp asks, posing it as a joke, but there's a serious undertone to his words—an uneasy edge to his laughter.

I shrug. "Guess we'll see."

He sucks his teeth and takes a step back, hands raised. "I don't want to get in the middle of it, but all I'll say is it's probably not the best idea to go starting shit in public. The spotlight is on you now more than ever, Princess."

"Tripp, that's our driver right there." He turns to look at the car I point out, and then I wave for the girls to follow me. "See you back at the house tonight?"

As we get into the car, Jessie murmurs to me, "You're not really gonna start shit, are you?"

The idea puts me off. It's not my scene at all to crash a party and start freaking out. I've always hated that kind of behavior. Really, tonight, I need to see for myself what John's up to, and then I guess my emotions will take it from there.

"If he's cheating on me, Jessie, the bad publicity's gonna hit him a lot harder."

Maya laughs. "Girl, you got that right."

—

With all the Coachella traffic—people still arriving for the concerts and others heading out to grab dinner someplace else—it takes an eternity to get to Riley's house. I almost tell the driver to take us back to our place instead, frustrated with the whole situation, and as my anger in the moment lessens, I wonder if it would be better to live in blissful ignorance. But that'd mean we left the festival for nothing, and at the very least, I convince myself, if I'm wrong about John and Riley and we turn up at her party to find nothing at all, well, we could always just pretend we showed up to have fun. I'm sure she'd *love* that.

A "just checking in" text from Win pops up as we're idling in another row of cars at an intersection, and for a second it pulls me out of my obsessive thoughts about John. I can't explain the skip of my pulse when I see Win's name, and I guiltily realize I didn't reply to his last message, which had only made me feel even more special. Wanted. Thought of. I wonder for a fleeting second if I'm the only girl he's double texting, and then I shut the thought down even faster. Of course I'm not. This is *Win* we're talking about.

Then again, I didn't think he was the type to double text anyone.

"Does this look like the right house?" the driver asks a few minutes later, slowing to a stop outside a villa that looks pretty similar to ours.

We both look at Jess for confirmation.

"Yeah," she says with a nod. "This is the one."

As we bustle out onto the sidewalk, Maya leans back in to say to the driver, "Can you wait here for us? We might need a quick getaway."

"Where'd you see them?" I ask, noticing the street is lined with other cars that no doubt belong to people at the party. I can hear the faint thump of music from inside the house.

"Over there, literally right by the front door. They couldn't have been more in plain sight." Jessie points to the topiaries on either side of the front door, and I glance through the windows of the house to see all the lights are on inside, the music only getting louder the farther we walk up the driveway.

"Nice. So if anyone was out here and cared enough to take a picture, you'd have heard about it online first." Maya shakes her head in disbelief. "Seriously, they're practically asking to be caught."

"Well," I say as we reach the front door and I curl my fingers around the handle, "let's give them what they want."

"You're so fucking badass," Jessie encourages me.

I throw her my best smile and push the door open.

It's not exactly the grand entrance we expect. No one even looks our way as we enter, too preoccupied in their own world, dancing and chatting and straining to listen to their friends' conversations above the noise of the karaoke machine and loud music. Red Solo cups litter the floor, party streamers everywhere, and it looks like someone exploded a Funfetti cake all over the huge white sectional.

"Jesus," Jessie says, coming to a standstill beside me. "Have these people never heard of a cleaning bill?"

I scan the room and the dozens of unrecognizable faces, hoping I'll see at least someone who'll guide me. We move through the downstairs of the house, my chest tightening with every room we enter without finding Riley or John, anxious with the knowledge every room we pass through is another room closer to us having to search upstairs. And upstairs is only bedrooms; it's always the same at every party like this. And nobody wants to find their boyfriend alone with some other girl in a bedroom.

Thankfully, as we enter a room with floor-to-ceiling windows overlooking the pool, a sound system playing loudly and all the furniture pushed aside to create a makeshift dance floor, I catch sight of a face

I recognize. It's one of Riley's close friends, a girl whose name I don't remember but someone I know I've hung out with before, and dancing beside her are two more girls I recognize as part of Riley's clique.

"Over there." I nudge Maya and point her and Jessie in the right direction, casting my eyes around for any sign of John.

"Wait." Jessie grabs my arm, pulling me to a stop before I can walk any farther. "Princess."

I can already tell from her tone of voice that what I'm about to witness won't be anything good. Following her line of sight, my eyes catch the flash of a crimson-red ringmaster's coat first, tailored to a flattering fit, cinched around the waist to draw attention to the sparkling red, barely there bikini underneath. She's wearing black fishnets on her legs and thigh-high black stiletto boots; there's a riding crop affixed to her waist, and two hands hold her tight right above it.

My gaze slides up, following those hands that look a little too familiar for comfort.

She's grinding on him, throwing her head back over his shoulder every now and then, so when I finally catch his eye and his pupils dilate with shock, she doesn't even see. John's movement slows, but as if to keep Riley from noticing, he continues to dance, eyes locked with mine while the rest of the room fades out around me.

So it's true.

Not that I ever doubted it for a second.

And I think that really says it all.

"That bitch," Maya says from a distance, even though I know she's right beside me.

"That asshole," Jessie adds, her words equally faraway.

I don't speak. Because what the hell do I say? Sure, it'd fulfill some deep-down sadistic desire to barge over to them right now and drag her off him by the hair—or the stupid fucking top hat balanced at an angle on her head—and maybe they deserve that. But in the moment, I can't bring myself to do it. The will simply isn't there. I can't muster up the energy with such a hopeless sense of devastation bloating me from the inside out, making my limbs heavy and drawing awareness to my suddenly too-hot cheeks. Embarrassment. Humiliation. Betrayal. It all cuts through me, sharp and unforgiving, because beneath it all, the one thing that hurts the most is the fact I really believed him, trusted him.

I took a chance on him when I shouldn't have, and he threw it right back in my face. As I spin on my heel and storm off, pushing my way through the party, Maya calls my name.

"Princess!" Jessie shouts too.

Outside, the desert air traps me with my emotions, suffocating and hot and way too much. So when I turn around and see John walking out the front door, arms open as if he's getting ready to embrace me and tell me it'll all be okay, we can work through this, I don't even give him a chance to speak. With Jessie and Maya acting as witnesses in the doorway behind him, I say my words loud and clear, making them nonnegotiable. Final. The end.

"Fuck you, John! I'm so fucking over this bullshit. We are done."

"Princess—"

I hold up a hand to silence him. "Don't even bother."

He tries again. "Please, just—"

"Seriously," I cut him off, closing my eyes for a second just to help me breathe. "How dare you fucking embarrass me like this! I went against my own judgment and gut and fucking trusted you! How could you do this to me!" I take another deep breath, completely certain. "It's over."

"You can't end things without hearing what I have to say!" he protests, arms out by his sides, spinning around to look for a second opinion, as if either of the girls would ever agree.

"She can do whatever the fuck she wants, actually," Maya says derisively, narrowing her eyes into slits as she and Jessie pass him by. She throws her arm around my shoulder. "Don't you ever even think about coming near her again, *Jonathan*."

"Come on, Princess." Jessie's voice is much softer as she places her hand flat in the center of my back and rubs in gentle circles. "Let's get out of here."

They lead me back to the waiting car while John yells out a string of bullshit behind us. All his words bounce right off me, none coming close to even scraping the surface of my thoughts. I don't think I've ever been so clear on a decision. We are over. Done. Relationship status: single. Nothing to discuss. Nothing complicated about it. I'm just completely numb. So fucking hurt I can't even feel anything.

"I'm proud of you," Maya whispers to me as the driver pulls away, dragging me closer to her on the back seat to land a kiss on my head. "Good job, P. It's about damn time."

I try to respond but I can't. Because as much as I know this is the right thing to do, I'm suddenly struck with the sense there's no going back on this decision. I've closed the door, locked it tight, thrown away the key, and forgotten the address.

And in the back of my mind, the same old fear kicks in. Will I *ever* find myself in real, true love?

21

Back at our house I ask the girls to give me some space for a while. I need time alone to let what happened today sink in, and to make peace with the fact I'm single once again.

Cheated on.

"Are you sure you don't want some company?" Maya asks, both hands on my shoulders as she looks deep into my eyes, probably searching for some hidden cry for help. Or even just a sign I need a hug. "It's better to have someone with you at times like this."

"Trust me," I tell her, even though I don't know if I can trust my own words now, "I'll be okay."

At the very least I've been alone through this kind of pain before. Thanks to John, I'm well versed in the disappointment department. I always see his potential, not his actions, and each time I get my heart broken.

Even so, Jessie goes off to the kitchen to prepare me an iced coffee and delivers it to my room a few minutes later, along with the tray of fruit slices left over from breakfast. I'm starfished on my bed when she walks in, arms and legs out by my sides, staring up at the plain white ceiling. It's a blank canvas, like my mind. Except with a blank canvas there's potential for something beautiful to be created; my mind feels like a bleak, empty end. Numb and cold, no art to be gained from this crushing sense of rejection. The only emotion breaking through is the embarrassment of it all. Am I really so horrible at judging people's character? Can I even trust myself to make the right choices anymore? Clearly I've fucked this up, so what about everything else? I've never felt so stupid in my life.

"We'll be downstairs if you need us," Jessie tells me sympathetically, stroking a strand of hair out of my face while she lies beside me for a while. "I'm sorry he hurt you like this, Princess. You deserve so much better."

"It's not your fault," I say weakly, my voice barely there, distant, just like my emotions. I'm not even mad anymore. I simply feel nothing.

After she leaves I tilt my head to look out the window at the hillside, listening to the sounds of the girls in the kitchen below. I hear them move out to the pool area, the occasional burst of laughter carrying on the air along with the splash of water, but mostly just the murmurs of talking, much more serious than our carefree attitude last night. Sadness sits in my chest where my heart used to be, but knowing Val's back and must be okay lightens my mood. Suddenly, I feel selfish for being so caught up in my own emotions, filled with a sense of self-loathing, because at the root of it all I guess this is kind of my fault for letting him back in.

Today really didn't live up to expectations.

It's not hate, but something else that fills me at the thought that John's ruined yet another big event for me. I was supposed to be here with my girls having a great time, and sure, he isn't responsible for Val's actions earlier pulling us out of the Coachella spirit, but even if that didn't happen first, I know I'd still be feeling numb right now.

It's nobody's fault except John's. I try to reason with myself internally while the other thought rings loud and clear. *And Riley's too. But you didn't cheat. You stayed loyal this whole time.*

That thought at least gives me fresh hope. I shouldn't just lie here wallowing in self-pity. I'm better than this.

I get up and stroll into my bathroom, grateful for the waterfall shower and jacuzzi tub. Catching sight of my reflection in the mirror, I realize I'm still wearing the cowgirl outfit, all the glitter streaked down my face now, making me look kind of messy. I need to wash it off. All of it—the glitter, the outfit, the hairspray, the makeup, the memory of today, and my whole damn relationship.

I just need to feel like myself again.

Hitting the shower on, I strip out of my clothes and kick off the boots, then step beneath the waterfall of warm water and close my eyes.

Breathe in . . .

. . . and out.

In . . .

. . . and out.

Whenever I travel my bathrooms are always stocked with the same products I use when I'm in LA. It helps me feel a sense of normalcy since I'm on the road so much. There's a collection of shower products unboxed and lined up in the shower ready for me. I distract myself by picking out the ones I want to use, the heady scents filling the air as I wash the glitter down the drain and lather the luxury shampoo into my hair. It calms me gradually, my tension and stress unknotting and easing with every passing second, until I feel refreshed and clean and much more like *me*. Worthy. Deserving. Better than this shit.

Then, stepping out of the shower, I wrap myself in a thick, fluffy towel and apply moisturizer and hair product, leaving my blonde tresses to dry naturally. I'm about to go back into my room and put on some clothes, maybe join the others by the pool, when something catches my eye.

Down on the floor, kicked into the corner of the room near the laundry hamper—just another one of his *totally mature* habits—is John's shirt from this morning. The one he arrived in, fresh out of Riley's house and into our kitchen to join us for a breakfast feast as if nothing even happened. A lump forms in my throat and sticks there as I imagine him waiting for us all to leave for the festival and then hopping into *my* shower to clean himself up, ready to race back out and meet *her*.

And then I wonder how many other times he's turned up acting totally normal when in reality, he's been living a lie.

Just like that, my bubble of rejuvenation bursts.

And I'm *mad*.

"Fuck you, John," I cuss at the shirt, kicking it even farther into the corner as fresh tears burst from my eyes. "Fuck you, fuck her, fuck your immature . . . fucking . . ." I reach down and pick up the shirt with every intention of dumping it in the hamper, but then something stops me. Instead, I shake it out in front of me and hold it up to my nose, breathing in deep to the smell of his aftershave, the fruity scent of his vape, and the undertones of something else. A feminine, floral scent. A perfume that doesn't belong to me.

I don't even realize I'm screaming until I've halfway torn the shirt, ripping it right down the center in anger. It's as if I black out, the emotion overcoming me in a strong wave of feeling, every past disappointment and tiny annoying detail I've brushed off coming right back around to hit me full force. I rip the shirt again, the satisfying *zzzip* of the fabric the only sound in my ears alongside my screams.

But I don't really hear it. Just like I don't really process what I'm doing as I bundle the shirt so tight around my hand it hurts and then launch myself at my stupid fucking reflection.

There's a crack at first, and then I hit it again, the overwhelming surge of energy so uncontrollable it burns with a sting that runs up my arms. Or maybe that's just the pain of my rage. As the mirror splinters into hundreds of tiny shards, I see myself in every one: broken beyond repair. This time when the tears fall they don't stop, and when I breathe out, I can't seem to pull my breath back in. Short, sharp, shallow gasps leave me lightheaded, and the next thing I know I'm on my ass on the cold tile with warm arms wrapped around me, cheeks wet with tears, face pushed into the satin material of someone else's robe.

"Valerie?" I pull back to look into her face. Her eyes are still kind of faraway but she's fresh and clean out of the shower, too, her balayage hair loose and damp around her shoulders, and the worry on her face mirrors my own from when I held her earlier.

"Babe, what the fuck?" she asks loudly, her voice slicing through my bad mood and breaking it down into more manageable doses. The pain of it all hurts just as much, but not all at once now, as I train my eyes on hers and try to keep a clear enough head to respond.

"Goddamn it, Princess, we thought you were dying in here, being attacked or something. Is everything okay?"

I look up at the doorway, where Tripp's leaning with his hands either side of the frame, poking his head around to check I'm all right. Val looks at him as she stands up, and I notice for the first time she has 911 ready to call on his phone as she hands it back to him, locking the screen.

"We were ready to call the freakin' cops," he explains as he takes the phone back, letting out a relieved sigh. "Shit."

"You really scared us." Val helps me up off the floor with both hands, reaching to grab my towel before it slips and reveals all to Tripp. Not that I care about that right now. Nothing could ever be more humiliating than knowing I fell for John's transparent bullshit once again. "What *happened*?"

"I don't . . . I don't want to talk about it," I manage, my words no more than a mumble, my throat still hoarse from screaming. I look down at my hand, the ripped shirt still wrapped tight around it, protecting my skin from the broken glass. Thank god. I don't even want to think about how I would've explained those injuries. "Sorry."

"Everything's okay," she reassures me, holding on to my waist, noticing my hands trembling. "You're shaking, take some deep breaths."

She's totally unaware of what happened with John, oblivious to the news and still dealing with her own issues under the surface. No wonder she's confused—it's only been a few hours since we were all happy and smiling, after all. So much really can change in a day. Funny how it's always the bad changes that come up fast.

"I need to lie down," I hear myself say, but even as I step back into the bedroom it feels like my limbs are moving of their own accord. My mind's just a passenger in my body, and as I land on the feather-soft mattress with heavy limbs and a heavier heart, I'm grateful for Tripp, who pulls the curtains over the huge windows.

I put my friends through that. Holy shit. I've never lost control that way before. Regret floods in as I think about how scared they must've been, how insane I must look to them, how humiliating it'll be to talk about this later.

"It's not worth it, whatever it is," Tripp tells me, squeezing Val's shoulder as if to urge her out of the room. "Get some rest, you'll feel better. Call if you need anything."

"Thanks," I manage, my voice barely a croak as exhaustion settles deep in my bones. Giving a hopeless sigh, I curl up in the fetal position under the covers, not even caring about my wet hair or the fact I'm only wearing a towel.

"If you need me, I'm just down the hall," Val says.

"Mm-hmm," I mumble into the pillows, too groggy to bother talking anymore.

The door shuts quietly behind them both, and for the next few hours I sink into a dreamless sleep, not even interrupted by the buzz of my cell phone on the nightstand beside me. When I wake up to a pitch-black room later, I don't realize the phone is vibrating until the light of my screen casts a blue glow across the soft sheets. I pull myself up in the bed and rest my back against the headboard, pushing my air-dried hair out of my face.

No surprise, there's a string of unopened texts from John right at the top of my notifications, the newest one from just two minutes ago. I don't even bother to check them. I almost forgot the sense of despair while I slept, but seeing his name again is the worst type of reminder. It brings a sick feeling to my stomach, flooding me with all those negative emotions all over again.

I clear my notifications.

Like I wish I could clear my head.

It's past midnight, no sound from downstairs. I guess everyone went to bed already, or maybe they're out partying like I should be.

Getting comfy, I click onto my recent calls and hover my thumb over Mom's name for a few seconds. I should talk to her—she always gives the best advice in situations like this. But instead my gaze slips to a different name.

And then I'm back on our messages, grinning like a fool as I sit alone in the dark reading through them. Not John but Win, one of the only men in this crazy life who hasn't let me down.

I don't know why I do it, but before I know what's happening, I'm calling him on FaceTime.

"This is so dumb," I mutter to myself, breaking free of my moment of insanity and finally moving to cancel the call. But—

"What's dumb?" His rumbling nighttime voice hits me directly in my core, the sound moving my body instinctively. My heart rate picks up as I tilt the screen to see him.

"Sorry," I lie. "I didn't mean to call."

"Shame," he says casually, and as the phone screen moves while he adjusts his position, I see his dark bedsheets and mussed hair. Clearly, I woke him up. "I was just thinking about you."

"You were?" I ask, feeling his confession like a lick of heat.

"No, Princess," he deadpans. "It's one in the morning. I was sound asleep in bed like any sane person should be."

I laugh reflexively, though really, it's humiliation I feel. *God, I hope I didn't sound too enthusiastic there.* "Sorry," I say again. "It really was a mistake."

"It's all good. I have my notifications silenced after ten, except for from you." He chuckles, almost seeming embarrassed, but then his expression turns quizzical. "Why aren't you out partying like a good little Coachella VIP?"

"Uh, it's kind of complicated."

He shifts to sit up straight in his bed. "Princess . . ."

"It's nothing, Win."

"Talk to me." His tone leaves no room for protest. The way he speaks makes it seem like he already knows exactly what I'm about to tell him. "Come on, you already woke me up—I could use some pillow talk."

"And I could use a hug," I grumble, not missing the amused quirk of his lips as he watches me gather my thoughts. He seems genuinely interested in hearing me out. So instead of brushing it off, I tell him everything, starting with the Val situation and ending on John's string of unopened messages—another of which pops up as I speak.

"Jeez." He lets out a low whistle. "You really could use a hug, huh?"

"It's been a fucking *day*, Win."

"Sounds like it."

"I don't know why he—" I don't get to finish my sentence before my voice cracks on another round of tears. "Fuck," I sob, wiping at my cheeks. "I'm so sorry I'm keeping you up like this. It's so not your problem. You should be aslee—" I finally glance at the screen and notice he's out of bed now, pulling on a shirt and flicking on the lights as he walks through his house. "Wait, what are you doing?"

"Coming to pick you up," he says like it's nothing. "You're not happy there."

"Win—"

"It's nonnegotiable," he says, not in any sort of controlling tone, but in such a way that makes it sound like the obvious, easy solution. Never mind the fact it's one in the morning and he owes absolutely none of his time or kindness to me. "Put your stuff together and get something to eat, and I'll be there as fast as the traffic will allow."

"Are you insane?" I laugh, barely believing this. "I'm in freaking Coachella Valley, Win! You're in Los Angeles—it's like a three-hour drive!"

"I can make it there and back in time for work tomorrow." He shrugs. "I already have the address, so just hang tight. You should probably let the girls know you're leaving."

My body's practically vibrating with the excitement of all this. "Are you being serious right now?"

He jangles his car keys in front of the camera. "Yep."

"This is *crazy*."

He chuckles. "Crazy isn't always a bad thing, Princess."

22

"You know I think you're actually insane for this, right? It's literally the middle of the night. You got here *so* fast."

Win laughs as he pushes the door of his Rolls-Royce Ghost shut and steps up to the entrance of the house. I try not to crush too hard on the lazy smile he gives me, nor the little wink before he pulls me in for a quick hug.

"There's no need for the speed limit on an empty highway—what more do you want me to say? I'm here safe, aren't I?" he teases, following me inside. I think this might be the first time I've seen him dressed in anything except a suit, and even now he's looking smart as hell in black sweatpants and a crisp, high-quality white T-shirt. "Did you let the girls know you're leaving?"

"Yeah, I did. Val's with Tripp sleeping off a hangover or whatever, and I had to practically beg Jessie and Maya to stay here and enjoy themselves when they heard I was leaving. Maya was literally seconds away from booking a car. I know they just want to make sure I'm okay, but I need them to forget about me and enjoy themselves. And obviously FaceTime me for the rest of the festival. Tomorrow's performances are going to be really good."

"If it's gonna eat you up to miss it, you could always stay."

I flash Win a dry look. "Thanks, but I'm coming back with you."

He's already lifting my luggage. "Great, because we should probably get moving ASAP."

"Should I make coffee before we get on the road?" I ask, grabbing my purse and the rest of my stuff and following him right back out.

"We can grab coffee on the drive," Win says, making me wonder for a second if he ever just takes a half hour to stop and sit down. The thought of him perched on a stool at a breakfast bar eating a bowl of cereal and scrolling on his phone almost makes me laugh out loud. It's so not Win at all.

I wave good-bye to the house—not that anyone else is awake to see me—and get settled in the leather bucket seat beside Win, catching the glint of his gold Rolex as he pulls into the dark night. He turns down the volume of the music and then he angles the vents so the AC's blowing on me too. It's a sweet gesture, and I love the fact he did it before I even knew I needed the cool air myself. I don't remember John ever making this little move.

God, I've got to stop comparing him to John.

Twenty minutes into the drive we pull up at a twenty-four-hour gas station, turning the heads of the two other people filling their cars at the pump. Win cuts the engine and unclips his belt.

"Something about that middle-of-the-night gas station coffee just hits different," he says jokingly. "What would you like?"

"I'll come with you and see what they've got," I say, and then glance out the window at a group of girls walking up the street toward us, their faces still painted from whatever Coachella party they're coming back from. Across the other side of the street is another group of friends yelling and laughing loudly as they film something on their phones.

"Actually—" I glance at Win, thinking of all the ways our grabbing coffee together this late at night could be misinterpreted. All it'd take is for one of those girls to snap a photo and we'd be all over the internet with brand-new rumors about our Coachella "walk of shame" by breakfast time, which is frankly the last thing I need on top of everything else right now.

"Don't worry, I got it," Win says, apparently understanding without me even needing to say anything. He gets out of the car and locks it behind him, leaving me grateful for the tinted windows as the group of girls walks straight past without so much as a glance.

Well, okay, that's a lie—they're *definitely* doing more than glancing at Win. More like ogling him as he steps into the gas station and the door swings shut on his tail.

I can't blame them.

After he returns to the car with coffee and pastries, we head back on the road toward LA, the sky only seeming to get darker, and our sleepy silence becoming more comfortable by the second. Win drives with a steady focus that leaves me feeling safe and at ease, and when we do talk we don't dwell on the events at Coachella; instead we discuss his business and I tell him about a new restaurant that opened up last month, going into detail about the dessert menu when he tells me he loves peaches too. He says we should go there sometime, and when he asks about my family, I remember one of the first times we went out for dinner together, when he spent thirty minutes asking question after question about my family back in Guam and trying to wrap his head around all my siblings' and cousins' names. I remind him of that, and he laughs hard before checking in to ask how my parents are doing.

"You love your family," he states—not a question but an observation, and it sounds like he respects me for it. "That's important, Princess. Really important."

"Do you talk to your family much?" I ask.

Win's grip on the steering wheel tenses a little. "We get on well when we do spend time together," he answers carefully. "Never really had that real close-knit, call-me-when-you-need-me sort of connection, though, unfortunately."

"You'd like that?"

"It's what I want, Princess." His tone's serious, no room for misinterpretation. "When I have a family of my own, they're getting everything, all of it. My time, my attention—nothing else is going to come in between."

I swallow hard. "That's exactly what I want."

Win looks at me for a second. "I'm so eager to find my person but at the same time I'm not going to rush the process. These things should happen organically. I have so many goals I want to achieve and I'd love to check things off my list with my person by my side."

"Yes!" I lean forward, animated. It's so refreshing to talk to someone who *gets* it. "Exactly. I don't want to rush into anything as important as settling down. But I've always wanted the fairy tale. I want to be a power couple, building an empire with someone special."

I think back to my conversation with John about running away from Hollywood and living a simpler life, like his parents. It's only now I realize I don't need to run away; I'm strong. I have butterflies thinking about finding my person and having my fairy tale come to life. As dark as life can get, I still want the LA spotlight to shine bright on me. This is my dream.

"Did anyone ever try to force you down that path?" Win keeps his eyes on the road but there's no mistaking his interest in my answer.

"No . . ." I begin, wondering if John was even capable of the things he daydreamed about, or if it was just another fantasy for him. Win glances at me again, and I decide not to say anything. "No, nobody has."

"Good," Win says with a small nod. He doesn't add anything else.

We drive on through mostly empty roads, and I take out my phone to FaceTime my mom. It's early hours in California but with the time difference in Guam she'll probably just be finishing with dinner. I should give her a quick update on why I'm heading home early and that Win is taking me back. He's as charming as ever, taking the time to ask Mom how she is and what she's up to. I notice the way he checks in on my dad and siblings, too, and it makes me smile. Although Win comes from a completely different lifestyle, he fits in so effortlessly with my family.

I fall asleep soon after, and I don't know how much time passes before I'm woken by the buzz of my phone vibrating on my lap. Squinting against the glare of the screen, I check and see it's John calling. My stomach drops.

"You're awake," Win says, and when he sees my expression his eyes drop to the phone too. I see the realization sink in. "I assume you don't want to get that," he says.

"Not at all," I reply.

Without another word, I swipe the call away and the vibrating stops.

And then it starts again. I cringe at the phone.

"Persistent," Win mutters.

I take a deep breath. "Should I just answer it and get it over with?"

"I'll handle it," Win says, checking his mirrors before pulling off the road. I nod my approval.

He parks and holds out his hand for the phone. I pass it over to him just as the call cuts out and another one begins.

"Thank you," I say gratefully as he gets out of the car.

We're in the middle of nowhere, barely any cars around and only land for miles and miles. It's eerie not being able to see what's in the distance through the dark. I watch through the mirror as Win walks around the car to look out into the night, talking quietly at first so I can barely hear anything. Then he rolls his shoulders and his voice gets a little louder. I hear my name as his voice sounds clearer.

"Don't you think you've caused her enough pain? You don't care enough to keep your shit together for one weekend. And now that you've humiliated her you won't even allow her the space to collect herself before you start harassing her," he's saying, his voice much lower than it usually is around me.

"She's sleeping and she's safe, and if you care for her at all, that's what should matter right now. Grow the fuck up, John."

There's a long pause, and I hold my breath to hear his next words. Win's furious when he speaks this time, the emotion dripping from his words. "I don't want your excuses. I know plenty of men like you, you're no different. I'm turning her phone off. If you know what's good for you, and your career, you'll stop calling her and wait for her to call you . . . if she decides to."

My stomach knots. Win pauses for a few seconds before saying something more, raking his hands through his hair and breathing out therapeutically as he stares at the empty land around us. I try to listen, but it's impossible, and while I wait my eyelids droop with tiredness. I don't realize they've fallen shut until the car door opens, waking me back up.

"Thank you," I tell him sleepily, but he brushes it off with a shake of his head.

"He won't be calling you again," is all he says.

I don't know what else to say. Pocketing my cell phone, I watch him as we drive. Win seems genuinely affected by whatever John said to him on the call. I think of all the difficult people he must've dealt with in his life running his various businesses, and I know firsthand these sorts of things never faze him. So why is he so worked up about this now? It's only John, for god's sake. It's only my relationship drama, which feels so trivial compared to Win's life.

Win's jaw twitches, and I look away. Whatever it means or whatever was said is a problem for another day. For now, I'm safe with him, and he's good to me, and that's what I think about as we drive and my eyes slowly close on another deep sleep.

23

Win's house is incredible. And I mean *showstopping*. As we step through the entrance I'm reminded of why I love his place so much. Nestled high up in the Hills, he's got a view for miles—I even spot my own high-rise, and a shiver rushes through me at the thought he's always watching over me. Not that he could see much except the rays of sunlight glinting off the windows of my building. I'm suddenly more aware of the space his body takes up as he leads us past sleek furniture and surfaces that shine, they're so polished and clutter-free. Minimalism suits him.

"Why don't you settle down in there and I'll get us a drink?" He gestures to the main living space, the best view in the house. There's a sunken couch looking out over the city, and the sky's a deep orange as the early-morning sun creeps onto the horizon.

"A drink?" I chuckle. "Win, don't you have meetings to be at soon? The sun is coming up."

He pushes his cell phone into his pants pocket and lifts the smooth crystal top of the whiskey decanter. "I postponed my meetings. Too tired after all that driving." He shrugs.

"And yet still awake enough to drink." I watch as he pours two fingers of whiskey into a tumbler and then presses his finger on top of a brand-new bottle of vodka, spinning it around to face me.

"Call it a nightcap," he says, and then he winks at me and my stomach flips. "A morning cap, I guess," he corrects himself. "You want a cocktail?" Then he shakes his head. "No, I know what you want."

I laugh as he grabs another whiskey tumbler and pours another two fingers for me. It's a running joke between us, how similar our tastes are. Even when we go out to eat Win never needs to ask what I want. He always knows what to order for me.

He joins me on the coziest couch a moment later, a tan leather love seat closest to the window with a huge gold lamp hanging over it offering the only light in the wide-open space aside from the soft glow of dawn.

"I don't think I've ever needed anything more than this," I say with a smile, taking a sip and savoring the taste as the smooth liquid passes my lips. "Thank you, Win."

"Enjoy." He grins as he watches me, eyes on my lips when I take another sip. But all too quickly Win averts his attention back to his own drink, which he balances on the arm of the couch as he gets comfortable beside me. "God, we're crazy, aren't we?"

We. I love how he couples us together like that. It makes this feel even more like a secret mini adventure, just the two of us.

"What excuse did you give for postponing the meeting?" I ask with a grin, immediately aware of the heat of his thigh against mine as he spreads his legs and leans back, dropping his head back to look up at the ceiling, sending the butterflies in my stomach wild.

"I don't need to give an excuse. Perks of being the boss."

He doesn't say it cockily, just as a matter of fact. Which it is. I try to imagine how freeing it would be to have the power to blow off a meeting just because I didn't feel like it. Kimi and Wayne would be on me immediately, and besides, I'd beat myself up with guilt. But god, sometimes I wish I could take a break unplanned.

"Your life's so impressive," I say dreamily, twisting to face him in the love seat and drawing my legs up beneath me. I rest my head in my hand, my elbow on the back of the sofa.

Win moves his head sideways to face me, rolling his eyes affectionately. "Don't say that. Everyone says that."

"Sorry." I giggle. "I meant it as a compliment."

"My life *is* impressive," he says. "From the outside. Underneath it all it can be lonely, I'm sure you know."

I swallow hard, my voice turning quiet as I say simply, "Yeah. I know." On the seat between us, my phone buzzes with another notification, and Win glances down. I swipe to clear the home screen. "Just a stream of never-ending social media notifications, nothing important."

"No escape, is there?" He takes a swig of whiskey, then another, finishing off the tumbler and setting it down on the end table. "Even through the night there's always someone wanting to feel a connection with you."

"Always," I agree. "Which I guess is kind of nice, to know I'm not alone. Always someone thinking of me." But the words feel empty in my mouth, untrue. "But are they thinking of the real me? That's the question," I admit.

Twisting around on the love seat, too, Win reaches out to pull my hand from where it's resting underneath my hair, using both his hands to massage my fingers idly. It's the most natural, casual movement, like something we always do. Except I'm acutely aware that this is so unlike any other time I've been with him. Much more intimate. I've never had so much of his attention, and the pressure of his fingers moving over mine makes my blood run hot, energy practically vibrating through me.

"It's the dream for everyone, right," he says, "moving to Hollywood, the life of the rich and famous, fast cars, a house in the Hills, condos in the city, private jets. No one talks about how once you make it here it's all so fucking lonely." He looks down at our hands, his still massaging mine gently. Then his thoughts seem to shift, his expression softening as if he's trying to hold back a thought. He nods to a door leading off the room we're in. "I'm thinking of building a library. I'd like to start reading some more. In that room over there, floor-to-ceiling bookshelves, a desk so I can write down my thoughts."

"That actually sounds perfect." I sigh wistfully. "Invite me over more often when it's done. I've always wanted a home library."

His hands stop massaging for a second to squeeze mine tight. "You're welcome in this house anytime, Princess."

I hold his gaze for a moment longer than normal and lean into him, hoping he can see I'm grateful for that.

Win glances over the living room, surveying the furniture. "I'd love for this place to feel more like a home. More like *mine*. Right now, it's just so . . . big and empty."

"Minimalist and tasteful," I correct.

He chuckles. "I'm not talking about the décor."

"Then what else do you mean?"

He sighs. I watch carefully as he scoots a little closer, repositioning himself so he's comfortable again. He keeps hold of my hand, waiting a second to answer as he contemplates his words.

"I mean, when all's said and done, some nights—*most* nights, actually—I'm back here all on my own, it'd be nice to appreciate it all with someone. And I mean one person, *my* person, not someone just checking in on the other end of the phone. Deeper than that. Someone who matters."

"Someone worth skipping work for," I say without thinking.

Win looks directly into my eyes. "Exactly."

The air stills around us for a second. Two seconds. For a stretch of time I couldn't count even if I tried. I'm far too distracted by his energy and the way his hands have stopped massaging but instead are now encasing mine with so much heat, his legs once again pressed against mine, his face so close either intentionally or not, but either way enough to make it difficult to see anything except the way his eyes trace my features, his gravity pulling me in . . .

I use my free hand to lift the cocktail glass to my lips, taking another sip just to cool down. I don't want to make a mistake here. If we take things too far, what if he regrets it later? Does Win see me fitting into his world? Could I be the one who matters?

I run my tongue over my lips. "This whiskey is amazing. You're gonna have to get me another."

His eyes hold mine but with a sad sort of expression. My heart sinks—I ruined the moment. "Sure, let me get that for you." He stands up and takes my glass, but this time our fingertips don't brush each other's. "Back in a sec."

He returns holding a fresh glass, and I try to ignore the way my pulse drums as he stands in front of me, his waist at my eye level, so close his cologne floods my senses. His gaze meets mine as he holds the glass out to me, and something seems to shift behind his expression for a second like maybe he's seeing—*feeling*—something else too. Before I can take the glass from him, he holds it up to my lips instead, tipping it carefully so I can take a sip with him still holding it. I watch him the whole time as I do, standing above me with the LA sunrise softening the sky behind him; everything feels totally surreal. I'm in Win's house. He just drove to Coachella Valley and back in the middle of the night to pick me up. We're drinking together on a love seat in front of the waking city. He's holding my whiskey while I drink it . . .

He's looking at me like *that*.

I can't drag my eyes away fast enough as I swallow the drink and finally take the tumbler from his hand. As if I've broken a spell, Win looks away, too, downing his next glass in one go. He sets it on the table and steps over to the window, hands in his pockets.

"Did you notice you can see your apartment from here?" he asks, back to normal now.

So he noticed too. "Yeah," I say, moving off the love seat to join him. "You can see *everything* from here. And I thought I had the best view of the city."

He smiles fondly, silence settling between us again as we look out over the Hills. When I yawn involuntarily, Win slides an arm around my shoulders and steers me gently back into the room. "We should get some sleep," he says with a glance at the pendulum clock on the far wall. "Can you believe we really drove through the night?"

"I'm gonna be honest, Win, I'm still in shock that you answered my call." I laugh.

"Some calls are worth losing sleep over," he says easily, guiding me up the floating stairs to the bedrooms. I don't know how to answer, so I follow him in silence, a private happiness tugging at my lips.

Upstairs, Win shows me to the guest room next door to his; the sheets on the bed are perfectly pressed and spotless. "No one ever sleeps in here," he explains. "Everyone else prefers the third-floor rooms that connect to the rooftop patio."

"And why don't I deserve that luxury?" I ask with a pout.

He opens the guest room door and steps into the hallway again, gesturing for me to follow. "You can sleep anywhere you like. Follow me."

"Win." I reach for his arm and laugh. "I'd rather stay down here—seriously." I glance around the large room, the sheets tucked in tight as if we're in a hotel, not his house. "I only need a catnap anyway. Weirdly, I'm not even that tired now we're back." I glance down. "I don't have anything to sleep in."

"I'll get you a shirt of mine. I have plenty," Win offers.

"Thank you."

"You want to watch a movie?"

Instant. Chills. "Oh, yeah, that sounds nice. In here, or . . . ?"

He closes the guest room door behind us. "I have surround sound in my room."

My heart thumps an extra-loud beat as I realize that means sharing his bed. "All right, lead the way."

His lips quirk in amusement as he leads me into his room. In here it's much cozier. I recognize the crumpled sheets and the art on the wall behind his bed from our FaceTime calls.

"Pick a side," Win says, moving over to his walk-in closet. He disappears into it for a moment while I linger beside the bed, trying to figure out which side he usually sleeps on from the way the sheets are messed up. Then, choosing the other side, I place my phone down on the nightstand and turn around in time to see him walking back toward me holding a brand-new pair of Calvin Klein boxers and a plain white T-shirt.

"Will these work?" he asks, offering them out for me to take.

"Perfect, Win. Thank you."

"The bathroom's through there."

When I'm done in the bathroom a few minutes later, I step out in the too-big shirt and boxers feeling a little self-conscious . . . until I see Win's face. He's sitting up in bed, the lights dimmed as he scrolls through Netflix, and maybe it's just thanks to the whiskey, but something about the way his eyelids drop as he drinks in the sight of me walking over to join him sends an electric current through my core. I have to focus on my breathing as I climb into the bed, hoping the heat in my cheeks isn't noticeable.

It's never felt this intense with John. Or with anyone, in fact.

I can't help but notice he spends longer than expected in the bathroom. As I lie there in his bed staring up at the unfamiliar ceiling, I wonder what he might be doing behind the closed door. It's feral, and I have to stop myself before my body reacts in ways I don't need it to. Not here. Not now. Not with so little space between us.

And yet the distance has never been more tantalizing when Win finally returns to bed and takes care not to shift too close into the center of the mattress. I can smell the fresh spice of some sort of bodywash or cologne on him, a rich new scent now, different from earlier, and it draws me in with a gravitational pull: first my legs, then my body roll over into his space, and before I know it there are mere inches separating us.

"How do you feel?" he murmurs out of the blue, his voice so deliciously close to my ear, husky and warm.

"About being here with you? Pretty damn safe," I answer. "Comfortable."

Win chuckles, and the movement brings his body closer. I feel the bare skin of his leg tickling mine. "I meant about the situation with your ex," he says. "But that's nice to hear. I think I feel the same."

"Oh." I cringe with embarrassment. "God, sorry, I think at this point my brain's just trying to block him out." And then my mind returns to that word: *ex*. John's my ex now. Again. "Hey, Win, thanks for everything tonight."

"It's nothing. It's what friends are for."

Friends. My mind holds on to the word, and I instantly feel dumb for thinking for a second someone like Win could ever want more from me than just that.

"You okay?" he asks, and I realize I've zoned out.

Perking up, I say, "Yeah, I was just thinking. How about we just watch a show, not a movie? I am feeling pretty sleepy."

"So which episode of *The Office* are we going for?" His eyes twinkle when I gasp.

"How did you know that's my favorite?"

He just winks, and my stomach flips, and then I'm snuggling in next to him and we're both laughing together at Michael and Dwight until my eyelids droop and I find myself naturally snuggling farther under the duvet with Win, no longer worried about putting any space between us.

Because we're just friends, right? He's just looking out for me because we sometimes do business together and we're *friends*, right?

And yet when I feel his hand fall into the dip of my waist as I drift off to sleep, something about the word doesn't add up. Win can't treat all his friends like this. He said he feels lonely here, but right now I feel the furthest thing from that. It's peaceful beside him. Safe with his hand on me. Easy. Simple.

It just feels right.

24

I woke up after noon, still exhausted from the superlate night. Though I never intended to fall asleep in his bed and thought it'd be kind of awkward to wake up beside him, Win wasn't even in the room when I opened my eyes. It was clear he'd spent the night with me, though, and that he'd only just left, because his watch and cell phone were still on the nightstand and his pillows had indents where his head had been.

I sit up and stretch on the huge mattress, losing myself staring out the window for a moment, when chimes sound from the ceiling above me. The next thing I know, Win is talking to me from . . . the clouds?

"Beautiful day, isn't it? Almost over, though, so I figured I'd better get up. How did you sleep?"

I look up, confused and laughing. "I'm sorry, what is happening? Can you see me?" Immediately, I reach for the covers, tugging them up to my chin.

"Oh, my bad, I should've mentioned." He chuckles. "It's the intercom system. Check out the little touchscreen above the nightstand beside you—it lets you talk to any room in the house. And unfortunately, no, I can't see you."

I relax a little, leaning over to check out the screen. Sure enough, a little keypad has a button for each room. "So cool," I say, more to myself than to Win. "Where are you right now?"

"In the kitchen. My chef is here making you breakfast as we speak. Come down, it'll be ready in about ten minutes."

"Oh perfect, okay, I'll be down in a few."

I pull my hair into a high ponytail and head downstairs to the dining room for a restaurant-quality breakfast.

It's pretty cute walking in and seeing Win in such an intimate setting, messy hair from the night before, our breakfasts beautifully plated. We don't talk much while we eat but it feels perfectly comfortable. I enjoy every bite while my mind runs away with daydreams of what life would be like if we were actually a couple.

"Hey, someone's calling you," he says, breaking through my thoughts. My phone buzzes on the table next to me, Kimi's caller ID flashing onscreen.

"Oh, thanks." I take the phone from him and swipe to answer it. "Hey, Kimi, how are you?"

"Uh, I'll feel better when I know your name's out of the rumor mill," she says wearily.

"What now?" Blood drains through me as I realize I haven't checked my email or socials yet—anything could be happening right now and I wouldn't have a clue, I'm so lost in a heavenly little bubble up here with Win in his fancy mansion.

"Don't panic." Kimi sighs. "A little birdy told me you left Coachella early—"

"You mean three little birdies who still happen to be soaking up the house as we speak?" I ask, nodding over at Win when he throws me a cautious look as if to ask if everything's okay.

"Yes, those three," she confirms. "Something about you escaping in the middle of the night, over something to do with John and Riley Vega, and now the two of them are posting some *very* touchy-feely stories together on Instagram."

"Gross." I can't help myself: it's the only word that pops into my head at the reminder of John and his shitty actions.

"Really, I just need to make sure you're as uninvolved in whatever went down there as possible—at least in the eyes of the public. You can't allow a guy to get in the way of your stardom right now, especially someone you're going to be working with. Where are you right now, Princess?"

I glance over at Win, who's sipping his coffee, and for a second I don't even want to tell her. It's been so nice to get some time away from all the drama, even if only for a few hours, that the thought of revealing where I am and bursting that bubble back to normality kind of sucks.

"I'm at a friend's house," I say reluctantly.

"In LA?" Kimi asks.

"Yeah, I'm in the Hills."

She pauses for a moment as if trying to figure out whose house I might be at. "Okay, well, how quickly can you make it downtown?"

I hang my head back. I knew there'd be some sort of duty to attend to. Nothing special ever lasts. "I don't know, Kimi. What for?"

"Do you remember a few months ago we had to turn down the invite for you to be guest of honor at that record store opening?"

I vaguely recall something about it. "Yeah, I guess. Didn't we say no because I was going to be at Coachella?"

"We did, and now look at where you're not. The last thing we want is to draw attention to the fact you disappeared early, right off the back of John and Riley posting all these coupled-up videos with each other. There are enough rumors out there already about the three of you—let's not start any more. You need this to repair any possible damage."

I grind my teeth, cursing John internally for still having such a hold over my life. "So, what, we're going to pretend as if I came back for this store opening?"

"Exactly," Kimi says. "I made a few calls this morning and the owners are delighted to have you attend. They would've had to go ahead with some actor who had three lines in an episode of *Game of Thrones* or something otherwise."

"But they're still going to be there, right? I don't want to steal an opportunity from someone just because I suddenly became available, Kimi."

"You know how it is and that's not your problem to worry about. You need to be there, and you need to worry about yourself. Their team can handle their side." She sighs, sounding a little annoyed with me.

"All right," I agree, knowing she isn't going to give in. I pull back to glance at the time on my phone. "It's already after noon. What time does this event start?"

"They need you there to open the store at two."

"Two! As in, less than two hours from now? Kimi, you know that's not going to happen. I'm literally in the middle of eating breakfast. It'd be impossible for me to get my hair and makeup figured out. Plus, I don't have anything with me I can wear."

She sighs heavily. "I'm backed into a corner here, Princess. Find a way. It's this or deal with weeks' worth of rumors about you and Riley headlining all the blogs."

I know what she means. If it looks like I left Coachella for no reason, the press will fill in the blanks for us. There's enough suspicion where John and I are concerned already; I definitely don't need people catching on to what really happened yesterday. I can explain away our time as recording together but if anyone catches on that it was more than that, it could destroy all my hard work over the last few months.

"Okay," I say with a sigh. "I'll be there. Send me the address and I'll see you in a couple of hours."

"See you there, Princess," Kimi says, and right before she hangs up she adds, "Make sure you're dressed like you planned this."

The call ends and I look down at my outfit then stare into my reflection in the wall-length mirror. "You've got to be kidding."

"Something wrong?" Win asks.

I sigh and press my hands to my temples, so utterly done with the situation. "I have to appear at a store opening at two this afternoon so people think I came back from Coachella for work and not running from John and Riley drama. Which means I somehow have to get myself from here, back home, into a perfect outfit, do my hair and makeup, and make it to the store through traffic, all within the next"—I glance at my phone—"one hour, fifty-five minutes. No—one hour, fifty-four minutes."

"That's rough." Win exhales, stepping over to rub a hand between my shoulder blades. It feels so damn nice, but my mind's too preoccupied to settle down.

"Not rough—it's *impossible*."

"Nothing's impossible, Princess." He pulls out his cell phone and scrolls through his contacts. "Let me see what I can do."

"What do you mean?" I ask, eyeing him suspiciously when I see the small smile dancing at the corner of his lips.

"I have it under control." He looks up. "Just trust me."

"You know I trust you."

"Perfect." Win releases me and hits Call on a number, bringing the phone up to his ear. "In the meantime, go take a quick shower. You can use mine or the guest room's. Take whatever you need. All the towels are fresh."

With more questions than answers, I decide I don't have time to stick around and find out what he's plotting, so I make my way back to Win's room and take the fastest shower known to mankind, deciding a messy updo will have to suffice. It looks kind of cute in a laid-back way. Even if Kimi thinks otherwise.

I make my way downstairs ten minutes later feeling—and smelling—much more fresh and clean. Win's waiting for me near the door, using the smart screen on his wall to open the front gates for a sleek black Range Rover. I watch it drive in on the little video camera.

"Did Kimi call a car for me?"

Win shakes his head. "This is one of my drivers. And you're not going straight to the record store—or to your apartment." When I raise an eyebrow in question, he elaborates. "I called ahead to Maxfield, it's not too far away. They have my credit card so just get whatever you want. Their personal shopper, Carli, is pulling some outfits for you right now, and they'll close off a section of the store for you to shop in peace, just in case anyone notices you scrambling for an outfit last minute. One less chance for rumors to spread."

My jaw is on the floor, and I shake my head slowly. "You are amazing. I'll pay you back for all of this."

Win shakes his head and nods to the screen showing the car on the driveway. "And then the driver will take you to your event. Just tell him the address when you get in. He knows all the shortcuts around here."

"You're a lifesaver. Thank you *so* much, Win."

He laughs. "Don't mention it."

"No, I owe you big-time for this. For today, and for last night."

Placing a hand on my back, he guides me to the door. "You owe me nothing. But we should go out to dinner sometime soon."

"Dinner that *I'll* be paying for, sure," I tell him, but even without looking I know the grin on his face says otherwise. He'd never let me pay for dinner; one time we were out for drinks and I took my card out to pay—I'd never seen such a look of disapproval. He told me I should never offer to pay with him again. With Win it's always taken care of.

Just like everything else.

25

I just finish a call with Mom the next day—updating her on the record store appearance and how Win saved the day, as usual. It was easy; I took photos for them, did a quick meet and greet with some fans. It was smooth, not much more to it. Jessie FaceTimes to fill me in on the Coachella gossip. I bring my phone with me into my bedroom and prop Jessie up beside me while I lay out some art supplies and start to paint overlooking the skyline. I usually end up painting these girls—I call them the HappiGirls—that always have a big forehead, big eyes, and big lips. Usually they're crying or look really disturbed. I don't know why they come out like that but they always do. Some people tell me I need therapy when they see them, which is kind of funny to me. But on second thought, maybe they have a point.

Anyway, despite how dark they might look, it's therapeutic; painting has always helped me relax and tune out the world. It's the same way I feel when I make music, but with way less pressure to create something people will judge. Although it's kind of impossible to ignore Jessie's wild laughter as she recalls all the crazy shit Maya did after I left the valley.

"Something hot and heavy was definitely going down in Val's room," she gushes, and I whip my head around to look at her.

"With Tripp?"

"Obviously." Jessie takes a sip of her cold brew back in her room in San Francisco, and I slump back in my seat with relief. "I had second-hand embarrassment for her, though. We could pretty much hear everything that was going on. Tripp was really going for it in there. The guys who came back with us got a real kick out of that whole situation."

"Oh my god. What guys?"

"Oh, just some randoms who kind of attached themselves to Maya. I was trying to pull her away from them but they kept following us around and then Maya got it into her head that one of them liked me, so then she was trying to set us up, I guess. You know me, and *that* didn't work."

I chuckle. Jessie's so bad at reading signals from guys it's a running joke between us. "You probably had her so frustrated." Then I pause. "Actually, let's be real, I bet she was having the time of her life."

"Three guys giving her all their attention? You freaking bet she was." Jessie giggles. "Pretty sure the one she was trying to set me up with had already forgotten my name by the time he left in the morning."

"Oh, so Maya had a lil sleepover too, huh?" I raise my eyebrows suggestively.

"I was surrounded, Princess." The deadpan look on Jessie's face makes me howl with laughter. "No, but seriously, they were both in their rooms getting their brains fucked out and then there's me sitting under the covers scrolling freaking TikTok trying not to overhear them, and all the videos coming up are, like, ads for vibrators and steamy book quotes and shit. Talk about calling me out!" She holds her head dramatically, and I laugh even harder at the mental image. Poor Jess.

We sit talking while I paint for another half hour, and when it's just me again and the room's silent, my thoughts wander back to the past few days and everything that went down between me and John. In a way, I'm glad I caught him, because it just confirmed to me that I was right to have a gut feeling something wasn't right all along.

Getting up out of my seat, another painting completed, I realize what I need to do next.

There's an old suitcase in my closet that I used when I first came to LA from Guam. I pull it out and memories flood in of me and Mom lugging it around between hotels and some of my first shows, the thing near bursting at the seams with all our belongings, which grew and grew over the months we spent trying to find my big break. Deciding it's too precious to use for this, I roll it back into the closet and pull out a newer Rimowa suitcase instead. It's one I used on my last tour, but it doesn't hold sentimental value like the first bag. This one's large and has wheels, and it'll be perfect for the job.

I open it on the floor of my closet and then make my way over to the section I always left empty for John. Over the months he slowly filled it with clothes and vinyl records and some of the cute little gifts I got for him, like the wooden picture frame with our names etched into it that he always said he'd find the perfect photo for and would put up at his place.

It's only now, as I pick it up and turn it over in my hands to see the hidden personalization on the back, a small note with a date from last year, that a little voice in the back of my mind tells me he probably had no intention of ever displaying it at his place—or even letting it leave this closet. My heart sinks. I know that's not true, but I can feel my eyes start to burn. I don't want to cry so I push the thoughts away. Could he seriously have been playing Riley and me off each other the whole time? The idea turns my stomach. I never imagined I'd be this naïve;

I've been in LA for long enough to know that there are as many snakes as there are ladders. This behavior just isn't John.

With a sigh, I wonder if I should even pack all this stuff for him or if it just needs to go in the trash. I grab a pile of neatly folded T-shirts and place them in the suitcase first, using them as padding for the frame. I reach for the stack of love notes I've given to him throughout our relationship. I wonder whether or not to let him have them or if they should stay with me for safe keeping. He doesn't deserve to reread them—who knows who he might show them to. After going back and forth, making up a thousand scenarios arguing both sides of whether to keep or pack them, I give up and reluctantly place them in the bag. Maybe him seeing it all will be a good reminder of what he's losing. A reminder of all his forgotten promises.

Don't overthink it.

Still, my cheeks heat up as I finish packing all his stuff, moving into my bathroom and collecting his things from in there. I take my time packing them in a new toiletry bag, fitting it in neatly alongside his clothes and records and all the other stuff. In my mind, if I take my time and do everything neatly he'll understand that I'm calm, I've made my decision, and I'm serious. This isn't some rash, spur-of-the-moment decision; I actually thought this through. I'm not throwing his things in a bag in some emotional rage. It's just over, done, and I'm showing him I'm mature enough to handle it respectfully—which is more than can be said for him.

When everything's packed and ready to go, I unlock my phone and pull up our text thread. He sent me another 11:11 message this morning, but there's been nothing since. I can't lie, seeing the message makes my heart sting. And though I don't want him to be blowing up my phone with apologies, and I know Win told him clearly to back off, it still kind of hurts to think he'd give up so easily. Am I really worth so little to him? This is not how I wanted things to go.

John: "If they can hurt you and then walk away, don't hurt yourself twice following after them."

I think about that for a moment. Is it possible I hurt him too? Did I cross the line going off with Win, sleeping in his bed that night—wasn't all that just as bad?

I can hear Maya's voice in my head screaming at me, *Are you kidding me? At least you had the decency to break up with him first, and you didn't even do anything with Win! John was literally making out with Riley in public, making a laughingstock of you and your fucking relationship.*

And that's when it hits. John really thinks he's the victim here. I'll never get through to him, and he'll probably never realize just how much he's messed with me. The whole damn world revolves around him, but as of right now, I don't live in his orbit.

I type out my message quickly, knowing what I need to say once and for all.

Me: Hey, no need to reply, I just wanted to let you know. I've made up my mind, John, and this relationship is over. I can't keep doing this to myself. I know my worth and I don't want to hate you, but I can't have you in my life anymore, in any capacity. I'm not interested in being friends or in anything more with you. When you're back from Coachella you can come pick up your stuff. It'll be downstairs with the front desk.

Before I can think twice, I hit Send.

And then I breathe out the biggest fucking sigh of relief as I crash back onto the soft pillows of my bed.

26

Ping.

Ping.

Ping.

I cover my eyes with my arm and groan, rolling over in bed to glance at my phone screen. It's lit up on the pillow beside me, another stream of texts popping up from Mom, my sisters, Maya, Val, Jessie, and probably Kimi and Wayne too. I'm just not in the mood for any of it—talking, texting, pretending like everything's fine. The painting I did while on the phone with Jessie almost a week ago stares at me from where it's propped up against the wall on the other side of my room: the face of a blonde-haired girl with tears in her eyes, bruised and broken and pleading at me, one simple message painted in stark black around her.

YOU DID THIS TO YOURSELF

I guess my emotions have gotten the best of me since I sent that final text to John a week ago. I didn't get a reply, and that's cool—I didn't want one. But the thought of him quietly picking up his stuff and not having anything to say really bothers me.

That isn't the only thing that has me feeling this way. It hurts, sure, but the whole damn situation is what I'm upset about, not some stupid fucking suitcase full of his stupid fucking stuff.

I'm so tired of feeling used and not good enough. I'm sick of investing in people and having them turn around and blindside me, dumping me like I never mattered in the first place. I'm sick of being vulnerable and having my trust destroyed over and over again. It makes me feel delusional—like am I crazy or are we not building real relationships? I'm exhausted. Sick of feeling like the butt of the joke when all I ever try to do is open my heart up to people and let them in.

Enough is enough. I am the priority. I'm letting calls go to voice mail and texts go unread. It's just me in bed with my journal turning my thoughts into lyrics and my emotions into melodies.

I've written three versions of this song already, and I think this one is perfect. So perfect that I recorded a rough version of it in my home studio—raw, acoustic, but exactly how I wanted it to sound. It's simply me and my emotions in their purest form.

I'm reading through the lyrics again, singing under my breath, when the familiar *ding* of my elevator sounds from my entrance hallway and then the sound of heels *click-clack*ing on the marble floor has me scrambling to hide my notebook. Whoever the fuck is intruding, I don't want to share this with anyone. It's too raw. Too real. Too—

"Princess, I swear to fucking god, you are infuriating!"

I hold my breath as Maya barges into my room, red in the face and almost spilling the two large iced coffees she's holding, one in each hand. She marches over to my bed and slams both down on the night-stand before standing tall with her hands on her hips.

"What the fuck?"

"What the fuck right back at you!" I exclaim. "How did you even get in here?"

"How do you think? Your doorman knows I practically live here, and even if he didn't, he sure as hell wasn't going to say no to me coming up here to check you're even still alive. Four days he hasn't seen you! Four fucking days, Princess! You really think he's going to argue with that?" She lifts her hands in the air as if to say, *Duh?*

"I—"

"Honestly," she cuts me off, kicking off her heels and getting into bed beside me, pulling the covers up and making my pulse jump as I discreetly shift to move the notebook out of her reach. "I know he was your first serious boyfriend here in LA and all, but really? All this over John? He's a fucking sleazebag. You're goddamn Princess, for fuck's sake. You're so much better than this."

"All right, enough!" I cut her off, slumping down under the covers with a scowl. "It's not even about him. I mean, it is, but it isn't *just* that, Maya."

"Then what the fuck else is it? Seriously, Princess, I'm so upset you feel you can't talk to me about this. I got you, through everything, and you know that. But one hundred and twenty-six missed calls and you still can't even send me a text to let me know I shouldn't be writing your freaking obituary?"

"I'm sorry," I groan, sinking down under the sheets even farther. "I just want to be alone."

"Nuh-uh." She shakes her head and reaches for her coffee, crossing her legs one over the other and reclining back against the headboard as she takes a sip. "You've done enough of that already. Now it's time to talk it out."

The thing about Maya is she doesn't take no for an answer. She'd make a great interrogator. Without much argument, I tell her everything—well, most things. I deliberately leave out the part about the new song I wrote. She listens intently, adding her input at all the right moments, saying something funny when it seems like I'm about to cry and backing me up when I ask if I did the right thing. I cry some more and she consoles me, hugging me tight while I rest my head on her chest and sob it out. And when I'm done crying, she hands me my iced coffee and watches with a smug grin as I moan in pleasure at the taste of it.

"I feel awful for you, P., I really do," she says sympathetically a few minutes later. "It's like all this shit is going down in your life, and meanwhile I'm over here having one of my best years ever."

"I'm so happy for you, Maya," I say with a small, sad smile. It's true. She's on top of her game this year. Her modeling career has accelerated to a whole new level, her paychecks are more than double what they were this time last year, and she's had none of this pathetic boy drama to deal with. She just lives in the moment and lets whatever will happen, happen. "God, I wish I was more like you."

"Don't say that."

"It's true."

"Princess." She grabs both my hands and makes me stare directly into her eyes as she pins me with a stern look. "Let's just think about that for a sec, shall we? Look at that phone over there." She nods to my cell phone as it lights up with yet another call. "Full of people who care about you. You have the best family, and they check in on you 24-7. Me? I haven't heard from my mom in maybe two weeks—actually, I think it's three—and when we do talk the disconnect between us is so obvious. It's basically impossible to have real and deep conversation. My family doesn't know the real me, they don't put the time in. They're too preoccupied with their own lives, they wouldn't understand even if I tried to explain. You don't have to do that shit. You can talk to your family about everything. You're *lucky*."

"I guess."

"And I get lonely, too, sometimes," Maya continues, still searching my eyes as if she's waiting for the light-bulb moment; the realization my life isn't all that bad, actually. "We all fucking do. It's what drives us to find new connections, right? It's what makes us believe we need someone else by our side and so we go out falling in love and trusting people with so much of ourselves, and if they want to screw us over for that, fucking let them! That's their issue. Fuck them."

The corner of my mouth lifts in a small smile. "You make it sound so easy."

"Oh, babe, it isn't. It really isn't. But that's why it's so freaking great when you see someone doing exactly that. Living their life and not caring what anyone thinks—that shit is brave! It takes a lot."

"Well, you've mastered it."

"Yeah, and look at all the things I haven't mastered." She shakes her head. "Princess, you don't just top the charts with your songs—you also run a fucking business! Like, you're beautiful and then you're there coordinating beauty brand launches and collabs and talking finances with your managers and knowing your own worth. That's incredible. I wish I could do that. I let my team handle everything and just do what I'm told, I can't wrap my head around it all. Not like you. You're in control in ways I'm just not."

"Don't do that," I say insistently.

"Do what?"

"Lower yourself to make me feel good. Maya, you know we're both in control, just in totally different ways, and that's good. We shouldn't all want to be the same."

"See?" She lets go of my hands to clap her own. "See! You get it. Beneath all this moping bullshit you know you're better than this."

"Hey, I'm allowed to feel my feelings."

"I'm not saying you aren't. Just don't cut everyone out while you're doing it. You're always here for us, let us be here for you, okay?"

"Okay, okay."

"And, hey, let's not forget you have a great relationship with Win to keep you nicely distracted."

At the mention of his name, I cringe, and Maya narrows her eyes in suspicion.

"What?"

"You're going to think I'm an idiot."

She drums her fingers on her chin as she waits for me to continue, and I let out a sigh.

"I haven't had the energy to deal with anything, Maya. I haven't been replying to his texts."

"Oh my god." She hangs her head back. "You've been ignoring him, P.?"

"He's only written a few times. And it's not like they've been anything other than our normal conversations."

"I don't believe that for a second."

"No, really." I fall back onto the pillows again and bury my face. "God, it's just all so confusing," I growl.

"What's confusing? The fact he drove to fucking Coachella and back in the middle of the night to collect you for a sleepover at his place?"

"Maya, he hasn't said a thing about that night since."

Which is the truth. Since I left his house for the store opening last week, it's as if that night with Win never happened. And it's stupid because every time I frame it like that, it makes it sound as if something *did* happen, when really, all I did was sleep over at a friend's house after he helped me out—in the most innocent sense, of course. So for the past week I've been in my head about how maybe I'm reading way too much into things and getting all muddled because I'm still sore over John. It's yet another area of my life he's butted into.

"Listen, I don't want to think about men right now. Just, I don't know, tell me something new and let's forget about Coachella—please?"

"Well . . . hold on a minute."

At the change in tone, I look up. Maya seems kind of apprehensive, and I frown. "What's up?"

"It's weird. And it's about Coachella," she says sheepishly.

"Maya, tell me."

"You have to keep it a secret."

My skin prickles as I realize she's being serious. This must be bad news.

"I promise," I say quickly.

Maya pulls out her phone. She doesn't say anything for a few seconds as she scrolls to find something onscreen, and then she holds the phone out to me, gesturing for me to take it. "Here. Listen to this."

I take the phone from her and hit Play on the voice message in Maya's chat with Val. There's the crackly noise of movement for a couple of seconds, and then Val's slurred voice sounds out.

"Tripp, I don't . . . know how to say—"

"Nope." Before I can register what's happening, Maya's stolen the phone back from me and hit Pause on the voice message.

"What—?"

"Sorry, Princess, I just can't. I actually don't think I should play it for anyone."

I shake my head, totally confused. "Maya, what are you talking about?"

"Ugh." She scrapes her hair back and blows her cheeks out, clearly affected by the voice message, whatever it said. "All right, so it was late the last night of Coachella, and I thought Val was in with Tripp because they were clearly together, you know, the night after you left. We could hear it through the whole house. Seriously. Anyway, so we just assumed she was with him and they were together in her room for a second night, right?

"And then I have this voice message come through and it's basically Val confessing everything to him, telling him it wasn't just sex and that she really is in love with him. I don't know, it sounded a lot to me like they'd been edging around this conversation already, like maybe he'd mentioned something to her before and she didn't give the answer he wanted. So she tells him how emotionally fucked-up she is and how lonely and complicated her life is, and she goes into some really deep shit in this message. It's definitely not something I was supposed to hear, so I don't want to replay it even though I know you wouldn't ever tell another soul because we both love her to death."

"No, I get it." I can see how distressed Maya is by the message, and it floods me with worry too. "But, Maya, is she okay? I mean, what happened after she sent it?"

"I don't think so." Maya chews her lip. "I've been debating whether to ask her about it since I first saw it, Princess. She put everything out there in this message. She's so fucking upset, and there's no way she knows she sent it to me. Truthfully, I've been hesitant to text her all week 'cause I don't want her to scroll back and see it in our messages. She'd be mortified—I know she would."

"Hmm, I'm not sure, she's probably been so upset thinking he hasn't responded," I say warily. "That was meant for Tripp."

"True. We need to figure out the right time to bring it up to her." Maya heaves a sigh. "Shit, Princess, between your issues and Val's, I haven't known what the fuck to do this week."

"Tell me about it," I agree. "I'll find a time to talk to her. They need to sort this out between the two of them, and that can't happen until she knows he never got the message."

I stare out the window over the skyline wondering what the hell to do. It all looks so peaceful out there, the clear blue sky uninterrupted by clouds and the buildings practically glittering under the sunlight, but, shit . . . on days like today it all seems to be just one pretty, shining distraction from some of the bleakest, scariest moments of our lives.

27

Maya stays over at my place after finally dragging me out of bed, and we hang out for most of the evening watching movies and making a couple more girls'-night-in TikToks that get pretty good engagement. We call Jessie and my family, and I get the play-by-play of everything else that went on at Coachella after I left. But the next morning Maya has to leave bright and early, after Kimi calls to confirm I'm still planning to do phone interviews about my latest song at their office today.

Amidst all the madness I forgot it was dropping today. That's the thing about making music in Hollywood: it takes months to go from making a song to finally having it released. I'd lose track of my drop dates if it wasn't for Kimi and Wayne. I'm always already on to the next idea, my mind flooded with new sounds and lyrics. Sometimes I'm even over the emotions that went into creating the song by the time it's released, and that's never been truer than it is for the one I'm releasing today.

Which, of course, is about John.

On my way to Wayne and Kimi's office I stop off to get a coffee in Beverly Hills, and run into a paparazzi guy. He's always hanging around this area and we've had a lot of interactions together before, so far all friendly—which is why I'm cool about him videoing me while simultaneously taking pictures as I walk out of the coffee shop and head back to my car.

"Princess, you look great today," he says, holding the camera up to my face and walking next to me.

"Aw, thank you."

"So what's been going on with your music lately? Anything new coming out?"

These are pretty standard paparazzi questions so I answer easily without thinking twice. "It's been so surreal! I'm so grateful for all the support on my latest releases, and actually have something new dropping today that I'm really excited about." I smile for the camera.

"Congratulations! I saw that and have been listening to the snippets on your socials. You sound great and I love the song. Did you know Riley Vega released a surprise song last night? It sounds just like yours. Do you have any comment about that?"

My face falls and I'm baffled. *What the fuck is he talking about?* I stop responding and pick up the pace, trying to get back to my car as fast as possible.

"Princess, do you have a comment?" he tries asking again. "Is this a collab, or whose song is it?" He's having a hard time keeping his camera steady while trying to keep up with me as I approach the door to my car.

"You seem surprised, Princess, what—" His voice cuts off as soon as I slam the driver's-side door closed. He walks around to the sidewalk, still filming me while I sit in disbelief before pulling up the video to see it for myself. *It's true. She released my fucking song and is trying to make it look like it's hers.* I open the thread of comments on her post:

Riley! That fame whore Princess is teasing your song but with her vocals, saying it's her next single!!! Lol what a loser!

Princess aka knockoff version of Riley.

I always knew Princess was a one-hit wonder and would do anything to have a taste of success again. Leave Riley alone.

Princess has always been garbage. Not a single original thought behind those eyes.

Lol. Not Princess recording and trying to release Riley's song as if it's hers.

Princess should go back to her island her career is dead and always has been. She has nothing on Riley, you go girl!

Enraged, I throw my phone across the passenger seat and it bounces onto the floor.

I put the car in Drive and head straight to Kimi and Wayne's office. I need to calm myself so I can brief them on what just went down. I count repeatedly backward from ten and practice deep breathing until I arrive at their building.

Bursting into the conference room, I find Kimi and Wayne already sitting there, ready for me.

"Riley put my song out. It's out, it's on Spotify. I found out from a paparazzo on the side of the street just now when I was getting coffee. I looked it up and it looks like it came out last night. What the fuck! What am I going to do? There are a million horrible comments on her post tearing me apart. You can forget about this song doing well, this is going to ruin my entire career. They think it's her song."

"Slow down," Wayne says, trying to process what I just told him.

"I wrote this song. Riley had *nothing* to do with it. But no one is ever going to believe me yet again. You should see what people are saying. There is no coming back from this."

"The master for that song is owned by both you and the label. It's been paperworked. You wrote on the song. Riley can't legally post that. Who knows how she got access to the files, but there's a simple solution here. We're going to send a cease-and-desist and the label will have the song and any videos with it removed in no time," Kimi says, maintaining a calm and collected tone.

"Okay." This logic calms me slightly. "But that's not solving the controversy that'll be spreading like wildfire with the fans and online. The internet never cares what the truth is," I press her.

Wayne chimes in. "We'll have the label draft a statement that we can release right way to protect you and clarify the situation. Yes, the fans love the drama and will probably drag it out for as long as they can, but the truth will be out there. This was your song, you wrote on it. You did not take it from anyone. We'll stick to our plan, prep the interviews, and direct them not to ask anything pertaining to this issue, and we will be on the calls with you to step in and shut it down if any of them tries to."

This makes sense to me but doesn't stop my rage for Riley from burning through me.

"Stay focused. You are a businesswoman. You are successful. This is what happens when you rise to the top, people will try to take you down and block your success any chance they can get and however they can. If they're threatened by you, if you're a true talent with great potential, these are the things you have to deal with. Do not let them take this from you. Power through," Wayne says fiercely.

"Okay, I can do that."

Riley can try to take me down all she wants. She won't get rid of me that easily.

We spend the rest of the time strategizing and getting me into the right frame of mind for the interviews. Wayne and Kimi update the label and make sure a statement gets drafted and prepared for immediate release. I'm so thankful for them but I cannot wait for this day to be over.

"We have *Variety* on line two, are you ready?" Kimi's voice grabs my attention.

I take a sip of my water, clear my throat, and reply, "I'm ready."

28

"The group of kids over there is looking at us," Val mutters, drawing my attention to the large group of teens hanging out a little farther down the beach, a cluster of them staring and trying to take photos discreetly.

"Used to it," I say with a shrug. "I'm surprised you're bothered at all."

"I'm not," Val says, "but I'm telling you they're about to come over—yep, here they come. Great." She sighs, and I look up to find two of the girls approaching us, excited smiles on their faces.

"It's cute," I say with a laugh, standing up to greet them and proceeding to pose for a selfie with one of the girls.

"You want a photo with me too?" Maya offers, looking up from where she's sunbathing with a magazine splayed over her face to block the sun completely, her latest method to combat premature wrinkles or something.

"Uh." The girls look at each other, giggling, and I laugh at Maya before saying, "I guess you don't know who she is, right?" When they shrug, I tell them, eyes sparkling with mischief, "Oh, she's just a friend, no one famous. Don't worry about it."

"Thanks for the photos," one of the girls says, already starting off across the sand toward their group.

"You're welcome." I smile.

"Hey, are they actually buying it?" Maya sits up instantly, slamming the magazine down on the towel beside her. "They really don't know who I am?"

"How would they know who you are?" Val teases, prodding Maya with her toe. "Miss Magazine Head over there."

"It's to stop the UV damage!" When she sees both of us laughing, Maya rolls her eyes and lets out a dramatic sigh. "Oh, whatever. Prevention is the best cure, bitches."

A few minutes later the group of kids clears off, and pretty soon after Maya leaves me and Val alone on the beach too. Unwanted thoughts of memory lane with John creep into my mind so I distract myself chatting with Val about pointless shit until the inevitable comes up.

Coachella.

"How are things with Tripp?" I ask casually, rubbing tanning oil onto my legs, as if I'm not really focused on her answer. Really, though, I'm eager to know all.

"What do you mean?" she asks.

Of course. She's still in denial about him.

"We need to talk." I raise my eyebrows at her. "I know about the voice message you meant to send to Tripp."

She nervously looks away. "Oh, what do you mean?"

"Babe, you accidentally send it to Maya."

She's silent for a while. "Oh."

I finish applying my oil and turn fully to look at her. "Val, I think it's so brave to be honest about your feelings, and I needed to tell you so you know he didn't ghost. Tripp is in love with you, it's so obvious. You need to tell him how you feel." My voice drops a little lower as I try to reach out. I can't stand the thought of her going through so much while feeling like she can't even open up to her *best friends*. "I'm here for you for whatever you're going through. I got your back, always. I've been worried about you and I think you need to talk to someone."

"Princess." She breaks her silence as she looks up at me finally. It comes out of nowhere as she says in an emotional rush, "You don't even know how stressed I've been this whole time. It's exhausting holding my feelings in, and I don't want to anymore. I'm in love with Tripp and I know he loves me, but I was so thrown off by why he wouldn't have anything to say back to my message. Thank you for telling me, it all makes sense now. And I know I need to talk to someone, I'm going to figure that out right away. I can't keep living like this. I'm not going to put it off any longer. I want to be healthy, I want to be better."

"Okay, good. This makes me so happy. I know you can do it, you're one of the strongest people in my life." I squeeze her hand and relief washes over me. "I'm always here for you."

Val continues, "Can I just say, I feel so fucking sorry for how John and Riley have treated you these past few weeks. Like, it's so goddamn cruel and totally unnecessary. Sometimes I wonder when the fuck it's going to end." She shakes her head. "God, I just wish things were different."

I let out a nervous chuckle but it doesn't really sound like anything more than a small noise in the back of my throat—which suddenly feels way too dry. *Why is she talking about this?* "Thank you, Val, but you don't have to feel sorry about that."

"Just—" She leans forward and grips my hand, the action so unpredictable, seeming so serious, my heart skips a beat. "Listen to me, Princess, I've been thinking a lot about things. Can you take my advice here for a sec?"

I stare back at her, worry flushing my skin. "Of course, Val. What is it?"

She glances around and then leans in close, keeping her words quiet. "Maybe it would be best if you started acting a little more . . . friendly, I guess, with Riley, in public, just in case."

I draw back. "What?"

"I know, I know," she says quickly. "It sounds fucked-up, but it might be good for people to think you two are cool again, what with"— she waves her hand around—"you know, the current situation."

"You mean John."

She presses her lips together tightly and gives a nod.

"Where's this coming from?" I ask, immediately suspicious. *Since when did Val become so invested in my relationship with Riley?* A million unwanted thoughts flood in. "Are you talking to her? Did she ask you to say this?"

"No." Val recoils as if I've physically hurt her. "Princess, I'm saying this because I care about you."

"And I care about you, Val—I wish you'd tell me what's going on. What you just said is so not like the Val I know."

She gives a bitter laugh, her voice faraway, on the verge of shutting down again. I don't miss the despairing drift of her words as she looks down at the sand and says with a weary sigh, "Well, I'm not the Val I know anymore, Princess."

I know I shouldn't do it, but I can't stop myself.

It's late evening and I've spent the past hour perfecting the song I wrote in bed last week, recording an acoustic version of it on my own, just my vocals and the piano, and it's the most raw, real song I've recorded in forever.

Since the Riley Vega TikTok incident kind of killed the last release, my label decided it was best if we leave that song alone. So the idea of posting the new one online—with no involvement from producers or managers, just me putting it out there in the world and seeing what listeners think—popped into my head, and I can't get it out. Clearly people like that, so most of my downtime between promo and planning for the big event in Miami next week has been spent perfecting it, listening back and rerecording certain sections, scribbling out lyrics here and there and writing over them with words that capture what I mean more clearly. It's been cathartic.

And now, as I sit here with my mouse hovering over the Post button, about to share my most personal song yet with the world, I pause for a second to consider what people will think.

But really, why does it even matter? Isn't that kind of the point—to release a song that's entirely made up of my unfiltered thoughts and feelings? A song that reaches out and grabs listeners' hearts in the most intimate, emotional place?

Without thinking twice, I click Post and the video goes live.

Here goes nothing.

I wait for a second, watching the view count jump up slowly as fans realize I've posted.

I'm still confused about why Val thought to give me that advice earlier as I look down at my phone screen an hour after posting the new song to see an unknown number calling. Unknown, and yet it looks familiar. The longer I stare at it, the faster the realization sinks in.

I know this number because I used to call it all the time.

I know this number because it's Riley's, and I've deleted and added it back more times than I'd ever admit.

What the hell?

I stand up from where I've been sitting on my couch and walk over to the windows, anxiety buzzing in my belly at the thought of answering.

With time running out, I grit my teeth and swipe to answer, bringing the phone up to my ear with a grimace. "Hello?"

"Princess?"

Unmistakably, it's her. The buzzing in my belly gets faster as more anxiety sets in.

"Hey, who is this?" I have no idea why I'm pretending like I don't already know.

"It's Riley," she says, and then quickly, she adds, "Don't hang up."

"Hey." I glance around the room as if looking for someone to share my confusion with, but of course, I'm alone. "This is . . . unexpected."

"Yeah, I know, babe, I'm sorry." *Babe.* I hate that. So fucking patronizing. "I've been thinking a lot, about how things have been between us since last year. We used to be so close, and it all just seemed to fall apart for no real reason. Do you remember a reason?" Before I can even find my voice to answer, she cuts in with, "I don't. So, I know you're performing at the event next week in Miami, and like—" She pauses to sigh, and I fall back onto my couch, certain I'm dreaming this. "Why don't we meet up while we're there, huh? Grab lunch together, do some shopping, just hang out like old times. I miss you and I know we can get back to that place where life just felt *fun*."

"Where's this coming from?" I can't help myself—I have to ask. Frankly, I'm too stunned to think of anything else to say. "Weren't you fucking my boyfriend at a party last week? And why did you try to say you wrote my last song? I'm so confused."

"Princess . . ." She drags my name out as if she's already tired of hearing about it. "I am so sorry, and I wish it didn't happen. When I'm drinking I just get wild, fucking messed up, and I do shit I don't even realize is gonna hurt in the morning. Because it hurt me, too, you know, realizing what I'd done to you and John. I never wanted to split you guys up. Truth be told, though, you're better off without him—everyone thinks that. As far as the song, I honestly didn't think anyone was going to take that seriously and I'm sorry for messing that up."

"Great, thanks." My voice lacks any emotion. This has to be the worst apology I've ever heard.

But at least she's apologizing. The thought pops into my head, and I straighten up, trying to focus back on her words.

"Look, I know this is out of the blue and you're probably wondering what the fuck is going on, but it's so impossible to get my thoughts clear on the phone, and that's why I think we should go out for lunch next week, you know. It'll give us both a chance to talk, and you won't be on the spot so much. Like, I get that this is *unexpected.*" She tries a laugh.

"You're right," I say reluctantly, looking around for inspiration to give me some kind of out. I don't really want to get lunch with her, but sometimes I can be quick to write people off. Even after all the horrible things Riley has done to me, I still have a soft spot for her for some reason. Maybe I should hear her out? Besides, there's so much shit circulating about me, Riley, and John right now that, at the very least, maybe it'd be good for us to be seen hanging out together to stop any more rumors.

"Please say yes, Princess. I'm sorry . . . for everything."

I swallow hard. She sounds genuine. Like the ghost of my ex-best friend Riley came back to haunt me through the phone. I'm so shocked for a second that the easiest answer spills from my mouth before I even know what I'm doing.

"Okay, sure. Let me get Kimi and Wayne to give your people a call and figure out a time and place."

"That's perfect." She sounds excited, and my stomach knots with nostalgia. It's been so long since I heard her speak to me like this that I actually feel . . . emotional? Maybe it's just the relief of knowing this could be the beginning of the end of our war with each other—that maybe in the future, even if we don't become best friends again, we can quit all the bitchiness and just start being supportive of each other again.

Wouldn't that be nice?

"Yeah," I say with a smile, relaxing into the idea. "Yeah, I'll get them to set it up. I'm looking forward to it."

"Me too!"

"Great, I guess I'll see you next week, Riley."

"Text me anytime, Princess. I mean that. And hey," she says before she hangs up, "thanks for this. You won't regret it."

I place the phone in my lap and stare out over the city, hoping like hell she's right.

29

"Oh my god, Win's calling."

The terminal at Miami International Airport is as busy as ever, a crowd of paparazzi and patiently waiting fans hanging around Arrivals hoping to catch a glimpse of one of the many celebs flying in for the boat show or for Riley's big event. Maya, Val, and I were escorted by security and had no time to say hi to the fans screaming our names before we were shown to our waiting vehicle. Now we're en route to our hotel, the colorful painted murals in Wynwood whizzing past on both sides of the highway through the dark-tinted windows of our ride.

"See! I freaking told you he didn't forget about you," Maya says beside me, throwing her hands up in the air. "Answer it, quick!"

"Win," I say, bringing the phone to my ear and using my other hand to shield my face from Maya and Val, who both react with laughter to my breathless-sounding voice. "Hey, how are you?"

"I'm good." His voice sounds thick and velvety through the phone, superchill, never fazed by much. "I just arrived in Miami, actually. I'm on the jet right now, taxiing down the runway."

Of course he got a private jet. I try not to be disappointed by the lack of an invite to join him. We flew here first-class, but that's not the point. Since Coachella I've been going back and forth in my head wondering if I read too far into things with Win, thinking he's probably got a line of other women he treats the same way. I'm his friend, nothing more. But, hey, at least he's calling me.

"Oh, we just left the airport," I say brightly, ignoring the girls' teasing to stare out the window. The blue waters of Biscayne Bay shine in the distance. "Headed to our hotel right now."

"You're staying in South Beach?" Win asks.

"Of course."

"I'll be close by."

"Did you end up buying the house on the water you showed me?"

"You know it." I hear the smile in his voice. "So, how are you?"

My heart somersaults. I'm suddenly confronted with the realization that for all the time I've spent wondering when Win will get in touch with me, I haven't gotten in touch with him either. Guilt creeps in as I say, "I'm great, thanks. Things have just been crazy these past few weeks, you know, with all the rehearsals and prep."

"I'll bet. I hope you've at least had time to be with the girls in all the madness."

I glance to my left. "I'm with them now, looking forward to lying by the pool later. Maybe we'll hit up the spa."

"Do you want to grab lunch together before then?" Win clears his throat. "I know some great places to eat."

My shoulders sink. "Ugh, I'm sorry, Win, I can't."

"You have other plans?"

"Yeah."

He chuckles. "You don't sound too thrilled about that. Is it work related?"

"You wouldn't believe me if I told you."

I can almost hear his shrug as he says easily, "All right."

I know he won't press me for more information—that's just not like Win at all—and so I elaborate before he can move on. "I'm actually meeting Riley Vega for brunch."

There's a pause as this information sinks in. Then he says simply, "Ah."

"Not my idea. She called me out of the blue last week apologizing, saying she wants us to be friends again, that sort of thing. Maybe I'm being naïve about it, but it was easier to say yes than to keep this awkward energy going on, you know?"

"I get it. I hope it goes well."

"Thanks. Maybe we could meet for lunch tomorrow instead?"

"I'd love to, but tomorrow's my yacht party. Actually, I was hoping you would join me for that. Bring the girls too—anyone who's a friend of yours is welcome. I'll have some of my business partners with me for a cruise around the bay, there'll be drinks and food, good music. I'd love to have you there."

I feel the butterflies dance inside me. It wouldn't be a trip to Miami without a boat party, after all. Answering for all three of us, I grin excitedly. "We'll definitely be there. Thanks, Win."

"I'll text you the info later."

"Perfect."

"If I get a chance tomorrow morning, maybe I'll come meet you at your hotel for breakfast instead."

"Oh," I say, pleasantly surprised. "That'd be really nice." I already know it's unlikely to happen, but just the thought plants a seed of excitement for tomorrow to hurry up and get here already—especially as I think of my dreaded brunch date later this morning.

"Okay, I'm about to get off the jet now, Princess, so I have to go. Enjoy this beautiful day. I'll check you tomorrow. Oh, and by the way, I saw you posted a new song. Brilliant. Making moves, that's the Princess I know. I can't wait to listen to it."

I can't help but smile, glad someone close to me acknowledged it. Of course, I was beyond grateful it did so well, so many people online loved it, but Win knows me, the real me, so it hits different. "See you tomorrow, Win. Have a great day too."

"Always a great day when I'm talking to you," he says, and then before I can even think of a reply, the call clicks off and I'm left staring at my reflection as the busy streets of Miami fly by outside the car window.

Meeting up with Riley after so long is weird, to say the least. For starters, the last time we saw each other, we were not accompanied by plainclothes security. Some things haven't changed, though. She still orders her favorite food: waffles and berries with extra syrup and a dusting of sugar. Midbite she says, "What's the point in working this hard if I can't enjoy a nice meal guilt-free once in a while?" and I totally agree. Like I always say, everything in moderation.

We spend most of brunch talking as if we have an audience, extra friendly and polite, making a real effort to listen to each other discuss the surface-level details: a change in manager for Riley, the collabs we're working on right now, the success of my latest song—"Oh my god, it was *so* authentic, Princess, I literally almost cried listening to it. That's when I knew I'd done the right thing reaching out to you"—and avoiding the topic of John with expert precision. By the time we've paid our bill and left the restaurant, it still feels like we haven't really tapped into the real reason we're here. I don't want to be the one to bring it up.

"You know, I haven't been back to Miami in so long. Life's too busy nowadays. I miss the days when we'd book a flight and come hang out here for a couple of nights—don't you?" Riley says, linking arms with me and glancing behind us to check security are still with us.

"It was always the best time," I agree, leaving out that my trips away with Maya, Val, and Jessie have always been much more fun. I wonder what they're all doing right now. I wish Jessie could be here with us, but school got in the way as usual.

"You wanna go shopping?"

I look out over the Bal Harbour shops, Saks at one end and then a whole bunch of luxury stores all around us, the center of the mall filled with little water features and tropical plants, and the open top giving a view of the perfectly blue, cloudless sky. "Sure, why not?" I say with a smile, though Riley's already dragging me with her into the Gucci store, making a beeline for a leather jacket just inside the door.

We spend nearly half an hour inside trying on clothes and matching them with purses, and the longer we take, the more I start to wonder when Riley should be heading back. We're in Miami for her event after all—surely she must have press or meetings to get to? Even I need to head out this afternoon for more rehearsals before I can relax at the hotel with the girls.

All I know is, if I was hosting the show, I'd want to be front and center of the action, not hanging around shopping malls trying to rekindle friendships that expired long ago.

As we're leaving the Gucci store with our new stuff, a couple of shouts sound from across the other side of the mall, and the next thing I see is the flash of a camera. My shoulders immediately tense up. "Paps," I say low, moving to rush away from them with Riley as a security guy steps in to keep us safe, but Riley's less quick to react.

"Let's just humor them for a sec," she says, as if it's no bother. "If we give them what they want, maybe they'll leave us alone."

Riley knows how this works; if anything, humoring them will only open up the floodgates for everyone else around us to start requesting photos, too, paparazzi or passersby. Before I can speak, she links arms with me and starts giggling maniacally at nothing, leaning in close as if I've just cracked an inside joke. She pulls me along with her directly past the small crowd of paparazzi, heading toward the stores on the other side of the mall.

"Hey, why don't we go do something cute?" she suggests, and I try my hardest to look natural, unbothered, as the cameras flash in our faces over and over, guys running around us from all angles, hoping to get the best shot.

"Such as?" I ask, trying a smile.

"Like—" She pauses as if thinking of an idea, but with the way her eyes land on the Tiffany store ahead, it seems she already thought of this well ahead of time. "Why don't we go get matching bracelets to commemorate today, the day we realized friendship was thicker than competition all along?"

I let out a disbelieving burst of laughter—I can't help it. "Friendship bracelets?" I ask, bemused.

"Yeah, my treat." Riley grins wide, acting as if there's nothing weird at all about this. "Come on," she says, tugging on my arm and leading me into the store, where a greeter's already holding the door open for us, eyes glittering.

"Good morning, ladies. Are either of you looking for anything special today?"

It seems bizarre, but Riley insists on buying the bracelet for me even though I offer a million times to pay for myself and tell her it really isn't necessary.

The glamorous woman behind the counter has bouffant blonde hair and smells strongly of Chanel No. 5. "Would you like these gift wrapped or boxed today, ladies?" she asks us with a smile.

"Oh, no thanks," Riley replies. "We'll wear them now." She glances out the window at the crowd of paparazzi waiting on the opposite side of the mall, lenses no doubt zoomed in to get the perfect shot, and then I notice she angles herself as if she's posing for them.

She's really enjoying this, isn't she?

"Literally so happy we're doing this," she says to me privately a second later, her tone genuine and the look on her face surprisingly sincere.

"Me too," I say automatically. The store assistant clasps the bracelet around my wrist and I turn it over to admire it. "They're stunning."

"They really suit us," Riley agrees.

A few minutes later we leave the store sporting the gold chain bracelets with matching little diamonds, mine on my left wrist and Riley's on her right.

"Hey, I have to leave soon since it's getting late, but let's make a pact to never let a guy come between us again," Riley says as we approach the valet. She comes to a stop right beside a cascading fake waterfall and reaches her arms out for a hug.

"I'd like that," I say. "No more drama, no more lies."

"You said it, girl."

I wait for a second, hoping she'll offer up something more, a question burning on my tongue. When she doesn't speak, I have to let it out. "But, Riley, can I just be clear on something? Are you *with* John now? Is that what all this is about, smoothing things out between us so there's no bad energy?"

She studies me for a second as if she's trying to figure out the right thing to say. I deliberately try to keep my expression neutral, wanting to know the actual truth, not just what she wants me to hear. I know Coachella wasn't the last time they were seen together—if the photos popping up via their social media and the paparazzi weren't a big enough clue, Maya and Val confirmed sightings of the two of them at parties together. It doesn't really matter to me that much . . . I think. But it would be nice to know where I stand, if this friendship is something Riley's set on pursuing.

"It's kind of unofficial," is what she chooses to say eventually, biting the inside of her cheek, lips pursed. "I don't know that I want a relationship to tie me down right now. It's a big time in my life."

But you're happy to hook up with him even when someone else is *in a relationship with him?* I can't stop the thought. "Right."

"Look, it's complicated," she says quickly. "And that's why I don't want it to come between us. We got these bracelets as a reminder none of this boy shit matters as much as supporting each other, right? I don't want to go back to that weird place of competing against each other again. This industry's difficult enough to deal with as it is."

I nod but don't say anything. It's like she's blacked out the memory of how we got into this weird competitive place to begin with. Because of *her* shady behavior.

When her phone buzzes, she lifts the corner of her mouth apologetically. "I gotta go, Princess."

"Of course. You do your thing."

We hug, and Riley squeezes me tight for a few seconds longer than

I'm comfortable with as the white flashes of cameras reflect off the wall of water beside us. And then, with a quick "Okay, I'll see you later. Good luck with the show and call me whenever. Thanks for today!" she struts off to her car without so much as a glance back. My gut pings, hoping for once that this feeling of dread is all in my imagination.

30

The first thing I do when I wake up in the hotel room the next morning is roll over in bed and stare out at the view. The soft white sand of South Beach stretches out below my balcony, looking like a miniature version of reality from this high up, and the teal blue ocean glitters beneath a helicopter and a couple of huge herons swooping low to dip into the water.

The second thing I do is reach for my phone and sigh.

Rehearsals went on for way longer than expected yesterday afternoon, lasting into the evening, and then, after a couple hours' break for dinner, we picked back up because the show needed some adjustments after we saw how much space we had onstage. I missed out on the chance to relax with the girls at the spa, and didn't even get to see them when we finally got back to the hotel late at night since they'd both gone to bed already.

I sit up and pull the sheets close to my chest, hugging my knees against the crisp breeze from the AC. I scroll through my notifications, a nagging sense of something being off about my meetup with Riley. She hasn't reached out. And neither has John. It just doesn't sit right with me, not after her speech about supporting each other and not letting boys come between us. Did she tell him that we'd made up? Did she tell him not to text me? Is he annoyed I met up with her?

Does it even matter?

Deciding it doesn't, I toss my phone across the mattress and slip out of bed, running a hot shower to relax after yesterday's long-ass day. When I'm done, I head down to breakfast, where Maya and Val have already grabbed us a table with a perfect view of the ocean and a steaming pot of coffee awaits me, its aroma an instant and welcome distraction. I pour a cup and take a sip, then slump back into my seat with a contented sigh.

"Bliss," I say with a smile, cradling my mug.

"Where the hell did you go last night?" Maya's quick to break the tranquility as she bites into her avocado toast.

"Where did I go?" I scoffed. "Rehearsals dragged on past midnight, *so* exhausting. Had to keep running it to get all the choreo and blocking right. We needed that, though, and thankfully I feel good about the show now. Praise the lord, it had me stressing for a sec."

"Sheesh," Val says, her voice noticeably groggy. "Between your rehearsals and Maya's fitting for the fashion show, I was here all alone for most of the day, bored as shit. I went to the spa and it was gorgeous, but damn, there were so many judgy supermodels in there."

"Hey." Maya swats at her with the menu. "Less supermodel hate, or I'll start bitching about all these whiny hotel heiresses who think nothing's good enough."

"Good morning."

All three of us whip our heads around at the velvety-rich voice that appears right behind my seat, the conversation suddenly forgotten when I realize who it is.

"Win!" I stand up and lean into his embrace, hit by the intoxicating drift of his cologne as I pull back. *Fuck, he even smells handsome.* "You made it!"

"Of course I did. What better way to start my first morning here in Miami than in the company of you three?"

He pulls out the chair beside mine, opposite Val and Maya, and seats himself casually, as if this is perfectly normal. Honestly, I didn't expect him to come at all. Usually when I make a loose plan with a guy something comes up or they forget or there are a million other reasons why it never actually happens.

But this is Win, and he's a man of his word.

I instantly wish I'd made more of an effort with my hair and makeup before coming downstairs. Self-awareness washes over me as I sit back in my seat and offer to pour him a coffee.

"So, what's the news this morning?" Win asks the table as he reaches for the menu, and for the next few minutes before the waiter comes to take our order we talk easily, swapping stories about what we all got up to yesterday and discussing our plans for the show.

"Where are you staying, Win?" Val asks pleasantly.

"Not too far away," he says, gesturing behind him. "I recently bought a house out here."

Maya lets out a low whistle. "Fancy. Didn't I hear you have a yacht out this way too?"

He smiles and tucks his designer shades into the collar of his shirt. "I sure do. Who told you that?"

There's a sparkle in Maya's eye as she watches him over the rim of her glass. "Now, that would be telling."

Instead of rising to her flirtation, Win glances at me, the smile on his face as calm as ever. I know Maya's only teasing, but a little pang of something uncomfortable hits me as I recall her saying she'd chase after Win if I didn't. *It was just a joke*, I remind myself, but still. I feel strangely territorial over him.

"So, I told Princess already, but I'm having a little party on my yacht tonight with a few friends and business people, and you're all more than welcome to join us."

"That's so sweet of you, Win," Val says.

"That sounds fun, we'd love to come!" Maya straightens up.

They discuss the timing and where the yacht is docked a little bit, but I'm not really paying attention. I'm still sleepy, and I can't tear my unfocused gaze off the sunlit ocean as it ripples in the distance.

Without warning, his warm hand touches my knee, surprisingly large and completely unexpected. I jolt back to the conversation, meeting eyes with Win.

"Huh?"

"You're still planning to come, right, daydreamer?" Yet his hand stays put for a few more seconds. His pupils dilate and my eyes are drawn to his lips, where his charming, amused smile alerts me to the fact he just asked me a question.

Embarrassed, I let out a small chuckle, feeling my cheeks flush. "Oh, for sure, I'll be there. Sounds like fun."

Goose bumps break out all over as he finally slides his hand away. *Daydreamer*. I kind of love the way he called me that.

"Good. I gotta use the restroom. Know where it is?" he asks.

"Over by the bar," Val says, pointing in the right direction.

"Thanks."

"Actually, me too," I say, standing up at the same time as Win. I push out of my seat and bump into him accidentally, my ass brushing against his thigh. Startled, he steps back quickly but reaches to grab my waist and steady me.

"Oh god, I'm sorry."

"No, no," he says quickly. "That was my bad."

His breath fans the hair on the side of my neck, making more goose bumps prickle over my skin. I become acutely aware of his hands, his fingertips squeezing my hips until he's sure I'm steady on my feet. I wonder if he's just as tuned in to the sensation of our bodies colliding as I am. There's such an energy between us I can barely breathe. As soon as I remember where we are and exactly who's watching—Val with a lifted brow, Maya with a knowing smirk—his hands have left me and he's pushing my chair back under the table, ever the gentleman.

Holy shit.

"So he just, like, showed up to have breakfast with you and then left to go about his normal day?"

"Exactly. It was so unexpected but, like, I loved it, you know."

"Yeah, I bet. Imagine that. Win showing up at your hotel to start his day with you." Jessie sighs dreamily through the phone.

I'm making my way back up to my hotel room, having just finished breakfast. The girls are headed to the pool, and Win's off to do whatever Win does.

"He's so reliable," I say in agreement, knowing Jessie's swooning just as hard as me.

"Seriously. Why can't all men be like him?"

"Right?"

I hit the button on the elevator to go up and then step inside, thankful when nobody follows me in. I saw a group of girls whispering about me as if they were starstruck down in the hotel lobby. They seemed harmless, but after the stalker situation I get really nervous about being followed, especially when I'm in hotels.

"All right, time to address the elephant in the room. How was yesterday?" Jessie asks.

"Just as weird as I expected," I say, glancing down at the friendship bracelet still on my wrist and back at Jessie, trying to read her tone. "We got matching bracelets."

"Oh, don't I know it." Jessie laughs dryly.

"Yeah." I let out a hesitant laugh. "I still don't really know what to think about it. Are you thrown off? I wasn't the one who came up with the idea."

"What?" Jessie laughs. "Not at all! A little bit of a questionable situation on Riley's part but the bracelet is actually really cute."

"Okay, good." I press my hand to my chest. "I was worried there for a sec. All this talk of rekindling our friendship and BFF this and that is so much to take in right now. I think I'm still in shock, to be honest." A laugh skips out. Then I realize what Jessie just said. "Hold up, how do you know about the bracelets? I haven't told anyone."

"I have your Google Alerts, remember? The pics of you two at Tiffany's are plastered on like every site. RileyxPrincess was also trending on X for a minute."

The speed with which the media spreads stories never ceases to amaze me. Guess I missed all that while I was in rehearsals for the show.

"Right, that makes sense. Riley wouldn't have had those pics set up for nothing."

"Did she mention John at all?"

"No, aside from not really giving me a straight answer about whether they're together or not and saying something about how she doesn't want him to come between us anymore. Why?"

"Yikes."

"Ugh, please, no yikes. I cannot handle any more 'yikes' right now."

"I'm just going to give it to you straight."

My heart lodges in my throat. "What now?"

Jessie takes a deep breath. "Riley and John had a massive meltdown on Instagram yesterday. It started with a comment or something, and then the next thing you know, she's on Instagram Live giving a speech about how she's sick of men ruining powerful female friendships with their inconsistent, slutty behavior—"

"She literally said 'slutty'? For John?"

"Yep."

"Wow . . . that is yikes."

"It gets worse. Obviously you haven't checked, and honestly, more power to you, because that place is a cesspit right now, but I'm just going to say it. She tagged you in a story and then reposted a bunch of photos from your outing yesterday, talking about how close you two are and how you've recently gotten even closer follow-ing—and I quote—'a few growing pains in your friendship' where you realized you'd both fallen victim to 'a certain manipulative guy.' So she's posting all this on Instagram while simultaneously having these very public, *very messy* arguments with John in some com-ments section, so he then retaliates by posting some stories of his own—not videos, but like reposting passive-aggressive quotes from a bunch of different accounts—and my god, it was fucking exhaust-ing. All the while I was trying to call you, but you weren't answering because—"

"I was in rehearsals," I say, completely drained. I can barely believe a word of what Jessie just told me. It feels like I'm not even in my own body as I step out of the elevator and onto my floor, half stumbling down the hallway toward my room. "A few growing pains . . . both fallen victim . . . Is she fucking delusional?" Tapping my key card against the lock, I push open the door and storm into my room, even more irritated by the slow-close hinges that stop it from slamming shut behind me. I need to make some noise right now. This is *insane*.

"Why?! I swear she thinks she's some master puppeteer dragging all of us into her drama. Doesn't she get tired? Isn't there someone else she can use for entertainment? I keep all this shit to myself, stay out of her way, and somehow I'm right back in the middle of fucked-up situations and I'm always one step behind. If I'm being real, I'm not even one iota surprised by this shit. This is Riley Vega, after all."

I pace the room in front of the windows, raging into the phone. "So she used me once again. All that bullshit about wanting to be friends again, to get back to a place where we weren't competing with each other—mind you, *she* started this weird competition, whatever this is. Oh, and of course, don't forget the fucking photos she staged!"

"I'm so sorry, Princess." Jessie sounds as devastated as I feel underneath all my anger. "For what it's worth, there were a lot of comments—and I mean *a lot*—wondering why you weren't speaking on it, and so many of your fans kept mentioning your new song lyrics and connecting them to the John and Riley situation. I think most people get that she's fabricating this whole thing."

"But why?" I say, exasperated. The temptation to log into my Instagram and check is too much, but I know it'd only be bad news. I wouldn't be able to control myself from speaking up in my current mood.

"I don't know, Princess," Jessie says. "All I'm saying is, that song you released on your own hit deep for a lot of people, and it really took off—more than a lot of Riley's songs. Maybe she got jealous of your success and freaked out thinking those lyrics would expose a little too much of the truth about who she really is."

"You think? She wouldn't set up this whole thing just to stop the rumors from spreading about her and John fucking me over?"

"It's the only thing that adds up. If anyone's going to fall down a rabbit hole online for you, you know it's gonna be me."

"I love you, Jessie."

"I love you, too, girl. Please, keep your ass off social media today and just . . . I don't know, talk to Kimi and Wayne and see what they think you should do."

"Honestly, right now I just feel like flying home and saying a big fuck-you to Riley's Cirque au bord de l'eau bullshit. She probably only wanted me to perform here to add some more weight to the lie."

"Makes sense."

"God, I hate this."

"Call Kimi and Wayne. They'll help you."

I nod even though she can't see me and take a deep breath. "All right, I have a call set up with them in a couple of minutes, anyway. Thanks for the update, I guess."

"I'm sorry, Princess."

"Don't be, Jessie. This is not your mess to be sorry for."

We hang up and I spend a little while trying to decompress before answering Wayne's call. Before I do, there's just one more important task to complete. Standing on the balcony of my hotel suite, the sparkling ocean below and the blue sky above, I rip the stupid diamond friendship bracelet off my wrist and throw it over the railing. Let someone else find it and sell it for some cash. Better yet, I hope it gets carried out to sea, never to be found again. I've made up my mind. I won't let her use me any longer.

"Fuck you, Riley."

This is the *last* time I'm falling for any more selfish lies.

31

The sun glitters off the ocean on the horizon, burning my eyes until I turn away from it and take another sip of Real—my favorite, because naturally Win would stock my favorite on his yacht. There's a perfect view of the downtown Miami skyline behind us and the palm tree–lined backyards of celebrity mansions on the island ahead. I push a flyaway strand of hair out of my face and look across the deck to where Maya's flirting with some guy in a sleek white business suit, looking as tipsy as I'm starting to feel.

Win's party's alive with people, although the music's chill compared to some of the party boats I've been on in the past, and the conversation is business focused, as expected. His yacht is beautiful, all polished chestnut wood and soft white leather, complete with a full bar, two bedrooms, an indoor seating area, and a deck big enough to perform a live show on. I just wish I was in a better state of mind to truly enjoy being here.

"Princess?"

The voice filters in above all the other conversations and laughter, and I pull my eyes away from Maya to find a tall man with graying hair and wearing a laid-back linen outfit approaching me with a charming smile.

"Hi, yes, that's me."

"I thought so. I saw you over here looking lonely, so I thought I'd come introduce myself and keep you company. I hope you don't mind."

I give a polite laugh. "Oh, not lonely, just taking it all in." Though I realize, actually, when my girls aren't by my side, I *am* fucking lonely. In a room—or a yacht—full of people, it's just me and my thoughts. God knows I don't need to spend any more time lingering on those.

"She sure is one hell of a boat, isn't she? Used to have one of these babies myself, but nowadays I spend more time on the golf course than out at sea." He smiles and holds out his hand, and I'm pleasantly surprised; it's not unusual for businessmen like him to assume I'm too delicate and dainty to shake hands. "Martyn Michaels," he introduces himself. "I own a pharmaceutical company based in San Francisco. Win tells me you have a connection in town."

My eyes light up. "Oh, that's awesome. And I do—my best friend's a biologist living there right now. She's the hardest worker I know."

"Well, we have plenty of dedicated biologists working for us. Maybe I might know her."

"Oh, Jessie's not working for anyone yet. She's still in school."

Martyn smiles, his warmth infectious. It clears my mind of all the negative thoughts I was having and sets me at ease, a good distraction. "Now, how does an LA star like you know a biology student in San Francisco?"

"Jessie and I go way back. We're both from Guam, best friends since birth, and got lucky enough to move over to the States around the same time as one another."

"It takes a genuine friendship to last so long. I'm sure Jessie feels very lucky to still have you as a friend after all this time, and considering how far you've come . . ."

"I'm the lucky one. She helps me more than I could ever help her."

An idea springs to mind as the words leave my mouth, and I don't waste a second thinking twice about it. "If you're open to it, I'd love to get your contact info and connect you two. It sounds like you run exactly the kind of company she'd love to work for. Maybe there's an internship opportunity?"

Martyn watches me closely for a second or two as if trying to figure out how the arrangement would work, and then he shrugs and chuckles. "Okay, why not? You obviously think very highly of her, and I admire a person who lifts others up."

"Amazing!" I reach for my phone, and while we're swapping details, I feel a presence approaching from behind. I know without looking who it is, and my guess is confirmed when Martyn looks up and greets him.

"Win, there you are. I was just speaking to the lovely Princess while I waited for you to be free."

"What an excellent way to spend your time," Win says so easily I almost blush. "Princess, Martyn and I have been talking about a potential investment opportunity down in the Florida Keys. A hotel recently came up for sale that he thinks would turn a great profit with a little work—a few design touches and some stronger marketing. I've been looking for a new project to sink my teeth into. What do you think?"

They turn to me for my answer, and I'm honestly flattered by how genuinely interested they seem—as if my opinion matters in this. It's really none of my business what side projects Win takes on, but the way he's looking at me, that smooth, trademark smile on his lips and his eyes sparkling in the sun, makes me feel important.

"It's a great idea," I say brightly. "Do you have thoughts in mind for the place already?"

"Maybe hiring a team of designers would be the best route to take, but I love the idea of turning it into an adults-only luxury hotel. It's right on the beach, with a sushi restaurant attached and incredible ocean views. Would you visit a place like that, Princess?" Win asks.

"Come on, Win, do you really need to ask?" I say with a playful nudge of his arm. "I'm an island girl—anywhere involving the ocean and seafood sounds exactly like where I want to be."

Win grins and slides his arm around my waist, holding me loosely, easily, as he addresses Martyn. "Princess is from Guam, a beautiful island in the—"

"Yes," Martyn says proudly, "we were just talking about this, and about Princess's friend Jessie, who's also from Guam."

"Ah! Jessie," Win says knowingly. "Now I think I know what you two were discussing. Jessie is getting an advanced degree in biology, right?" He turns to me, and I nod, unable to form words at the feel of his hand still lingering on my back, his body so close to mine. And the fact he remembers so many little details about my life, my friends . . . everything I tell him and more. The movement pulls me closer into him, so it feels like I'm being *protected* by him somewhat. And my heart's sprinting inside my rib cage at our proximity.

"She does," I confirm. "And I think she and Martyn would have a lot to discuss."

Win looks at Martyn. "You took her info?"

Martyn nods. "I look forward to speaking with her."

"Wonderful." Win looks back at me, impressed. It's an emotion I can't place that crosses his features next, but it feels a lot like surprise mixed with awe and something even hotter. His hand slips away so he can take a drink, and when Martyn asks him a question, I hear it like a faraway thought, not fully engaged. My eyes don't leave Win, though, until my phone buzzes in my Loro Piana pouch.

Not wanting to seem rude, I step away from them for a second to check the notification onscreen. It's a text from Kimi, and it makes my heart leap.

Kimi: Turns out you did the right thing releasing that song last week. The streaming numbers are going crazy, the label wants to make it a single, put money behind it and take it to radio. It's going to have a big push—congratulations!!

I can't stop the little yelp of happiness that leaps from my mouth. One of my deepest, realest song to date is being picked up as a single and going to radio?! Releasing this on my own was a risk but I trusted myself and it worked! I'm stunned. The smile spreads across my face as fast as lightning, and then I start to feel it, the buzz of alcohol like an undercurrent in my veins, swaying the edges of my vision. In the back of my head is the conversation with Kimi after I pulled my stunt, and how unhappy she was at the time, but it seems like she's fine now.

"Everything all good, Princess?" Win asks, placing a hand on my shoulder.

I spin around, unable to stop myself from blurting, "Yeah! My label is picking up the acoustic song I released on a whim and making it a single! They're putting money behind it and apparently a big push!"

"That's amazing!" He celebrates with me, clinking our glasses together.

"Hold up, did I hear that correctly?" Maya interrupts, cutting across the deck to swoop in and link her arm through mine. "*The acoustic song is going to be a single*, Princess?"

"Yes!" I show her Kimi's text excitedly, and she does a little happy dance with me, both of us vibrating with energy.

"Win, have you heard it?" Maya clutches Win's arm, always way overconfident. "Princess released it completely untouched by anyone else. It's so fucking good"—she glances at Martyn—"excuse my French. Sorry."

He smiles and steps away. "No need to apologize. I'm heading to the bar, Win. I'll catch up with you later."

"Thanks, Martyn." Win nods. Then he turns to me. "This sounds amazing, Princess, we need to celebrate! I can't wait to hear it, I haven't had the chance to listen to it yet."

Maya squeezes me a bit tighter. "I've always admired your strategy and work ethic, Princess. If Kimi and Wayne quit work tomorrow I know you could run your whole business perfectly fine."

Win smiles at Maya's comment, though his eyes are glued to mine. "I believe that. Princess has a killer work ethic and her presence is undeniable. The streams are incredible."

"Thank you, Win," I say sheepishly. "I just hit Upload and snapped a photo of it for my Instagram story, and that was really it. I'm shocked at the response."

"And yet it's touching the emotions of thousands," Maya says theatrically, clutching a hand over her chest. "You know why that is, Princess? It's 'cause you kept it real, no filters necessary. People eat that up. It connects with the heart."

"Yeah, I think you're right. There's been so much going on I just needed to release it all creatively. I've been way too stressed lately."

"I feel that *in my bones*," Maya says, nudging me, less than subtle. She's been raging about the John/Riley drama since I filled her in on the details of their *very* public fight on our way to the yacht party. Thankfully, she bites her tongue from saying any more, though she gives me an incredibly pointed look. I wonder if Win ever gets affected by social media stuff; probably not. He's always been so private online, basically nonexistent with one account, Instagram, a very rare work-related post here and there, not following too many people. Untouchable. Just like in real life.

"Okay, I'm gonna leave you guys to it." Maya throws a glance at the guy she was just talking to, and I follow her gaze to see him staring at her from across the deck, eyes rolling over her body. "You've got some great contacts, Win," she says audaciously, moving away from us. "Catch you later."

I laugh in disbelief as I watch her strut off, and then turn my attention back to Win. He's still watching me closely. "It's a great party," I say, just to say *something*. "If I owned a yacht like this, I'd be out here every day."

"Well," Win says, his eyes still glued to me, "some things just keep me coming back to LA, time and time again."

The heat of his stare makes me aware of the gnawing sensation gripping my core, the rocking motion of the yacht on the water, and the buzz in my veins from the three—or was it four?—drinks I've already had. In a second, Win seems to snap out of whatever thought he was having, and clarity sets in as he moves me to stand with him up close to the railing, looking out over the ocean and the Miami skyline. With his hand dancing close to my lower back but never quite touching, just lingering there, as if he's ready to catch me if he needs to, we talk for a few minutes longer about nothing in particular, pointing out birds in the water and which celebrity owns which waterside mansion. It feels a lot like we're skirting around the real topic, something unspoken, almost forbidden. Then he leaves me with another drink, and my mind drifts to other pointless thoughts—such as what exactly keeps Win coming back to LA other than business, who else he's invited on glamorous yacht parties here in Miami, and why I can't ever be around him without feeling like I just got charged by some irresistible type of electric force.

You should go to him.

The thought pops into my mind uninvited. Whether it's the alcohol talking or just all this pent-up, confused energy, I don't know, but my eyes instinctively dart to the back of the yacht where Win disappeared a moment ago, to the closed cabin door nobody else seems to be lingering by.

Just talk to him and tell him how you feel. He's all alone right now; What's the worst that could happen?

Slowly, my body responds, and I move across the deck, past the groups of people talking business and Maya flirting with her white-suited catch of the day, toward Win's cabin. My pulse matches the beat of my footsteps: slow and precarious at first, but gradually increasing in speed until it's fast and dangerous, spurring me on.

"Oops, shit!"

I'm stopped immediately by a body bursting out of the bathroom. The door swings shut behind her, and the girl stumbles into me, hair spilling over her face. She drags it back and looks up at me.

"Val?"

"Oh my god, I was just coming to look for you!" She seems totally unaware of my worried expression. "So, I talked to Tripp and I'm so unbelievably relieved. He feels the same way and we're . . . drumroll please . . . official."

"Aww, Val, that's the best news!" I pull her into a tight hug and my worry falls away.

"I have the worst damn sea legs right now," she says into my ear as we pull away from each other. "I have so much to catch you up on but long story short I was talking through a bunch of my family stuff with Tripp, and he's been the best to help me navigate it all. As awkward as it is to admit, I know I've been handling the stress in all the wrong ways.

I'm going to just take a breather to rest and focus on my self-care." She's glowing as she talks; I haven't seen Val like this in a long time.

"That's amazing, babe! Tripp is seriously one of a kind. Such a keeper." I'm bursting with happiness for Val; she's really getting her life together. I need to get on the same wave.

"I'm going to head to the front and take some pictures, find me in a bit." She blows me a kiss and walks away.

I'm watching Val walk away when my phone buzzes in my hand, notifications piling in. Pictures of John and Riley making out on Miami Beach. I can't scroll fast enough trying to read the article and get through all the photos of them. My world starts moving in slow motion. This cannot be happening to me right now.

They're basically fucking each other in these pictures.

On the beach.

This morning.

My head spins with so much new information and the high of everything good that happened today comes crashing down in an instant—without warning my racing pulse doesn't feel like such a buzz.

I look over at the door to Win's cabin. Suddenly, it feels so out of reach. So far away. So restricted. Off-limits. Not where I belong.

Because I'm naïve, stupid Princess who just got used again. Riley and John were never arguing, even if that's what it looked like. She used me as a way to orchestrate this whole drama, pretending like we were fresh new besties and John didn't matter to her, and I really believed for a second she wanted to be on my side again, supporting me while I supported her—even if it was mostly one big show to make herself look good. Even a half hour ago I never suspected she might actually be in on this with John; that their blow-up argument yesterday was rehearsed and calculated; that they're still fucking each other behind the scenes.

And getting caught together on Miami Beach? It's like the bitch *wants* me to know.

You're so out of touch with other people's feelings you're probably misreading this situation with Win too, the voice inside my head mocks. *He doesn't really care about you, just like Riley didn't, and John before her, and all those other guys you dated just to feel something real.*

Nothing's real.

Everyone's out for themselves in this life.

You'll always be alone.

It's the worst timing. It could only happen to me. Just as my stomach roils and my throat retches, the door to Win's cabin opens wide and he steps out into the seating area, right in time to see me throw up the contents of my stomach all over his immaculately polished wood floor.

"Fuck." I'm not even aware I'm crying until tears are blurring my vision, making it difficult to see the mess I made or Win's expression as I stand up straight. I swipe my eyes with the back of my hand and finally see his confusion as he looks from me to the pile of vomit and back again, his frown line making it clear he's as confused as I am about why I'm back here.

"Oh man, Princess, are you okay?" He strides over and smooths an arm around my shoulders, moving me away from the mess and seating me gently on one of the leather benches. "Are you feeling a little seasick?"

No, it's just the thought of how I'm fucking incapable of finding love without being used or humiliated. "I guess," I croak, feeling my stomach roll again. "Sorry, Win."

"It's not your fault." He squeezes my shoulder. "I'll be right back. I'll find someone to clean this up, and have the captain take us back to land."

"Don't end your party for me—" I try to say, but he's already out of earshot, and I don't have the energy to protest further. Right now, I *do* want to be on land, preferably hidden under the covers of my bed, and definitely not here in Miami where everything just seems to be getting worse and worse.

It's not your fault. His words resound in my head.

Yes, it is, I hear my mind answering back.

This is all my fault.

Every last thing.

32

"This is *not* your fucking fault." Maya yanks a handful of tissues out of the box on my hotel bed and holds them out to me. I scrunch up the tissue I was just using and throw it onto the little mountain forming beside me before taking the fresh ones. I dab at my face, which feels raw from all the crying. "Win probably hasn't even connected the dots and thinks you were just coming into the cabin to use the bathroom or something. It's not that deep, and even if it was, he's a good guy. If he really cares about you, none of this will matter to him in the slightest."

"But that's the fucking problem, Maya," I sob, fresh tears spilling over as the same damn negative thoughts circle back around in my head. "I don't think he does care about me. Maybe I've been misreading this whole situation with him, just like the Riley/John thing. Totally fucking misreading it."

"You've got to be kidding me. That man drove to Coachella and back in one night to pick you up! And as for Riley, babe, you quite literally figured out what she was doing. I mean, fuck the friendship bracelets and fuck her stupid fucking publicity schemes. You. Saw. Through. It."

"Yeah, I thought so. But seems I was wrong about that too."

Maya sighs heavily. "What do you mean?"

I shake my head. "So much shit came out about those two and I saw it all on the boat."

"Explain."

My body tenses, not wanting to speak it out loud. "Photos of John and Riley making out this morning on South Beach."

Maya studies me carefully, concern mixed with confusion. "Now why the hell would Riley have John with her in Miami when just yesterday she was blowing up the internet with their explosive fucking breakup?"

I hold my hands out. "Exactly. Do you see why this is such a mindfuck?"

"Jesus Christ, Princess. So, what, it's pap pics of them making out on the beach in public?"

"Yup." I drag the word out.

My phone buzzes with a new text. It's John.

John: Princess . . . I know you've probably seen the photos by now, but they aren't what they seem. It's too late for us, and I fucked that up, but I need to explain . . . please trust me when I say it's not what it looks like . . .

My head swims. I don't know what to believe—what's before my eyes, or what he says. I want to give him the benefit of the doubt, because deep down I know he wouldn't hurt me like this. Riley? All bets are off.

"Fuck this." Maya's anger seeps through, and she stands up from the bed, pacing in front of me and gesticulating with her hands. "After that whole show of acting like you were best friends? After timing this whole argument with John to hit at the exact moment you were in rehearsals and couldn't respond? After trying so fucking hard to look like the innocent one in the situation 'cause she couldn't handle the fact your realest song yet was about the pain her own tragic, shitty actions caused?"

"I'm so done with trying to figure it out. I give up." I get up, too, and walk over to the wall mirror, groaning when I see the state of my smeared makeup and puffy eyes. "I mean, look at me. I look as if I haven't slept in weeks, and I feel ten times worse than that. How the fuck do people do it, live day after day in the spotlight dealing with this type of bullshit, never able to tell their side of the story, and not let it destroy them?"

"They don't." It's an instant answer, and I turn around to look at Maya. "Take Val as the example. She was born into this, and life hasn't been easy on her. Thank god she's working on herself now but look at the road she had to take to get to this point."

"I know."

I watch as she places the tissue box on the little coffee table beside the two plush armchairs near the windows and then takes a seat, crossing her long legs one over the other.

"You know, there is one thing I know for sure," she says matter-of-factly, looking over her shoulder at me and nodding to the other seat as if I should come join her.

"What's that?" I ask.

"My new friend took me on a little walk around the deck while we were chatting, just after Win left you alone to go to his cabin, and I definitely heard him listening to your new song in there when we passed by. He had it on a low volume, but I don't think he realized his window was open a crack. I could hear everything."

I sink into the other armchair, giddy momentarily. "He was?"

"I swear. Win was listening to it on his own in his little cabin, it was actually so cute."

"Yeah, but why would he rush to listen to it like that?"

Maya laughs, resting her head in her hand and looking at me as if I'm some cute little kid. "Don't you get it yet? I'd like to think I'm a pretty good judge of character, and I can tell when a man likes someone as more than just a friend. I think Win went into that room to find some hidden message in your new song, maybe he was hoping it'd be about him. You heard what I said to him: it was a real, deep, unfiltered exploration of your feelings. He probably heard that and wanted to know what was on your mind."

It all fits together like puzzle pieces inside my head, building a bigger picture that makes perfect sense. The mutual respect. The constant compliments. The check-in texts and calls. The Coachella trip. The sleepover at his house. The special treatment he gives me. The way he joined us for breakfast. The fact he always follows through on his word, unlike any other man I know.

"Oh my god."

Maya nods. "Princess, Win's *obsessed* with you."

The thought sits on my mind, freezing me from taking action. It feels too good to be true, especially in the midst of all this other bullshit. For the rest of the evening I take a few distracted calls from Kimi and Wayne, explaining how I don't want to go through with the show tomorrow and never want to work with Riley again, and then I hide away in my hotel room, wrapped in a big white towel after taking a long bath, half watching *Friends* from my bed, the dark expanse of the ocean calming me through the open balcony doors. I order room service but just push my food around my plate, my appetite totally lost. I end up tossing and turning, desperate to meet sleep, but it never greets me. All I can think about is Win. His carefulness, his soft gaze, his honesty, his unwavering belief in me. I grab my phone, shutting out any second thoughts that creep in, and FaceTime him. "Win . . . hi."

He's outdoors, the night sky and palm trees in the background as he walks with purpose while he talks. "Princess." He sounds relieved to see my face, even though my room is dark. "You okay?" he asks, his voice instantly soothing.

"Much better. I'm so sorry for earlier. I don't know if I'm being crazy or irrational, but I need to talk to you."

"Tell me you're okay first?"

I nod. "I know this is random but I can't stop—" I pause. "I just need to see you, Win."

Without hesitation he asks, "What's your room number?" He enters through some doors, and then he's inside a hotel lobby that looks all too familiar.

My breath stops in my throat, so my words come out on a gasp as I give him my room number.

"See you in a minute." He hangs up.

Holy fuck.

I spring out of bed immediately, adrenaline jump-starting my pulse. *Win's coming to my room! I called him, but what the hell am I going to say once he's here?* "Shit, shit, shit." I grab the bundle of used tissues with my makeup smeared over them and throw them in the trash can, then run over to the mirror to check my face. I already took off my makeup, and my hair's up in a messy bun, but at least I'm wearing a cute silk nightie, even if it does reveal a little too much skin. No time to change now, though.

"Princess?" His voice comes through the door a second later, followed by three short knocks.

Heat pricks my skin *everywhere. Fuck.*

I take a deep breath once, twice, as my hand lingers over the door-knob. Then I pull it open slowly, swallowing hard.

Win's leaning into the doorframe, one arm up above his head, suit jacket open and his top button undone. His tie's slack around his neck, loosened, and his hair looks disheveled, as though he's been running his hands through it all night. But his eyes . . . *oh my god*. Hooded and hungry, he stares at me in silence for a moment, and all else fades out.

"Hi," I barely whisper.

Stepping forward so quickly I blink and miss the movement, Win places his warm lips over mine and steals any words from my tongue.

The kiss is unlike anything I've ever experienced before. One hand finds my jaw and the other moves to my waist, his hips bumping against me as he shuffles us back into the room. His cologne floods my senses, the skin of his cheek rougher than I expected even though it's clean-shaven, and when he sighs into the kiss, I feel it flooding through my entire body, filling my head with intoxicating airiness and melting deliciously down through my blood.

He presses me into the wall and my back knocks the light switch, and then Win's closing the door with one hand and then bringing it back to push his fingers through my hair. He grips a fistful, pulling my head to one side to expose my neck, and my body reacts instantly to his lips and tongue pulsing along my jaw in hot, wet kisses. He groans, and I gasp as I feel his hardness pressing into me, the silk and his suit trousers an antagonizing barrier between us. I want to feel him. I want to be as close to him as possible. I want—

He nips the skin at the base of my neck, his hand on my waist moving up to squeeze my breast through the silk, thumb pinching and hot breath pouring over my chest.

Fuck, I want *this*.

"Win . . ." I moan, gripping the lapels of his jacket and pushing it off. He shrugs his shoulders to help me remove it, but I'm already working on undoing his tie. As both fall to the floor, he presses his forehead against mine to stare deep into my eyes, breathing heavily.

"Princess."

It's like we're seeing each other for the first time, no walls between us now, nothing hidden anymore. My heart drums in my head, my ears, my chest—everywhere—as I stare back at him, wondering what on earth we should do next. Knowing there's only one solution to extinguish this burning *need*.

I kiss him again, once on the lips, and then my kisses move down and I drag my tongue and teeth over his neck, unfastening each button of his shirt as my lips descend across his chest, farther . . . and farther . . . He lets me reach the fifth button before placing his index finger under my chin and lifting my head up to meet his eyes. They're still hooded, kind of hazy with passion, and so I reach up on tiptoes to kiss him on the mouth, letting my tongue go in the hope he'll reciprocate.

But he doesn't.

"I've wanted this for so long," he says, breathless.

In the heat of my arousal, I let the words spill out. "I want you."

Win stops me from reaching in for another kiss, tilting my chin up again to hold his stare. His hand on my waist trails down the length of my nightdress, meeting the lacy hem and moving dangerously close to the space between my thighs. He draws little patterns on my bare skin with his fingertip, only increasing my desire. "I can't go another minute longer without letting you know how much you mean to me."

I swallow audibly, all my attention captured by his words.

"Do you know how important you are to me?" he whispers, eyes searching mine through the dim light.

Slowly, I shake my head.

"I see you, Princess. I see who you are deep inside, the love you have in your soul, the attention you give to others . . . the way you look at me. I see all of it. My fucking superstar. I notice everything you do, and it keeps me awake at night to know I can't tell you all this."

"Why can't you tell me?" I ask in a voice that doesn't even sound like my own. This whole thing feels like walking on air. Dreamlike. Impossible. *All I've ever wanted.*

"Because I don't know what to do," Win says with another incredible groan that hits me deep in my core. "I mean, look at you. You're *perfect.* And I'm not going to hurt you by being unable to give you my full attention. There's a lot on my plate right now, and I have so much respect for you, Princess, but I won't *use* you. Even if it kills me to wait."

"It doesn't have to be just sex, Win. It could be so much more."

"Believe me," he says, eyes staring deeper than ever and his words earnest, "it would *never* be just sex between you and me. You would have *everything.* In a heartbeat. For as long as you wanted it, until the end of time."

I can't reply at all. The way he says the words hits me with a fresh wave of emotion I've never felt before. It strikes me all at once this might be the first time anything a man has said to me has ever felt *true.*

Win continues to stare for a long moment. "I don't know what to do. Maybe I've had too much to drink tonight, but I couldn't go another minute without letting you know how important you are."

Before I know what's happening, he straightens up and steps away from me, adjusting his waistband and running a hand back through his hair. Emptiness washes over me, making me suddenly aware of all the places his body connected with mine. He takes a couple of deep breaths as he paces around in a small circle, and then he says, "Can we step outside? Get some air, maybe?"

I look toward the balcony doors, trying to hide my disappointment. Some air is the last thing I need. I want him to wrap his arms around me and trap me in his atmosphere. I want him to mold us together and never let go.

Instead, I say quietly, "Sure."

It doesn't help that his eyes slide over me salaciously as I move, lingering on my chest and taking their time over my legs. He waits for me to walk out first, and then he follows, coming up close as I walk to the edge of the balcony and lean against the glass wall. I stare out at the ocean, closing my eyes and taking in a deep breath of fresh air, so I'm not prepared for him to be quite so near to me when his hands snake around my waist and he presses his weight into my back.

But, god, it feels *right*.

"I listened to your song," he says, his voice gravelly against my ear.

I bite my lip to avoid letting him know Maya already told me as much. "You did? What did you think?"

"I think it's the best song you've released so far. You have the most beautiful voice, I can't get enough of it. Even in its rawest form it's perfect. Just like you."

A blush creeps up my neck. I wonder for a second what would happen if someone were to spot us up here, even though we're far from the sand. Paparazzi sometimes hang around hotels like this one, and zoom lenses can make photos of even the highest balconies crystal clear. There would be no doubting the connection between us if we were captured, *eternalized*, in this moment right now. Should I even care? With Win I'm safe; I don't have to worry about people knowing my hotel with him around. I don't need to panic over the stalker coming back or a crowd of fans invading my privacy. He would handle it. That eases my mind, my body, my heart.

"You're worried about something," Win says, and his hands move from my waist to my shoulders, warm palms sliding down slowly, grounding me in my own skin. "Just relax. Whatever it is, I'm with you. Try to push it out of your mind."

I breathe out to release the anxiety. Win would never set me up for paparazzi shots. Everyone else in this damn industry might be so desperate for fame and success they wouldn't spend one second considering the damage they cause others—too distracted stepping on anyone to get what they want. But I'm safe with Win. And with his chin resting in the crook of my neck, arms wrapped around my waist again, and the heat of his front warming my back, I feel good. It feels *natural*. More normal than I've ever felt with anyone else.

"Can I ask you a question?" he murmurs.

"Yes." The word comes out on a dreamy sigh.

"Who did you write the song about?"

I think of the lyrics: the story of a girl moving on from her cheating ex, telling him this is the last straw and he can keep his new girl because she's found someone better now. Someone who respects her. Someone who makes her feel powerful. Someone who's always there, without fail, every time she needs him.

My throat goes dry as realization hits.

That *someone* has always been Win.

"Princess?" he says gently, dragging me out of my thoughts.

I swallow hard and twist my head to look at him, bringing our faces level. Admitting who I wrote the song about feels like too much of a confession, and even with everything he just told me, I don't know where the truth will lead.

I *can't* make myself vulnerable to rejection again.

"Would it change anything if you knew, Win?" I ask, my voice barely a whisper.

There's a long pause before he answers, his eyes sparkling in the dark of the night. The sea breeze lifts strands of my hair, which lightly brush against Win's jaw as the distant thump of club music carries across from Ocean Drive. In so many ways, I wish I wasn't here right now, wish all this drama with John and Riley didn't exist, wish fame wasn't such an unforgiving obstacle course and love didn't have to hurt so much. But I'm not one to cancel. I would *never* cancel a show, even when my whole life is falling apart behind the scenes. I'd never let my fans down—if anything, I'm more fueled to put on the best performance of my life. They'll never see me coming.

I've worked too hard. I'm not going be to trapped by her games. If Riley thinks I'm not going to show, she never really knew me at all.

But if I hadn't gone through all that shit, I wouldn't know to appreciate this moment: just two people finding safety in each other, high up above this big, beautiful, messed-up city.

Win kisses my cheek and I turn to face him. The look in his eyes holds the promise of a new beginning.

ABOUT THE AUTHOR

Pia Mia was born on the Western Pacific island of Guam. At thirteen years old, she moved to Los Angeles and launched a career in music, and she is now a multi-platinum recording artist, songwriter, actress, entrepreneur, and creative who has collaborated with notable talents, designers, and international brands. *Sand, Sequins & Silicone* is her first novel.